Praise for the Hamilton High Series

Reynolds' treatment of youth and their challenges, from sexual abstinence to mixed-race parentage, is compassionate, never condescending; the dialogue, situations, emotions, and behavior of the well-defined teen characters ring true. [*If You Loved Me* is] An engaging, thought-provoking read . . .

Shelle Rosenfeld, *BOOKLIST*

"Out of all the books I've read (and trust me, I've read tons of books), yours have impacted me the most. They are filled with reality and hope and strength, and make me feel stronger."

Gillian (email)

For all the sadness in it [*No More Sad Goodbyes*], Autumn and her baby's story is ultimately one of love and hope.

Claire Rosser, *KLIATT*

"I have just finished reading *Detour for Emmy*. I wanted you to know that in all my years of school that book is the first book that I have honestly read from cover to cover. I have never in my life read a book, and I can't wait to read more of yours."

Amy, North Toole County High School

Touching on the adolescent themes of teenage sex, adoption, and abortion — this [*No More Sad Goodbyes*] topical novel is poignant and inspiring.

LAMBDA RISING

"I want to tell you that I find your books very interesting and reading them has helped me get through a lot in my life. Thank you."

Julie, La Puente High School

"Before I read *If You Loved Me* I had never bothered to check out a book at a library, but now I can't stop reading. Thank you for changing the way I lived my life."

Maria, Bell Gardens High School

"Your book [*But What About Me*] touched me because it felt like I was the only one going through these things, but when I read your book I knew that I wasn't alone."

Kendra, Waukesha, WI

Shut Up!

Shut Up!

Other titles in the
True-to-Life Series from Hamilton High
by Marilyn Reynolds

No More Sad Goodbyes

Love Rules

If You Loved Me

Baby Help

Too Soon For Jeff

Detour for Emmy

Telling

Beyond Dreams

But What About Me?

Also by Marilyn Reynolds

*I Won't Read and You Can't Make Me:
Reaching Reluctant Teen Readers*

Shut Up!

By Marilyn Reynolds

True-to-Life Series from Hamilton High

Morning Glory Press

Buena Park, CA

ISBN 978-1-932538-88-5 (pap); 978-1-932538-93-9 (hdbk)

Library of Congress Control Number 2008933535

Library of Congress Cataloging-in-Publication Data
available upon request.

MORNING GLORY PRESS, INC.
6595 San Haroldo Way   Buena Park, CA 90620-3748
714.828.1998, 1.888.612.8254   FAX 714.828.2049
e-mail: info@morninggglorypress.com
Web site: www.morninggglorypress.com
Printed and bound in the United States of America

The day before my Mom ships out to Iraq she tells me,
"I don't want us to be worried about what will probably never happen, so I'm not going to go into a lot of
details. Some of the others in our unit have everything all
spelled out, but I don't want to do that right now. Do you
know what I'm talking about, Mario?"

"I know what you're not talking about."

"Well . . . here's the one thing we have to talk about
– just this one thing."

I listen, waiting for the next words, wondering when
they'll come.

Finally she says, "If I don't come back, if I die over
there, you've got to be the maximum brother for Eddie."

"Mom . . ."

"I know you'd do that anyway, without my asking, but
he's not as strong as you . . ."

"He's only nine . . ."

"That's not what I mean. It's . . . he's just more . . .
tender."

We're quiet again and then she says, "That didn't come
out right. I know your heart is as sweet and tender as they
come."

"Now you're making me sound like a ripe watermelon."

"Don't joke, Mario. Not right now."

"Sorry," I say . . . "Sure, I'd take care of Eddie. You
know that."

ACKNOWLEDGMENTS

For much-needed reality checks, many thanks to:

Nancy Blackburn and Mac Slater, and their students at Esperanza Junior/Senior High School, especially Zach Cole, Brandon Flores, Robert Ivy, James Lewis, Steve Lopez, Mario Navarro, Alton Stewart, Steven Treadway, Sergio Velez, and Timothy Williams.

Deb Young and her students at Roanoke Benson High School, especially Kara Kolb.

Jennifer Harmon and the Adolescent Parent Program students at Walnutwood High School, especially Erika Rivera, Liliana Calderon, Stacey Delgado, Carolynn Samaniego, and Stephanie Nasca.

For close readings and plenty of general help along the way, thanks to:

Mimi Avocada, Dale Dodson, Kathy Harvey, Karen Kasaba, Judy Laird, Leesa Phaneuf Reynolds, Matt Reynolds, Mike Reynolds, Jeannie Ward, and my fellow writers in the UUSS Write to Life Group.

A special thank you goes to Libby for her generous gift of a quiet writing space—a space where Mario and Eddie could materialize.

Dedicated
to the silent boys who hold secrets
shut up in their hearts.

Shut Up!

CHAPTER

1

When I think back about all that went wrong, it seems like our troubles started back in September. That's when our mom, Max, went off to Iraq. Or maybe it was when Max first joined the National Guard, or maybe even before that, when my dad left my mom. But I think September was the start of the really bad times.

It's the first day of school for Eddie, and the last day before our mom ships out to Iraq with her National Guard Unit. Eddie's only nine, so little stuff keeps him happy – like being all Wal-Marted out in new clothes. There's a band of white across the back of his neck where his new haircut shows skin that the sun's never seen, and he's even already brushed his teeth without being nagged about it.

Hamilton High classes don't start until tomorrow, so I'm still in my boxers and tee shirt, helping pack crates of kitchen stuff to take to storage later today.

Max is smoothing Eddie's collar for about the hundredth

time. She pauses, wiping her eyes.

"*Ai Mijo*, I can't believe you're already in fourth grade," she says. "And you, Mario . . . you're taller than I am! And all buff," she says, grabbing my bicep. She's smiling and getting teary at the same time. "My little *niños* . . ."

"Hey! Max!" I say, giving her a light swat with a dish towel. "Don't go getting all emotional on us."

She laughs.

"I'm not getting all emotional. I'm just getting partly emotional."

"You're such a stickler for words," I say, taking another swat.

"Best form of communication ever invented," she says.

"Communicate this," I tell her, letting go with my specialty Pumbaa rumble fart.

She flings open the door and fans at the air while Eddie collapses on the sofa in laughter.

"Don't laugh," she tells Eddie. "It only encourages him!"

Eddie laughs harder. Which gets Max laughing, too. It's hard not to laugh when Eddie laughs because he's got this sort of cross between a giggle and a roar way of laughing that's like nothing else I've ever heard.

Max flops down beside Eddie and pats the place beside her, motioning for me to sit down.

I stuff the last plate into a storage box and sit next to her on the sofa – the sofa that's going to be picked up by the Salvation Army in about an hour.

Max puts her arms around both of us and pulls us close. Eddie's small for his age, and it's still easy for him to snuggle in under her arm. Me, though, I'm bigger than she is, so the closest I can get to a snuggle is to scrunch down and lay my head against her shoulder.

"Listen," she says. "You two clowns are going to have to get serious when I'm gone. That's first thing tomorrow morning. You know? First thing tomorrow morning, at 5:30 a.m., you've got to get serious."

"I don't want you to go!" Eddie yells, his voice going all crackly the way it does just before he starts crying.

I don't want her to go, either, but I'm too old to yell that out, or to let my voice go crackly.

"Why do you have to be in the stupid old National Guard anyway?" Eddie says.

Max tells Eddie, again, why she joined the guard. She had a hard time supporting us after our dad left. We had to move out of our house to a small apartment in a not very good part of town. Even after the move, Max's Macy's paycheck would barely cover our rent and food. She had to figure out a way to make more money. One thing she did was go to school to become a dental assistant. The other thing she did was join the National Guard.

"Can't you unjoin?"

Max pulls him closer.

"We all have to make the best of this, *Mijo*. You've got to be maximum now, too."

Eddie nods, wiping at his eyes.

Back when Max was still going to school plus working and doing her monthly duty thing with the Guard, Eddie and I both used to complain that she wasn't home as much as other kids' moms. Once, after a long bout of complaining, she told us it was time to get over it.

"I'm glad I got you guys out of the deal, but I'm sorry I chose such a minimum dad for you. The thing is, with such a minimum dad, I've got to work my butt off to be a maximum mom."

Which is why I nicknamed her "Max." Her real name is Maria. Maria Barajas, Eduardo Barajas, and Mario Barajas. That's us. My dad is Jacob Barajas but he's gone so long I hardly remember what he looks like. It's not like there are a lot of his pictures sitting around, either. I mean, a guy who runs out on his pregnant wife and seven-year-old kid doesn't exactly deserve a framed photo all over the place.

Max gets up from the sofa and starts searching around in a shopping bag that's sitting on the kitchen counter. She pulls out a battery-operated red racecar toothbrush.

"Maybe this will help you remember to brush your teeth," she says to Eddie.

Eddie takes the toothbrush from Max and examines the details.

"Cool," he says.

Eddie's notorious for not bothering to brush his teeth. Maybe the racecar toothbrush will help, but I doubt it.

"Twice a day, Eddie," Max says. "I don't want to come home and find you with a mouthful of rotten teeth."

Eddie's already got the toothbrush out of the plastic package and is vroom-vrooming around the room with it. It's loud enough to be a race car.

"Aunt Carmen won't be reminding you to brush your teeth, or take your vitamins, or eat your vegetables, or do your homework, or any of the things I always remind you about," Max says, shouting over the noise of the toothbrush. She turns to me.

"I've put a six-month supply of vitamins on your dresser, Mario, and I want you boys to take them every single day. No skipping!"

"I never skip my vitamins," I yell over the roar of the race-car toothbrush.

"No, but you've . . . Eddie, shut that thing off!"

He gives it one more vroom, then flops down on the couch next to me. I stick my finger out for him to pull. He pulls. I fart. We both crack up. Really, I owe my talent for farting at will to Eddie.

Eddie was born without any real fingers on his right hand. He's got a little stub thing where a thumb should be, and two sort of half-fingers that were attached to each other where his index and middle fingers should be.

When he was four he had an operation to separate his finger stubs. He was in a lot of pain for weeks after the surgery and the only thing that could take his mind off the pain and get him laughing was farts. He was only four. It's not like he had a highly developed sense of humor. We'd play that warthog section in "The Lion King" over and over for him. And I'd also do my part to entertain him. Once when he woke up in the middle of the night, screaming with pain, Max called me into his room and asked me to fart for him. Now she says she wishes she'd doubled up on the pain meds instead of encouraging my farting skills, but I know she was grateful at the time.

with him. Still, there was that no pets rule. Max borrowed a cat carrier from a friend and we drove Simba all the way up to Redville, to live with *Tío* Hector and *Tía* Josie. They always have a few cats around to keep the mice out of their barn, so they didn't mind adding one more to the rodent patrol. Eddie cried and carried on when we left, but Simba seemed pretty happy to be outside with trees and birds and grass to roll around in, and a barn full of interesting prey.

"Simba could stay in our room all the time. Aunt Carmen wouldn't even know he was there," Eddie says.

Max nails Eddie with her "no more foolishness" look, then turns to me.

"You guys have got to be responsible for yourselves now."

"We are, Max," I tell her. "We're plenty responsible. That's why we should just stay here 'til you get back. It'd be better than going to Carmen's."

"Mario. *Mijo.* We've been all through that. Unless you want to change your mind about staying with Hector and Josie up in Redville . . ."

"Where the biggest excitement of the year is who takes first prize in the garlic recipe contest? Where half the time the fog's so thick the soccer team can't even see the goal?? Get real!"

"Right. So you'll stay with Carmen and make the best of it."

"It won't be good," I grumble, lifting my head from Max's shoulder and moving a few inches away.

Max gives me a long look, and I can tell I'm in for one of her "let's get this straight" talks. Here it comes.

"Let's get this straight, Mario. I'm doing what I've got to do. If I'd known when I signed on with the Guard that someday I'd have to leave you guys for a year to go off and fight a war, I wouldn't have signed up. But I did sign up. I made a commitment and I'm bound to keep it. You understand?"

I nod.

Eddie sits quietly, picking at a piece of lint on the sofa. He knows better than to interrupt Max in the middle of a "let's get this straight" talk.

"Okay. So I've got to do my duty, just like thousands and thousands of other soldiers are doing. You've got to live with some adult who is your official guardian. You're not willing to go to *Tío* Hector's, so Carmen's it."

"I just don't want to leave Hamilton in my senior year. There's soccer, and the firefighters course . . ."

"Right. And you can stay at Hamilton High because Carmen's doing you a favor. Maybe you could show a little appreciation."

I sigh.

"The good thing about being at Carmen's is that you'll practically be on your own. Just follow her house rules. She's busy at the bank, and she's found some new love, Stanton, or Fenton – something like that. Anyway, she won't be paying a lot of attention to you two as long as you keep a low profile."

"Okay. Okay!"

Even though I don't do anything but sit there, Max's "let's get this straight" talks wear me out. And even though I say "okay," just to get Max off my back, I don't mean it. I've never really gotten along with Carmen. I don't do very well with bossy people and she's about as bossy as they get. Moving in with her and having her be our official guardian seems way not okay to me. Max is right, though. I don't have a better idea for a place to stay within the Hamilton High School boundaries.

Eddie picks at the lint for a while longer, long enough to know Max's finished her talk.

"If I can't take Simba with me, can I at least take his picture to Aunt Carmen's?"

"Of course you can take Simba's picture."

"Aunt Carmen's not allergic to pictures of cats," I tell him.

"How come Robert's not Carmen's boyfriend anymore?" Eddie asks.

"She's too bossy," I say.

Max ignores me.

"He was kind of nice," Eddie says. "He played Monopoly with me once."

"Well . . . he seemed nice for a while, and then he didn't," Max says.

"Why wasn't he nice?" Eddie wants to know.

Max just looks at Eddie, like she's trying to decide what to say.

"Why wasn't he nice?" Eddie asks again.

"Well . . . he'd get mad at Carmen over any little thing, and he'd say bad things to her."

"Why?"

"I don't know, Eddie. That's just how he was. Sort of like Mark was, too."

"But Mark was nice," Eddie says.

"At first he was."

"Why does Carmen always make her boyfriends mad?"

Max starts talking fast, the way she does when she's tired of questions.

"It's not what Carmen does. She's just not that choosy about men in the first place. That's how she's always been."

"But she gets boyfriends," Eddie says. "If you had boy-friends maybe you'd have gotten a dad for us, and then we could stay home with him when you leave us."

I look over at Eddie. Is he wanting to commit suicide, or what? This is a very sore topic with Max – how Eddie's always looking for a dad. Once, when he was about four, he asked the mail carrier if he'd come live with us and be our dad. The guy was a real geek, too. That's how desperate Eddie was. I guess I'm lucky I knew our dad for a while. Life with him wasn't all that great, so I'm not looking for a replacement. Eddie, though – he always seems to think he's missing something.

Max takes a deep breath and I expect her to tell Eddie, "I'm not settling for some idiot in pants just because you think you want a dad." I've heard that speech so often, I've got it memorized.

This time, though, Max doesn't say anything. She pulls Eddie close to her and holds him tight.

"When're you coming back, Mommy?" Eddie's voice sounds all muffled because he's got his face buried against Max's chest, but I can tell he's trying not to cry. He only calls her Mommy if he's really sad or scared or hurt or something.

"Like I've been telling you all along, *Mijo*, I'm not sure exactly when I'll get back. A lot depends on how things go over there, and that's unpredictable."

"But by Christmas?" Eddie says.

"I hope so. I just don't know."

"Well then, for my birthday?"

"We'll see."

Max moves gently away from Eddie and stands up.

"Come on. Let's get going."

She checks Eddie's backpack to be sure he has his lunch, then turns to me.

"You should come, too, since you'll be walking Eddie to school from here on out."

"Sure," I say.

I put on shorts and flip-flops and follow them out the door. There's really no reason for me to walk with them. It's not like I don't know my way to Eddie's school, since it's the same school I went to from kindergarten through the sixth grade. But I'm sorry I bugged Max with all my complaining about staying at Carmen's, and anyway these last few days, wherever Max goes, me and Eddie go, too. It's not like I'm a mama's boy, or don't have my own life, it's just that today is my last chance to be with Max for a while. It could be my last chance, forever. That's what I know. I don't think Eddie knows that, or if he does, he won't think about it.

I can't help thinking about it sometimes. I mean, people do get killed over there. I'm pretty sure Max won't be one of them, but I'm hanging out with her as much as I can for now. Just in case.

The phone rings just as we're leaving and Max runs back inside to answer it. Eddie and I wait around outside.

"Don't take our chairs away," Eddie whispers, as if Max could hear him clear out here.

"Chairs?"

"You know," he says, nodding in the direction of the storage shed behind the garages.

"Oh, those chairs. There's no place for them at Carmen's anyway."

Back behind the storage shed is where we used to hide when Max's friend, Leah, would bring her nieces over for a visit. They were little, younger even than Eddie, and they'd want us to play pretend games with them. Like "how about you be the prince and I'll be Snow White," the five-year-old would say. And then Eddie was supposed to be one of the dwarfs or something. And if we didn't play with them Max would start ragging on us about being nice to company. So finally we figured out we could play hide and seek with them. I'd be "it" first, and then Eddie. Then when one of the nieces was "it" we'd hide back here behind the shed and they could never find us. Maybe it was mean, but it was better than being the prince, which was bound to happen after about ten minutes of hide and seek if we didn't stay hidden.

"We can keep our hiding place, even if we don't live here anymore," Eddie says.

"I guess."

By the time we get to Palm Avenue School, two other kids, friends of Eddie's, are tagging along with us. Brent is a kid I know because he's been over at our apartment a lot. Well, to what used to be our apartment. I don't know the other guy, who's talking a mile a minute about some computer game he just got. His mom catches up with us.

"Eddie says you're leaving soon."

"Tomorrow morning," Max says.

"That must be so hard," the other mom says.

Max just nods. I know she doesn't want to deal with the subject of leaving again, now that Eddie's mind is finally off it for a while. She reaches into Eddie's backpack and brings out his back-to-school notice.

"Room 27," she reads.

"Me, too!" Brent says. The two of them run up ahead, all excited that they're in the same class together. We find their classroom, which turns out to be Ms. Sumner's class.

"Hey, you got lucky, Buddy," I say to Eddie. "Sumner was my fourth grade teacher, too. She's very cool."

Eddie looks worried, but he's way too old to cry in front of his friends. He gives us a quick wave and follows close behind Brent toward the classroom. He pauses at the door and looks our way.

"Bye, Mommy," he says.

3

Max and I are carrying the last two boxes to the car when Walker pulls up in front. His girlfriend, Courtney, is with him.

"Hey, Max!" Walker yells. "Can Mario come play with us?"

She sets down the box she's carrying and walks over to Walker's side of the car. I stack my box on top of hers and follow.

"Hey, Runner," Max says. That's what she's called Walker since the first time he came to a birthday party for me, back when we were about Eddie's age.

"He's too hyper to be a 'Walker,'" she'd told me. "He's a 'Runner.'"

"Guess where we're going?" Courtney says to me.

There's an ice chest and beach towels in the back seat of Walker's car, plus two boogie boards, so it's not too hard to figure out they're on their way to the beach.

"Can Mario come, Max? Can he? Can he? Please?" Walker

says, doing his little-kid-pleading voice.

Max laughs, then looks my way.

"What do you think? I can manage the rest of this."

"Last day of freedom," Walker says.

"Thanks, but I better stick around here," I say.

"Jenna's coming with us," Courtney says.

Walker reaches for his ever-present tin of Altoids and shakes them at me with a leering grin.

I picture Jenna in a bikini and it's all I can do to keep from climbing into the car. But tempting as it is, I don't want to leave Max on her last day at home.

Walker looks past me to the boxes in the driveway.

"You moving already?" he says.

"Reporting tomorrow," Max tells him.

"Well, shit!" he says, catching Max's raised eyebrows. "Shoot, I mean. Shoot! Why didn't anyone tell me you were leaving so soon?"

"Like I haven't been complaining about moving for the last month?" I remind him.

"Yeah, but I didn't know it was right now. That's bunk!"

Walker gets out of the car and gives Max a big hug.

"Stay safe, Rambo," he says.

"I plan to," she tells him.

For an instant I think they both might cry. But before that can happen, Walker quick gets back in his car and revs the engine. Max and I both step back, and he takes off.

"You could have gone," she says.

"I know," I say, picking up the boxes and carrying them to the car. "I didn't want to, though."

"Who's Jenna?" Max asks.

"Just some girl."

"Are you interested in her?"

"Maybe a little," I say.

Talk about an understatement. "She's practically all I ever think about" would be more like it.

Max gives me one of her penetrating, assessing looks. "What's she like?"

"She's kind of nice, I guess."

"She'd better be," Max says. "You'd better be, too. Remember . . ."

"Max! Don't start!"

"What?"

She starts laughing. So do I. If she can read me sometimes, I can do the same with her. I know exactly what was coming next. It was going to be the responsible-sex-always-use-a-condom lecture. I've heard it a thousand times in the past five years. If I ever even get a phone call from a girl, Max launches into the condom lecture.

"I'm serious, Mario," she says. "You've got to be responsible."

"Trust me on this one. We don't have to rush out and buy condoms right now."

Of course, getting the chance to use a condom with Jenna would be a dream come true. Actually, it would be a wet dream come true. But that's nothing a guy wants to tell his mother.

We jam the last of the boxes into the back seat.

"Can I drive?"

"Sure," Max says, handing me the keys.

We've got some cheapo insurance policy that says I can't drive without my mother in the car until after I'm eighteen, so I don't do a lot of cruising around town. I slide behind the wheel of the old Jetta, adjust the seat, rev 'er up, and start singing "*La Bamba.*"

When the Jetta was new, about eight years ago, Max thought it was like the hottest car on the road – bright red, with stick shift – it was "the bomb." Every time we went anywhere, even just three blocks to the store, we'd have to sing "*La Bamba,*" in honor of the Jetta.

It was Max's first new car ever. She bought it after she finally got a decent paying job in a dentist's office. The red's not as bright as it used to be, and you've got to baby the clutch when you shift from second to third gear. It's definitely not "the bomb" anymore, but we still call it that, anyway.

By the time we get to the corner, Max joins in, "*Para bailar la bamba, Para bailar la bamba . . .*"

Don't ask me what it means. I think it's something about a dance and being a little bit funny, but to me it's just a car song.

We're so busy singing, neither of us looks back at our old apartment, or thinks how nothing will ever be the same again. I don't think about that until later. You can't really think about anything but singing "*La Bamba*" when you're singing "*La Bamba.*"

After dropping the last of the boxes off at storage, we take a few more things over to Carmen's – raincoats and sweaters – stuff we won't use for a while. Max folds them up and puts them in the chest of drawers we brought over earlier – the one that now has our six-month supply of vitamins sitting on top of it.

Carmen's house has two bedrooms, but the extra one is set up as an office, so Max got creative.

"The room turned out nice, don't you think?"

"Yeah," I say, forcing a smile.

"No, really," she says. "From a dirty old storage room to this?" She encompasses the room with a sweep of her arm. "This is as good as any of those TV makeovers."

Usually I'd make some sarcastic remark but today I only want to be nice to Max. If she wants to think the room turned out great, let her. It's not exactly a place I'm wanting to show off to my friends.

The "bedroom" is painted turquoise blue (Eddie's choice), with a bunch of soccer posters (my choice) tacked up on the walls. The floor is just unfinished plywood, but Max found a rug at a garage sale that covers most of it.

Max does her mind reading trick.

"Okay, so we didn't manage the kind of makeover you'd see on one of those "Queer Eye for the Straight Guy" programs, but you've got to admit it's a lot better than it was."

"Right, Max. Lots better," I say, giving her a real smile this time.

"And the beds are pretty comfy."

"Right again, Max," I say.

She lies down on the bed Eddie will be using, and I stretch out on mine. There are only about six inches between the beds, just enough room for us to get in and out without having to climb over the beds.

Max reaches across the bed for my hand. We lie there, not looking at one another, and not speaking, for what seems like a long time.

"There's so much on my mind right now, Mario."

"Mine, too," I tell her.

She sighs a deep, sad, sigh – the kind I almost never hear from her.

After a while she says, "I don't want us to be worried about what will probably never happen, so I'm not going to go into a lot of details. Some of the others in our unit have everything all spelled out, but I don't want to do that right now. Do you know what I'm talking about, Mario?"

"I know what you're not talking about."

"Well . . . here's the one thing we have to talk about – just this one thing."

I listen, waiting for the next words, wondering when they'll come.

Finally she says, "If I don't come back, if I die over there, you've got to be the maximum brother for Eddie."

"Mom . . ."

"I know you'd do that anyway, without my asking, but he's not as strong as you . . ."

"He's only nine . . ."

"That's not what I mean. It's . . . he's just more . . . tender."

We're quiet again and then she says, "That didn't come out right. I know your heart is as sweet and tender as they come."

"Now you're making me sound like a ripe watermelon."

"Don't joke, Mario. Not right now. I need to say this."

"Sorry," I say. I lay staring at the dingy ceiling, thinking we should have painted that, too.

"Without me, legally, you would both go to your father. You'll be eighteen pretty soon, so that wouldn't be such a big deal. But Eddie's got a long way to go."

"Dad wouldn't even want us! He never has."

"No, but he'd be legally bound to take care of you, so he'd be the person to decide what would happen. You could fend for yourself, but I could just imagine Jake sending Eddie off to stay with one of his low-life relatives. That would be a disaster. Promise me you'll take charge if anything like that were to happen."

"I'd take care of Eddie. You know that."

"But it would require a big sacrifice. Not many students take their little brothers off to college with them, or out on dates, or . . ."

"Max! Come on! You're not going to get out of taking care of us that easy."

She moves over to my bed, lying close beside me, holding tightly to my hand. For the first time in my life she seems, I don't know, sort of breakable. The moment passes, and with a quick squeeze of my hand she jumps off the bed.

She takes a brown envelope from the tote bag she's been carrying around all day. It's got my name written across the front in bold, black letters.

"Keep this in a safe place," she says. "It's got copies of your birth certificates and Carmen's temporary guardianship papers, my life insurance policy, your immunization records, your health insurance cards – all of our important papers. Carmen's got the original guardianship papers, but you might need your own for school or something."

I take the envelope from her and shove it under my jeans in the bottom drawer of our chest.

"Oh, yeah, one more thing. It's also got information about your email account, and your password, in case you forget."

We both laugh at that. My password consists of the numbers of my date of birth. I may not be able to remember many important dates in history, like when did WWI start, or when was President Kennedy assassinated, but you can be sure I don't forget my birthday.

"Come on, we've still got lots more errands to take care of," Max says, fumbling around in her overloaded tote bag for her keys.

On our way out of the house, Max points to a laminated list of rules attached to the refrigerator with magnets.

"At least Carmen knows where to put things to get your attention," she says.

We pause to read it.

All dishes must be washed and put away as soon as you're finished eating.

No friends in the house unless I'm home.

Eddie's bedtime, 8:00.

Mario's curfew, 11:00.

Any changes in the time schedule must first be cleared with me.

The bathroom is to be kept open for my use between 6:30 and 7:00 every weekday morning.

No phone calls after 9:00.

Computer use for email to your mother only. No exceptions.

No shoes, clothes, books, etc., to be left sitting around.

"That's doable," Max says.

"The big boss lays down the law," I say.

"Come on, Mario, it's pretty much how it's always been with us. We just didn't have it spelled out on the refrigerator."

"An eleven o'clock curfew?"

"You're usually home by eleven, except on weekends."

"What if she wants me to be in at eleven on Friday nights? Things don't even get started until eleven on the weekend!"

"Relax, would you? Carmen likes to have things spelled out, so she knows what to expect, that's all. I'll talk to her about the curfew thing."

When we pick Eddie up from school, he's all enthused about a project his class is going to do to help at a big food bank near the homeless shelter.

"Ms. Sumner showed us some pictures of kids who don't even have any homes!" he says. "That sucks!"

"Big time," I say. I don't point out to him that we don't exactly have a home anymore, either.

After running about a thousand errands, Max takes us to dinner at our favorite restaurant. It's an "all-you-can-eat" Italian place – Dimitri's. We've been going there since before Eddie could eat with a fork. I know it sounds funny that a Mexican family's favorite restaurant is Italian – funnier still, I guess, that our very favorite meal at home is macaroni and cheese from a box, and our next favorite restaurant is Siam Thai. But hey, we live near L.A. We appreciate diversity.

We've barely started eating when Eddie starts with the jokes.

Besides farts the other thing that totally cracks Eddie up are his own stupid jokes. Right now his specialties are doctor jokes and animal jokes, especially elephant jokes, but that could change any day. He wants to be a comedian when he grows up, so he's always practicing.

"This guy goes running into the doctor's office and he says, 'Doctor, Doctor! I swallowed a bone!' and the doctor says, 'Are you choking?'"

Eddie's already laughing so hard he can hardly get the punch line out. But finally, after a lot of gasping and false starts, he manages.

"And the guy goes, 'No, Doctor, I'm serious! I really did swallow a bone!'"

Max gives Eddie an indulgent smile, and I just take another bite of garlic bread.

"Don't you get it?" Eddie says. "The doctor asks if the guy is choking on the bone, and the guy thinks he's asking if he's joking. Get it? Choking – Joking?"

Eddie starts laughing all over again. Max keeps smiling, and I just keep on eating. The thing is, Eddie likes to make me laugh as much as I like to make him laugh. But I always try not to laugh at his jokes, just to frustrate him. I guess it's that brother kind of thing.

"Okay, okay. How about this one?" he says, his voice getting louder and louder.

"Eddie, you don't have to shout. Some people have come here for a nice quiet dinner," Max says, nodding in the direction of an older couple two tables away.

Eddie glances their way. He leans in closer and whispers, "Why are elephants smarter than chickens?"

He sits looking back and forth between me and Max.

"Because they have bigger brains?" she says.

"No, that's not it. What do you think, Mario?"

"I don't know."

"Well, guess. You have to guess."

I take another bite of spaghetti and chew slowly, watching Eddie squirm. Then I give in.

"Let's see. Elephants are smarter than chickens because they go to better schools?"

"No, think about it. They have to be smarter, because you've never heard of Kentucky Fried Elephant, have you?"

This time we all laugh, which makes Eddie laugh even harder. Even the people two tables away laugh. All of the laughing makes me hungrier, and I go get another helping of lasagna.

Back at the table, Max pulls out a new digital camera. She takes a picture of us, and shows us in the viewfinder. Eddie's got spaghetti on his chin and my eyes are closed.

"What a handsome pair," she says, laughing.

She hands the camera to me.

"This is for you and Eddie, so you can send pictures with your email. I want to see you both at least once a week, and I want to hear from you every day."

Eddie reaches for the camera and tries to take a picture. Max hands me the instruction book.

"The camera is for both of you, Eddie, but Mario's going to keep track of it. Just ask him whenever you want to use it, and I hope you'll use it a lot."

Later, Dimitri himself stops by our table to say goodbye to Max, and to wish her luck. She takes his picture, and then he takes one of the three of us. Max even takes a picture of the menu, which I think is sort of extreme, but it pleases Dimitri.

"You boys come in next month – on the house," he tells us.

"That's so sweet, Dimitri," Max says.

"*De nada*," Dimitri says, getting a quick laugh from Max.

Next month. Things are going to be totally different next month. We've been sitting here eating and joking around like always – but there is no always.

Back at Carmen's, Max parks back behind the garage, in

the junky part of the yard. Not that any of the yard is like something you'd see in a magazine spread, but behind the garage is really junky.

Max gets the jack from the trunk so we can put *La Bamba* up on blocks.

"I don't think we need to do this, Max. I'll be driving it in a few weeks."

"It may take longer than you think to come up with the $500 for added insurance," she says, setting the jack under the back bumper.

"Yeah, but Sammy's going to increase my hours next week, and I've already saved $120."

"Well . . . in the meantime, if it takes longer than you've planned, at least the tires won't be rotting out from under the car."

Max cranks up the jack and I put a heavy wooden block under the right side of the rear axel, then the rear left. With the back tires off the ground, we move to the front.

Even if *La Bamba*'s not really the bomb anymore, it's way better than the bus. I don't know when I'll ever get up the nerve to ask Jenna out, but when I do it can't be like, "meet me at the bus stop." So I want to get the insurance paid as soon as I can. That's the deal I've got with Max – if I pay for the extra insurance, the car's mine to drive.

Sammy, my boss at Java Jive, said he'd use me 24-7 if he could. He says I'm the fastest specialty drink guy they've got. It's important to be good at the specialties because, except for the construction guys that show up when we open the doors at five in the morning, hardly anyone orders a plain cup of coffee. Once the hard hats are gone, it's all mocha, double-whipped, non-fat, double shot, half decaf . . . you get the idea.

Max and I check to be sure the blocks are secure, then go inside and wash up. Carmen's sitting at the kitchen table, paying bills. She looks up and smiles.

"Welcome home," she says. "Are you all settled in now?"

"Yep. Right down to the vitamins," I say.

"Eddie's got the Monopoly game set up in the living room. He's been waiting for you."

"We'll be right there, Eddie," Max calls. "I want the cannon."

"I want the ship," I yell.

Max sits down next to Carmen.

"Good place to post the rules," Max says.

Carmen laughs. "I may not know much about boys, but I expect they'll be using the refrigerator fairly often."

She points to a pad of paper sitting near the telephone.

"Make a list of whatever you want from the store, Mario, and I'll do a grocery run tomorrow. I've got plenty of milk and orange juice and cereal. And Maria says you both like string cheese, so I got a package of that. But I've probably missed some of your favorites."

She smiles at me like she means it.

When Max mentions the curfew to Carmen, she takes a fine Sharpie and writes, "weekends negotiable" next to the curfew rule. I feel better.

"They'll be fine here," Carmen says.

"I can't thank you enough," Max tells her.

I go into the living room where Eddie's got our tokens set out on the board and is practicing rolling the dice.

"Come on, Mom," he yells.

In a few minutes Max comes in with chips and sodas and joins the game. Carmen watches for a while.

"How are things with . . . what's his name again?" Max asks.

"Denton. He's great! He's not at all like Robert was. Denton's a real gentleman – like opening doors for me, and all. He treats me like a lady."

"Where'd you meet him?"

"A friend from the bank set us up. She told me Denton'd

had some hard times back in Minnesota, but he's getting a fresh start out here, with his new landscaping business. When I told him about Eddie and Mario moving in he said he'd like to help them out. Maybe set up some basketball practice with them. Wasn't that sweet?"

"Come on, Mom," Eddie says. "Your turn."

Max rolls the dice and lands on Community Chest. She collects $10 for winning first prize in a beauty contest.

"You must have been wearing your camo outfit," I tease her.

Eddie rolls the dice and Max goes back to her conversation with Carmen.

"What kind of hard times did Denton have in Minnesota?"

"I don't know. All I know is I really like him, and he likes me. I'm tired of guys like Robert, and Mark, and Carlos. I want someone who respects me, who I'd like to spend the rest of my life with."

"And you think this Denton guy's it?" Max asks.

"I hope so. I just really want a partner in life."

"Well, good luck," Max says, turning her attention back to the game.

I can tell by the tone of Max's "good luck" that she thinks the chances are slim to none that Carmen has found Mr. Right. It's the same tone she uses when she wishes me luck on a test I've not studied for.

We're at that place in the game where you can predict who's going to win, but the people who aren't going to win don't want to give up. In this case, I'm going to win. Max would probably concede, but Eddie will play until his last dollar is gone.

"Let's get a picture," Mom says.

I get the camera from our room and snap Max and Eddie leaning in together, with Max holding the beauty contest winner card on her forehead. Then Max takes a picture of the two

of us, and Eddie takes a picture of me and Max. You know
how that goes when you're not paying for film – hundreds of
pictures.

The phone rings and Carmen rushes to answer. We've finished the game by the time she hangs up. She comes back in
all smiles.

"That was Denton," she says. "He's coming over after
awhile."

"Oh, good. I'll get to meet him before I leave," Max says,
handing Carmen the camera. Carmen poses us at three sides
of the Monopoly board, facing the camera. She snaps a picture, then looks in the viewer.

"Mario, lean in a little closer to your mom. Eddie, give us
that great smile of yours."

Another snap. Another look in the viewer.

"Umm, Mario, hold the dice like you're getting ready to
roll them."

Snap. View.

"Just one more," Carmen says, but I don't look up for the
last one. Enough is enough.

When Carmen and Max start talking about the family
in Mexico, Eddie and I go out back to play ping-pong. Carmen bought the table for her old boyfriend, Robert, because
he was always going to a friend's house to play ping-pong and
she wanted him to spend more time at her place. I guess her
plan didn't work. Anyway, the table's sort of warped now. The
handle on one of the paddles is split, and the one remaining
ping-pong ball doesn't have much bounce, but it's something
to do.

Eddie serves first. Because of his hand he's got this very
weird way of holding the paddle, but it works for him and he's
ahead three to two when it's my turn to serve. I hold the ball
and paddle out in front of me, take careful aim, fart, wait for
Eddie to crack up, then serve.

"No fair," Eddie says, laughing.

I do the same thing again. It's a technique that gets me five points in a row. Eddie's still laughing when he gets the serve, which doesn't do much for his game. I'm about to let loose with another one when I see this blue pick-up truck turn into the driveway. It pulls up right next to the ping-pong table. A very tall guy in khaki pants and a blue knit shirt that matches the color of the truck gets out and walks over to me.

"Yo. I'm Denton," he says, sticking his hand out. "Frank Denton, but everybody calls me Denton."

"Mario," I say, shaking hands with him.

The guy's got huge hands and a crunching grip he doesn't mind using, and he's got to be way over six feet tall. He walks around the table to Eddie.

"I'm Denton," he says, offering his hand.

Eddie sticks his stub-hand out. Denton takes it without a second glance and gives what I hope is a gentler handshake.

Denton goes back to the truck for a grocery bag. When he closes the door I notice the "LUSH LANDSCAPING" sign printed across it in big white letters.

"Look at this," he says, pulling a big bunch of broccoli from the bag. "One of my customers has more vegetables in his garden than he can possibly eat. This stuff is delicious, not like that stuff you get in the stores."

I have a hard time coupling the words "delicious" and "broccoli."

"Your serve," I remind Eddie.

"You boys ever play any basketball?"

"I'm more into soccer," I say.

"Hey, I can give you a few basketball tips that'd put you right into the A team."

"That's okay. I'm pretty busy with soccer."

"Soccer. Basketball. I guess it's your choice. Basketball's a better game though. Requires more skill. I played pro for two years, until I hurt my knee and the doc said if I didn't give it up I'd end up in a wheelchair."

"What team?" I ask.

"A small team in Minneapolis. You wouldn't have heard of it, but I'd been scouted out by the Lakers. I was two days away from signing a contract when this happened," Denton says, rubbing his left knee.

"Tough luck," I say.

"How about you, Eddie, you like basketball?"

"Yeah," Eddie says, all smiles.

That's news to me. The last I heard, he thought basketball was stupid and he only ever wanted to play soccer. Like me.

"I want tips," Eddie says.

"Sure, Kid. We'll put a hoop up on the garage and get down to business. I understand you're going to be living here. I guess we'll be seeing a lot of each other. I'm here fairly often myself . . . See you boys later."

Denton carries his bag of groceries into the house.

"You ever gonna serve?" I ask Eddie.

He slams one over, which I miss – the next one, too. I don't exactly know why I'm all of a sudden in such a bad mood, but I am. I don't exactly know why I don't like Denton, either, but I don't. Was it his crushing handshake? His attitude about soccer? His bag of broccoli? Maybe it doesn't have anything to do with Denton. Maybe it's just that Max is leaving and we're stuck here.

"Let's go in," I say to Eddie.

"But the game's not over."

"It'll soon be dark," I say, putting my paddle on the table and walking back to the house. Eddie follows.

Denton, Carmen, and Max are in the living room, talking about the broccoli.

"It's really good with cheese sauce," Denton says.

Max sees us come in and smiles. "If you can get these two clowns to eat broccoli you'll be a miracle worker."

We all laugh, but then Denton goes into this lecture about

how broccoli has all these antioxidants and everybody should eat broccoli, blah, blah, blah, and then he starts talking about what a great vegetable garden his client has, beets, beans, onions, kale (whatever that is), carrots, radishes . . .

"Hey, why don't I just take you to see this place?" he says.

"I'd love to see it," Carmen says.

"No thanks," Max says. "We've still got some details to take care of here, and I want to get to bed early tonight."

"I'll tell you goodbye now," Max says, going over to Carmen and giving her a big hug. "Thank you again, for watching out for my boys."

"That's what sisters are for," Carmen says.

Max grabs the camera to get a picture of them before they leave.

"No pictures," Denton says, turning his back to her.

"It'll only take a second," Max says. "Just stand there by the door."

Carmen stands close to Denton, smiling for the picture, but before Max can snap it, Denton's slipped out the door.

"Oops," Carmen says. "I forgot. Denton told me he hates to have his picture taken."

Max and Eddie and I watch an ancient "Leave it to Beaver" rerun and start another Monopoly game. We play until past eleven – something Max has never ever let Eddie do on a school night. But she's never ever left us for a war zone before, either.

5

At 5:30 in the morning, Max comes into our room and wakes us up. She sits at the foot of my bed, facing me and Eddie.

"I've got to go now," she says. "Email me every day! Send pictures!"

"We will," I say.

"Promise?"

"Promise."

"I want to know all of the details of your lives, just like I would if I were home. I'll email you, too, whenever I can, and I'll call when I can. Take care of each other. Don't ever forget how much I love you. If you're ever feeling bad, or things are in the pits, just tell yourselves, 'Maximum Mom is out there somewhere sending megatons of love my way.' Everyday, every hour, every minute, I'll be sending love your way."

We get up and walk with her to the front door. She pulls us both close and holds us tight in one last long hug, then hoists her duffel bag over her shoulder and opens the door.

Eddie makes a last minute lunge at her, holding on with all his might.

"Don't go, Mommy," he cries.

I reach around Eddie to hug her again, too, then I peel him away. We watch from the front door as she gets into her friend's car. One last wave, and she's gone – down the street, around the corner, and out of sight. Tears run down my cheeks like giant raindrops. And Eddie's crying so hard, with such a high, piercing sound, the neighbors' dogs start howling.

When I get back from school in the afternoon, Eddie's standing in the driveway, watching Denton bolt the basketball hoop to the garage.

"Mario! Guess what? We're getting a basketball hoop!"

"I can see that."

Denton pulls at the hoop to be sure it's secure, then steps off the ladder.

"Let's give it a test. Where's your basketball?" he asks me.

"We don't have a basketball."

"No basketball?" he says, like I'd told him we didn't own toothbrushes, or some other necessity of life.

"We could use your soccer ball," Eddie says to me.

"First lesson," Denton says to Eddie. "Nothing works with basketball except a regulation basketball. Practice with a soccer ball? Makes about as much sense as practicing with that ping-pong ball over there – messes with your form."

"But we don't have a basketball," Eddie says.

"Well, we'll just have to fix that, won't we?" Denton smiles at Eddie. "Let's go get one."

"Now?" Eddie says.

"You know a better time?"

Eddie runs to catch up with Denton, who is already getting into his truck.

"Coming, Mario?" Denton asks.

"I've got to be at work in fifteen minutes," I tell him.

"See you later then," he says.

I see him reach over and secure Eddie's seat belt and watch them back out the driveway. Eddie's got this huge grin on his face and I think he's probably running through his mental joke file, getting ready to entertain Denton.

It seems strange, walking back to Carmen's after work, instead of to our old apartment. Eddie's in his pajamas, sitting at our study table, drawing cartoon characters with some special colored pencils Max gave him just before she left. I'm still amazed at how fast he draws, and how he manages such detail with his three-stubbed hand.

Eddie draws some of the same characters over and over again. One of the first ones he came up with was "Schimba." It has some Simba characteristics.

When he first showed me this character, I'd asked him why he didn't just name the character Simba.

"Because he's half cat and half human, so the "c" in his name is for cat, and the "h" is for human," he'd said.

Besides Schimba, Eddie's got a "Schar" character, and a "Phwumbaa," too. You probably already figured out that Schar is the half-cat half-human equivalent of Scar. But in case you're not as much of a "Lion King" scholar as my brother, I'll just tell you that Phwumbaa is his half-human, half-warthog guy. Eddie likes to use them to practice his jokes. He always uses "Schimba" for elephant jokes. Like he'll hold the Schimba drawing up in front of his face and say in his lion cub voice, "Why are elephants big, grey and wrinkled?"

Then he picks up the Phwumbaa drawing and answers in his deep warthog voice, "Have you ever tried ironing one?"

He does those big-eyed kids, too, like in the *manga* books – big round faces with big round eyes. All of his cartoons are bright with color – background, foreground and everywhere in-between. If I tried to put that much color on a page it would be a mess, but Eddie makes it all look good.

I look over Eddie's shoulder for a few minutes, then get my notebook from my backpack and check the assignment page. The first day of school, and already we've got homework. I drag my government textbook out and open it to chapter one.

"Mario?"

"That's me."

"Where do you think Mommy is right now?"

"Well . . . she's been gone from here . . . " I pause to count the hours from 5:30 to now. "She's been gone from here about fifteen hours, so, I don't know. Maybe she's flying over the ocean somewhere now. I'm not sure."

"She's not in Iraq yet?"

"She could be, I guess."

"Do you think she was in Iraq by 4:00 this afternoon?"

"I doubt it."

"'Cause when Denton took me to Target for a basketball he was listening to the news and it said four people were killed in Iraq today."

I close my government book and look at him. He's got that scrunched up worried look on his face.

"She wasn't there yet. Besides, she says she's going to a safe place."

"For sure she wasn't there yet?"

"For sure."

I'm also sure I'm out of the mood for homework.

"Let's turn the lights out," I say to Eddie. "We were up really early this morning."

I turn off the lights, strip down to my underwear, and lay on top of the bed. It's too hot to get under the covers. The crickets are click-click-clicking outside the window. I like hearing them. All the years we were living in our upstairs apartment, I was missing the crickets' songs, and I didn't even know it until just now.

I remember the night my dad left us. My mom had just told him she was pregnant and he was hella mad. I was watching television and they were arguing out in the kitchen, but my dad was so loud I heard everything he was saying.

"I didn't even want the first one," he yelled, "and now you're trying to shove another kid off on me?"

Even though I was only seven, I could figure out who he meant by "the first one." It shouldn't have surprised me to hear that he hadn't wanted me – he didn't exactly treat me like I was a national treasure. Still, hearing it like that made me feel kind of trembly inside. I went into my room and curled up on my bed, listening in the dark to his angry talk.

I don't remember the rest of what they said that night, except he told Max he wanted her to "get rid of it." She had a choice. She could either keep him or keep the baby. After a while, I stopped listening to their voices and listened instead to the high, steady hum of crickets clicking outside my window. I liked that sound. There was no hate in it. I drifted off to sleep, comforted by the humming, clicking crickets. When I woke up in the morning, my dad was gone. A while later, we got Eddie. Like Max always says, it was an excellent exchange. Eddie turned out to be a lot more fun than Dad ever was. According to Max, Eddie's a throwback to her Puerto Rican grandfather who had bright blue eyes that got all sparkly when he was happy, which was almost all the time as far as Max ever knew. Like Eddie.

"Mario?"

"What?"

"Denton says I'm getting really good at basketball."

"Good."

"I like it better than soccer."

Maybe that shouldn't irritate me, but it does. I mean, I've been playing soccer with Eddie since he was barely able to walk. And he was always pestering me, show me this, show me that, I want to be as good as you. And one day of basketball tips with Denton, and he doesn't like soccer anymore?

"Mario?"

"What!"

"Denton's really good."

"Whatever! Just listen to the crickets, would you, and go to sleep?"

"Are you sure Mommy wasn't in Iraq at four o'clock this afternoon?"

"Positive," I say.

First thing in the morning, we take a few pictures and attach them to an email for Max.

From: Mario Barajas <mario3@yoohoo.com>
Date: September 13, 7:02 AM
To: Maria_27@hitmail.net
Subject: what's up?

hey, maxi-mom! what's up? how was the trip? first day of school went fine. i know if u were here you'd ask me what class i liked best, and what I liked least, so i'll tell u i like peer communications best, and government least. walker's in two of my classes and i know right now what you're gonna say-- stay away from trouble--don't sit near walker. i'll keep that in mind. here's eddie.

"Hey Eddie. Come write your joke for Max."

"I'll just tell it to you, and you write it," Eddie says.

"No, come on. You write it."

Carmen comes into the room and scoots me off the computer chair without as much as an "excuse me." I know it's her chair, and her computer, but still . . .

"Tell me your joke, Sweetheart. I'll write it for you."

"Okay," Eddie says, giving me a "nyah nyah nyah nyah

nyah" look and sidles up close to Carmen.

"Ask her why mother kangaroos hate rainy days."

Carmen types the question out quickly, then waits for more.

"Why do mother kangaroos hate rainy days?" she asks.

"Because the kids have to play inside!"

Carmen and Eddie both crack up at that, then Eddie dictates a bunch of other stuff about how Denton's teaching him how to be really good at basketball, and how after school today he gets to go to the fair with Denton.

I get into the shower, making the water hot enough to sting. I'll tell you one thing, Max would never baby Eddie like that, typing his emails for him.

Walker catches up with me after sixth period Friday afternoon.

"8:00 show time tonight. First four episodes of OC. Loge seating. Come early for a swim. Jenna'll be there so suck an Altoid."

Walker's got a thing for those Altoid mints that come in little tin boxes. He says he and Courtney never kiss without first popping Altoids. Like I care? But he's always giving me advice about how to "move things along in the Jenna department." He says I've got to stay Altoid kissable, just in case. Walker's been a lot more successful with girls than I have, so I listen to his advice.

"I've got to work until eight," I say.

"Whatever. But if you want the prime seat next to Jenna, the earlier the better."

Walker's house has this amazing surround-sound home theatre, with a screen that covers one whole wall in their den, and it's like movie festival time every weekend. Walker's girlfriend, Courtney, is always over there, and sometimes Jenna comes with her. If I wasn't working so much, trying to pay for the car insurance, I'd be hanging out at Walker's a lot.

From the time I get there until about seven, Java Jive is crammed with people wanting every kind of coffee drink ever invented. Then all of a sudden the place empties out. Sammy and Leticia and I wipe everything down, restock counter supplies, and then stand around watching the ceiling fans turn.

Sammy says, "You two may as well leave if you want."

I get my apron off and sign out before Sammy can change his mind. It's still hot out but I don't care. I jog all the way to Walker's. Most of the soccer team is already there, along with half the girls from drill team. A bunch of people are playing water volleyball, and Walker's fat bulldog, Rhino, is barking at the ball like it's some kind of threat to the property. It's not exactly the intimate foursome I'd imagined.

"Mario! It's about time you showed up," Walker yells across the patio at me.

"Borrow trunks?" I yell back.

"Sure. In the pool house."

I poke around in a giant straw basket of loaner bathing suits. Just when I think I'm going to be stuck with a Speedo, I find one of my own that I must have left here earlier in the summer. I change and go out to where Walker and Courtney are sitting at the edge of the pool, dangling their feet in the water. Jenna and Trevor, another guy from the soccer team, are floating in pool chairs a few feet away. Jenna flashes me a big smile. I smile back.

"You're just in time to be the tie breaker," she says. "Come on over."

She doesn't have to ask twice. I sit down next to Walker at the edge of the pool, about as close to Jenna as I can get without jumping in. I dangle my feet in the cool water, giving them a refreshing break after my hot, four mile jog.

"What's the fastest animal in the world?" Jenna says. "Two of us think it's one animal and the other two of us think something else."

"Ask Jeeves," I say, which gets a big laugh from Jenna. That's one of the things I really like about Jenna. She's always laughing and happy.

"We're not asking Jeeves," Walker says. "It's an opinion poll, and you, you lucky dude, you get the final opinion."

"I say it's the cheetah," Jenna says.

"Me, too," Courtney says.

"Walker and I say it's the gazelle," Trevor says.

"So, come on Mario. What do you say?" Jenna asks.

"The hummingbird," I say.

Jenna laughs.

Walker groans.

"Hummingbirds can't run," he says.

"You said fastest, you didn't say anything about running."

"No, but I said animal. A hummingbird's not exactly an animal."

"So if you're playing that twenty questions game, and the subject is hummingbird, and you've got to say it's animal, vegetable, or mineral, what do you say?" I challenge.

"Right. You say animal," Jenna says, taking my side.

"That's bunk!" Trevor says, laughing.

Jenna splashes Trevor, who dumps her from her pool chair. Courtney jumps in and dumps Trevor. Walker and I jump in, just because. After a time of the five of us splashing and dunking and yelling and screaming, somehow Jenna and I each end up floating on a pool chair. The volleyball game is ended. Courtney and Walker snuggle up on the chaise, in their after-Altoid mode. Trevor is nowhere to be seen. As Jenna's chair drifts slightly away from mine, I pull it back toward me.

It's getting dark now, and the outdoor lights have just come on. Everything's automated at the Wheeler house. Lights come on and go off by themselves, as does the air conditioner, the heater, and the coffeemaker that sits on the counter in the kitchen. Even Rhino's food is released automatically at the same time each day.

I tell Jenna how way back when Walker and I were in the second grade, I used to like coming to his house just to watch stuff happen by itself. I'd be the first one up in the morning to see the coffeemaker start up, and long before dark I'd sit outside waiting for the lights to come on. Oh, yeah, and there was a lamp in the living room that was on a timer. I liked to watch for that, too.

Jenna laughs. "You must have been a weird little kid," she says.

She says this like it's a compliment, not a criticism.

"How about you? Were you a weird little kid?"

"I'm still a weird kid."

We both laugh at that.

"I only came over tonight because I thought you'd be here." I tell her, surprised that such words even escaped from my mouth.

She smiles. "I hoped you'd be here, too."

While we float around next to each other, I try to think of something else to say. All I can think of, though, is "I want to jump your body," and I'm afraid that might be a little too crude.

I show off my jack-knife dive. Trevor follows me and does a total belly-flop. So far, so good.

Most of the crowd leaves for another party across town, but I stay at Walker's with Courtney and Jenna. At the end of the evening, after we've watched the "OC" shows, and asked Jeeves (it's the cheetah) and helped Walker clean up around the pool area, Courtney gets a call from her mother, reminding her of her curfew time.

I walk with Jenna out to Courtney's car.

"Can I call you tomorrow?"

She rummages around in her purse, finding a pen but no paper.

"Here," I say, holding my hand out to her.

She holds my hand steady and writes her number in bold

letters in the palm of my extended hand.

I guess to someone like Walker, who's had lots of girl-friends, the whole phone number writing thing wouldn't be a big deal. But to me it is, and my right hand, the one with the number, throbs with heat and hope the whole way back to Carmen's house.

6

Carmen's sitting in the kitchen, in her bathrobe, when I come through the back door. From the look on her face, she hasn't stayed up to offer warm milk and cookies for a nighty-night snack.

"You're late!"

I glance at the clock. It's barely past midnight. She calls that late?

"What do you mean, I'm late?"

She points to the list on the refrigerator, where it says "Mario's curfew, 11:00."

I point to the line that says "weekends negotiable."

"But you didn't negotiate! You didn't even bother to call!"

"Gimmee a break! I didn't know I was supposed to negotiate!"

"Well you are supposed to negotiate. Anytime you're going to be out past curfew, you call, damn it! That's just being courteous."

"Okay!" I say.

"Oh, I really don't like that tone, Mr. Mario Barajas. You're grounded for two weeks! Maybe that will help you remember the rules!"

Carmen stomps out of the kitchen, down the hall and into her bedroom, slamming the door behind her.

I go into the living room and flip on the TV, hoping for – I don't know what – something distracting. I get war news. I can't deal with that! Wrestling – that works for a while but then the meanest guy starts reminding me of Carmen, so I shut off the TV and go to bed, my head still spinning.

Grounded for two weeks for getting in just after midnight? That's so extreme! Maybe I should have negotiated but Carmen's like soooo over the top! I'll be eighteen in six months, and she's treating me like I'm some twelve-year old!

I knew it would be like this. She's never liked me and she'll use any excuse she can to make things hard for me. I oughta get out of here – move in with Walker. When Max first heard she was shipping out, Walker's parents said I could move in over there. They wanted me to stay with them. They think I'm a good influence on Walker, which tells you how bad Walker is.

It would have been great to stay there, with the ongoing film festival and girls in and out all the time. If I was living at Walker's and Jenna came over with Courtney, maybe we'd just happen to sit down next to each other on the big leather sofa in the den, and maybe we'd sink down into it, and maybe . . .

But if I stayed at Walker's, that would have left Eddie alone at Carmen's. I couldn't do that, because even though Carmen likes Eddie, she's still hella uptight. And even if Eddie irritates me sometimes, we're brothers, and brothers have to stick together. So I can't exactly move in with Walker and leave Eddie here, especially since I promised Max I'd look out for him.

I close my eyes and concentrate on the sound of the crickets. Even though I've memorized Jenna's number, I leave my right hand outside the covers, so the number won't rub off in my sleep.

All morning long, at work, all I can think about is calling Jenna. That's maybe not a good thing, because I gave this guy an extra twenty in change while Jenna was on my mind. Luckily, he was an honest guy and gave it back, otherwise it would have been twenty out of my pocket.

The trouble is, as much as I want to call her, I can't think of anything to say. At my morning break I stand near the phone, trying to think of something that would come after "hello." I do the same thing at my lunch break.

No one's home when I get back to Carmen's after work. I change clothes and go for a run. I run a lot, mainly because I need to maintain stamina and endurance for soccer season. On my run I talk to myself about not being a wuss with girls in general, and Jenna in particular. When I get back to Carmen's I jog straight to the phone and call Jenna's number, even though I'm still clueless about what to say. Jenna answers on the first ring.

"Hi, this is Mario."

"Oh. Hi Mario."

"Hi."

"Hi."

"Well . . . I just thought I'd call and say hi."

"Yeah. Well . . . thanks . . ."

"Well . . . Okay . . . See you later . . . Bye."

Dang! I need to take lessons from Walker, or someone who knows how to talk to girls! Last night I thought Jenna sort of liked me, but she's probably changed her mind after that lame phone call.

I just sit there by the phone, replaying the conversation in my mind, over and over and over, trying to come up with witty remarks that I might have said. I've been sitting there long enough that my sweaty tee shirt is all stiff and dry when the phone rings. It's Jenna.

"Hey, I wasn't through talking to you," she says, laughing. "I had to call Walker to get your number."

"Yeah?" Another of my brilliant comebacks.

"Are you a shy-guy or what?"

"Sort of," I admit. "With girls, anyway."

She laughs again. "Shy guys are hot."

"I'm really, really shy."

Pretty soon we're both laughing and talking like it's the easiest thing in the world. I tell her about my plans to get into the fire-fighting program, and she tells me about how cool our senior year will be – all the parties and dances and big graduation events. I've never been much into that stuff, but maybe it would be okay, with Jenna.

I've barely hung up with Jenna when the phone rings again. It's Walker.

"Way to go, Dude!"

"What?"

"You know! Jenna called me to get your phone number. You better go buy a case of Altoids because your dull, sexless life is about to change!"

"Come on, Walker. We talked for about five minutes. I don't think that's grounds for a case of Altoids."

"More like twenty minutes, you mean. I know, because I've been trying to call you for at least fifteen minutes and all I got was a busy signal."

"Walker . . ."

"No shit, Dude, I'm telling you it means a lot when a girl like Jenna goes out of her way to get some dude's phone number."

"Maybe it does, and maybe it doesn't," I say, not wanting to get my hopes up and end up all broken hearted.

"Trust me, it means something. I know about these things."

To hear Walker talk, you'd think all the girls at Hamilton High have the hots for him. The thing is, that's close to the truth. So maybe it does mean something.

In the steaming hot shower I think about Jenna. The sound of her voice, her laughter, the soft warmth of her hand when she steadied mine to write her number, how she thinks shy guys are hot, and . . . it wasn't only the shower that was hot and steamy. I used my left hand, because part of Jenna's number is still on my right palm.

I try not to do that thing too often, even though Walker says it's just good practice. But sometimes, like tonight, I can't help it. It just feels too good.

I'm watching some lame sitcom, wishing Carmen had cable, when Eddie comes in with Carmen and Denton. He's all jazzed about winning a cheapo plastic prize playing miniature golf.

"I beat everyone, even Denton!" he says, all sparkly eyed.

"Cool."

"Denton says maybe next time we can go to a real golf course, 'cause I'm too advanced for miniature golf."

"Great," I say.

Carmen walks over to where I'm sitting and looks down at me.

"I told you, you are grounded!" she says.

"So? I'm here aren't I?" I say, my eyes still on the TV.

"We tried to call all evening long and the phone was always busy."

I look up at her. "I was talking to some friends. Is there some law against that?"

Denton comes over to stand beside Carmen. He totally towers over her.

"You're grounded, Mario! No phone calls when you're grounded!"

"That's bunk!"

"You better drop that attitude, Buster," Denton says.

I don't even look at him. It's bad enough that Carmen's my official guardian. I don't have to follow orders from some has-been, maybe never-been, basketball player.

"Keep it up and you'll be grounded for a month!" Carmen says.

"Whatever," I say and go back into our room.

I stand at the window, looking out into the night. The moon is bright and full and I wonder if it's a full moon where Max is right now. I'm trying to feel the megatons of love she's sending my way, but all I can think about is how Carmen's being such a bitch! No phone calls because I'm grounded? That's total bullshit!

After too long staring out at the moon and thinking over and over how I hate being here, I get out my books and check my assignment sheet. It's only the end of the first week of school and I'm already behind in my homework. I really need to get caught up. I've got to maintain at least a "C" average to play soccer, and I've got to do better than that to qualify for the pre-firefighting course the captain wants me to take next semester.

For a while, back in middle school, Max kept talking to me about being a lawyer, like my cousin Vincent. By the time I was a sophomore in high school, though, it was pretty obvious that I wouldn't be getting lawyerly grades. Besides, all I've ever wanted to do was be a firefighter. It may sound sort of lame, but I want to do something to help people. And I know for sure I couldn't last in a job where I was inside some office all day. Whatever the reason, I just know that's what I want to be.

I've already done pretty well in some preliminary tests at

Hamilton Heights C.C. Not only that, but I passed a tough physical training course that's like a requirement for the certification program. Captain Shelby, the veteran fireman who heads things up, told me I was their top candidate – "a shoo-in for acceptance," he said. So I guess I'd better get serious about keeping up with my homework.

I'm halfway through answering the questions for chapter one of the government assignment when Eddie comes in.

"Why's Aunt Carmen mad at you?" Eddie asks.

"'Cause she's a witch."

"She says you're not following the rules. Mom said we were supposed to follow Aunt Carmen's rules."

I put down my pen and turn to face him.

"I am following the rules. Don't you start with me."

Eddie gets into his pajamas and climbs into bed.

"Hey, Eddie. Brush your teeth."

"I'm tired."

"No, go on. You have to follow the rules, too."

He drags himself out of bed and goes into the bathroom. I pick up my pen and try to focus on question number four. I hear the racecar toothbrush make one, quick, vroom, and Eddie's back to bed.

"I want Mommy to come home," Eddie says.

"No shit."

"You're not supposed to say those words."

"No SHIT! You're supposed to brush your teeth for at least three minutes, too."

I reread the page where I think the answer to number four is.

"I can't sleep with the light on," Eddie says.

"Damn it, Eddie! Just pull the pillow over your head and go to sleep!"

A few minutes later, still stuck on number four, I look over at Eddie. He's got his head under the pillow. His right arm is hanging over the side of the bed, and I can see he's got a picture of Max clutched between his stubby fingers. I can tell by the way he's breathing, that kind of catchy way, he's trying to keep from crying.

I look one more time for the answer to number four, then give it up. Maybe it's the full moon, or maybe it's for real, but life doesn't seem so great to me right now.

Under the desk lamp I can still see the faint letters of Jenna's number. At least there's that.

"**D**id your mom tell you I called last night?"

"She's just my aunt – not my mom. But yeah, she said you called. I wasn't really sleeping."

Jenna just smiles and I get all funny feeling inside.

"Maybe I'll stop by your work tonight."

"Cool," I say. Then the bell rings and we go to our seats on opposite sides of the room.

Walker, who sits in the next row right across from me, gives me a nudge when I sit down. Out comes the tin of Altoids. It's way past time for Walker to get some new material.

At exactly 7:30, Jenna walks through the Java Jive door. She looks straight at me and smiles.

Two people are waiting in line and I finish with them in a hurry. Jenna steps up to the counter and asks for a blended vanilla mocha cappuccino with whipped cream. I show off my specialty drink skills by having her cappucccino ready in less than a minute – a personal record.

Sammy gestures to the top shelf, which needs to be refilled with harvest season coffee.

"I'll be back in a sec," I tell Jenna.

I rush to the back, grab armloads of coffee and stack them on the high shelf before Jenna has a chance to finish her drink.

"I'm off in ten minutes," I tell her. "Can you wait?"

"Sure."

After work Jenna gives me a ride back to Carmen's. We sit in front of the house, talking. It's so easy to talk with Jenna – not like any other girl I've ever known. I tell her that because, well, it's easy. I tell her about Max having to go off to Iraq, and about how I didn't want to move in with Carmen.

"I'd like to move in with my aunt," Jenna says. "My mom is a total control freak."

As if to prove the point, Jenna's cell phone rings.

"But Mom, you said nine-thirty."

"But . . ."

"Okay."

She ends the call and puts the phone back in her purse.

"See what I mean? She tells me I can have the car until 9:30, and then she calls at 9:00 saying to come home right now. It's all about controlling me."

"My Aunt Carmen likes a lot of control, too," I say. "I try to stay out of her way."

"That doesn't work with my mom. She's always in my face."

"Pretty face," I say.

She smiles. "Is that shy-guy talk?"

"Maybe I'm not so shy with you," I say, sliding a little closer to her. She puts her head on my shoulder and sighs.

"I've got to go or I'll be grounded."

"Yeah, okay," I say, moving closer still.

"Really."

I reach over and open the door.

"Thanks for the ride," I say, getting out of the car.

She smiles, waves, and then she's gone. Why didn't I kiss her? I could have leaned over and kissed her but I didn't. Why not? What's wrong with me? Way far into the night I relive the scene in the car – how I could have put my arm around her, and pulled her toward me, and kissed her. At least I could have kissed her.

7

For weeks after Max leaves, Eddie and I keep finding hidden treasures with notes. On the first cold morning after school starts, I reach into my jacket pocket and pull out a cellophane-wrapped oatmeal-raisin cookie. "For the anti-chocolate maxi-brother" is written across the front of the wrapping. That's because Max, unlike nearly everyone else in the world, understands that I hate chocolate.

When Eddie's digging around clear at the bottom of his backpack one day, he finds a watch with a timer and an alarm. "Timing is everything to a comedian," the note said.

There were other hidden treasures, little things, but things that made it seem like Max was still with us in a way. I guess we've found all the hidden treasure by now, though, because it's been a long time since anything new has turned up.

After being at Carmen's awhile, the best I can say is that there's always food in the refrigerator and she's not home a lot. When she is home, she's the devil rule monitor. Take this morning, for instance – Wednesday. I thought Carmen was finished in the bathroom – she'd already taken a shower. So I get in there at around ten minutes to seven. I'm in the shower for all of about thirty seconds when she starts yelling at me to get out.

"It's not seven," she screams. "You don't get the bathroom until seven!"

"I thought you were through," I yell back.

"I've got to dry my hair!"

She bangs on the door.

"All I'm asking is that I have my own bathroom between six-thirty and seven. Is that so hard?"

I finish as fast as I can, wrap a towel around my waist and rush past her to our "bedroom."

Eddie is lying in bed, staring at the ceiling.

"Better get up," I tell him, with a nod to the clock. "Carmen's on one again."

"Wipe up that water you tracked down the floor, Mario!" she yells from the hallway.

I make sure our door is closed tightly and then I let loose with a rumble.

"My comment to Carmen," I say.

I expect to get a big laugh from Eddie, but he hardly seems to notice. Could he be outgrowing his sense of fart humor? Hard to believe.

I pull on some clothes, go back out to the hall, wipe up the few drops of water that sent Carmen over the edge, then go back to our room. Eddie's up now, getting dressed.

"Hey, Eddie, I'm emailing Max. You got anything to add?"

"No, it's okay," he says.

"No jokes?" I ask.

He shakes his head.

I hate when Carmen reads over my shoulder when I email Max, so I always wait until I hear her back out the driveway before I turn on the computer. Emailing Max is part of my morning routine now – as automatic as brushing my teeth.

I log in using the password I created last week, after I figured out Carmen's been getting into our email stuff. I'd been kicked back watching TV when she came in from the market. Before she even put her grocery bags down she told me, "You'd better go read *To Kill a Mockingbird* or you'll never get finished on time."

Right then I knew she'd been reading our emails because I'd written to Max that I was a little behind in the *To Kill a Mockingbird* assignment and having a hard time getting into it. I'd never even told Carmen what I was supposed to be reading, and I always kept my books in my backpack unless I was using them, which honestly wasn't very often, so how did she even know what I was supposed to be reading unless she'd been snooping around in our sent emails? I guess it was kind of stupid of me to be using my birth date in the first place. Anyway, I set up a new password — a random mix of letters and numbers. Not that we're writing anything to be ashamed of. I just don't like Carmen sticking her nose in our private business.

Clicking the icon for "new," I write:

From: Mario Barajas <mario3@yoohoo.com>
Date: October 28 7:06 AM
To: Maria_27@hitmail.net
Subject: What's up?

Hey, Maxi-Mom! wasup? did you get our mac-n-cheese mix? guess what--i should be able to pay the car insurance in two more paychecks. cool, huh? things are okay here. i got a b on my government test. peer communications and computer science r ok but the rest are just the same-o-same-o. eddie's fine, but he's too lazy to add anything this morning. he got an a on his last math test. that's it. stay safe. megatons – mario

P.S. I've been running early every morning, so I'll be in shape when soccer starts.

There's plenty more I could write, like even though I got a B on my government test, I'm way behind in homework. My grades aren't all that great so far.

When Max left, she said she wanted to know everything we did while she was away. I'd like to tell her about Jenna, how much I like her, and how happy I am that she likes me, too. But I don't know how to say any of that in an email. And I could tell her what a witch Carmen is, and that Eddie had to stay after school last week because he hit some kid in the nose. I mean, Eddie? Who's never been in a fight in his whole life?

Speaking of Eddie, I usually meet him after school on Tuesdays, my day off. Sometimes I go to his classroom to see Ms. Sumner. When I stopped in last week, she said Eddie seemed "a bit preoccupied," and wanted to know if everything was all right with him. After, I got to thinking about it. He's not telling many jokes these days. Maybe he's not laughing as much, either. And there was that fight. But I can't really say any of that stuff to Max, because I don't want to worry her, so I just keep things short.

I re-read my message, attach the latest pictures, and click "send."

I'd like to take a minute to check out Walker's new blog, but Carmen'd have a fit if she caught me using the Internet.

"You can only use my computer for email to your mother," she told me when we first moved in – like it wasn't enough to have it all spelled out on the refrigerator.

"I don't want you doing any of that Internet porn stuff in my house," she'd said. Like I'm some kind of a horn dog or something. But that's Carmen. She expects the worst of me. When it comes to her Mr. Perfect boyfriend though, she's blind. I bet she'd be surprised if she did a history of websites visited on old Denton's laptop. I got a glimpse of something on his screen the other day when he was hanging out here waiting for Carmen to get home from work. It was some kind of "tender young bods" thing that he closed as soon as I came into the room.

I get the orange juice carton from the refrigerator, shake it, and take a quick swig. Next I pour cereal into a bowl, cover it with milk, and flip on the TV. ". . . triggered a roadside IED killing twenty-three . . ." I quick switch to cartoons.

In case you don't know, IED stands for Improvised Explosive Device, and it's not nice. Max keeps telling us she's in a pretty safe place – not to worry. She says it's safer to be with the National Guard than with the Marines. Maybe so, but it scares me to hear about car bombs and suicide bombers and IEDs because I know someone's being killed, or maimed, and I really can't think about Max being blown to pieces. Except I just did.

I dump my cereal into the garbage disposal, rinse the bowl and put it in the dishwasher.

"Hey, Eddie," I yell. "What's taking you so long?"

No response. Stepping into the hallway to call him again, I hear the vroom-vroom of his toothbrush. I bang on the bathroom door.

"Come on. We gotta go."

"Just a sec!"

I shove my books into my backpack and check the clock. Eddie's toothbrush is still vrooming away.

"Let's go, Eddie! Max was only kidding about rotting teeth. I'm sure they're clean by now."

Finally, the sound of the toothbrush stops and Eddie comes out.

"Get something you can eat on the way."

He gets a fruit tart from the kitchen and shoves it into his jacket pocket. We barely get out the door when this skinny, half-grown cat comes winding its way around Eddie's legs, meowing in the loudest, most ear-piercing sound I've ever heard come out of any cat.

Eddie unwraps his fruit tart and starts feeding small pieces of it to the cat.

"You know this cat?" I ask.

"Blue," Eddie says.

"Blue?"

"For his eyes."

I take a closer look. Definitely blue eyes. I've never seen a cat with blue eyes before.

It lets out a stream of piercing meows and Eddie hands it another small bite.

"You shouldn't be feeding him."

Eddie shrugs and gives the cat another piece.

"C'mon Eddie. It's hard enough to get along with Carmen as it is. She'll be totally stressed if this cat keeps hanging around."

"He's hungry," Eddie says, crumbling up the rest of the fruit tart and dropping it onto the cement.

"Here you go, Blue Kitty."

The cat licks up every last, tiny crumb.

"Now what're you going to eat?"

"I'm not hungry," Eddie says. "Blue's hungry."

When we get to the corner where I turn off for Hamilton High Eddie starts in about how he doesn't want me to work late tomorrow night.

"I always work late on Thursday nights. That's my regular schedule," I tell him. "Why are you already thinking about tomorrow night, anyway?"

"Please," he says.

"Hey, it's good for me to get those hours. Pretty soon I can start using the car. I'll take us to the beach, and the mountains . . ."

"I wish Mommy'd come home," he says, and walks off toward his school.

Second period, PC, I take the sign-up sheet for our projects from Woodsy's desk. She's really Ms. Woods, but everyone calls her Woodsy. She's probably one of the best teachers here at Hamilton. You only have to be in her class for about five minutes to know she cares about people and treats everybody with respect. Anyway, I check the sign-up sheet to see what group Jenna has chosen.

Out of eight possibilities, binge drinking, teen pregnancy, drug abuse, abortion, new age restrictions on driver's licenses, compulsory military service, gun control and suicide, Jenna has written her name under the teen pregnancy category. If I were ranking topics of interest to me, teen pregnancy would rank last. But in a ranking of all of the girls in this school, or town, or world, Jenna Porter ranks first. I like her soooo much. So I add my name to the teen pregnancy list, just to be around Jenna.

Here's how things are with her now. She picks me up from work whenever she can get the car, which is usually a couple of times a week. We talk on the phone every night, even though Carmen has a thing about limiting calls to ten minutes and Jenna's mom says she'll take Jenna's phone away if she uses it to call boys. On weekends we hang out whenever we can. She's got an eleven o'clock curfew, though, and I work until nine, so it's not like constant togetherness. I'm saving like crazy to get the car insurance taken care of. Things will be easier for us when I'm able to use the car whenever I want to. And here's just one of the things I like about Jenna. She doesn't even care if I drive a beat-up old Jetta. She says she'll be happy just to be with me.

Without going into details about the night last week when we parked up in the foothills, or the time we were together at her house when no one was home, I'll just tell you that we're way past the kissing stage and I'm pretty happy about that. I've even started carrying condoms, just in case.

So anyway, I sign up for the teen pregnancy group, put the sign-up sheet back on Woodsy's desk, and take my seat in the back of the room next to Walker.

"What'd you sign up for?" he asks.

"Teen pregnancy."

He goes up to the desk, checks the list, laughs, and comes back.

"You're so transparent," he says, sliding back into his seat.

"And you're such a snoop . . . What'd you sign up for anyway?"

"Binge drinking. I'll do the research, then give a how-to demonstration."

"Better bring your barf bucket," I tell him.

Sometimes I wonder why Walker and I are still friends – he loves to get all sloshed up and I can't stand it. He's like a total rapper and I'm classic rock. His parents bought him a brand new Ford Mustang for his birthday and I've got to save up $500 before I even get to drive Max's beat up Jetta. We might not even be friends if we met now. Ten years of hanging around together though, that counts for something. And soccer. That counts, too.

I look over at Jenna who's talking and laughing with Courtney. Walker says after you've been with a girl for a while she doesn't look as good as she did at first. But when I look at Jenna I still see a girl who's drop-dead beautiful in a sweet sort of way, and who I'm in love with, in a horny sort of way.

Walker nudges my arm and looks in Woodsy's direction. I guess she's talking to me.

"I'm so pleased to see that you've chosen the teen pregnancy group, Mario," she says. "So many boys think teen pregnancy is only a girl's problem. I'm glad to see that at least two boys in this class know better. You and Norman will offer a broader perspective to that group."

Walker's head is on the desk, cradled in his hands. His

shoulders are shaking with silent laughter. He looks over long enough to mouth "Norman," then hides his head again, trying to stifle snorts of laughter. Some friend.

After class, on our way to government class, Walker's still laughing.

"You and Nerdy Norman, the two male experts on teen pregnancy! And all for the sake of Jenna," he says.

CHAPTER

8

I go straight from school to Java Jive. Usually I work until eight o'clock on Mondays, Wednesdays and Fridays. Tuesdays I'm off unless somebody calls in sick and I have to cover for them. Thursdays I work until ten. Sammy was true to his word about giving me more hours. Some days I even go in at four-thirty in the morning and work until it's time for school, then go back in the afternoon. Except for missing my morning run, I like to go in early because it gets me closer to the *La Bamba* insurance pay off.

Things are slow this evening, I guess because of the new Starbucks just around the corner from us. Walker comes in around 5:00. Luckily, Sammy's gone to pick up some supplies. He doesn't like Walker hanging around. Says Walker's a smart-ass, and smart-asses make his customers nervous.

Walker works at a McDonald's just a few blocks away. Part of the deal when his parents bought him the Mustang, was that he'd pay for his own gas, and half of the insurance, so even though they're rich, Walker has to work. His dad says it builds character.

"What's up?" I ask him.

"Break time – thought I'd see how things are going in the coffee trade."

"Dead."

"They're lined up around the block at Starbucks. Maybe you oughta go apply."

I get a whiff of Walker's breath.

"Researching your binge drinking report?"

He laughs. "How about that teen pregnancy topic? You getting together with Norman in the library?"

"Jenna and I are doing our own research," I tell him.

"You wish," he says.

Six customers come in together. Maybe they got tired of waiting in the Starbucks line. I step up to the counter and take their order.

"Back to the Golden Arches," Walker says, stopping by the condiment table before leaving.

After all six customers have their drinks – tall non-fat decaf latte, double-double espresso with whipped, iced caramel cappuccino, etc., I check the condiments. The sweetener packets are gone, replaced by McDonald's salt and pepper packets – Walker's idea of fun.

After work I grab four Java Jive cups, large size, and fill them with water. I wedge them into a cardboard Java Jive tray and sign out. I keep my dorky little Java Jive cap on and walk down the street to McDonald's. Walker is at the front counter, calling out orders. He gives me a quick nod when I come in, then does a sidelong glance at Trina, one of the managers. The glance means he can't talk now because Trina's watching. That's okay. I didn't come to talk. I walk to the middle of the room, carrying my phony coffee containers, then, in my loudest possible voice I yell,

"Walker Wheeler! Walker Wheeler!"

I look all around, as if I don't know who Walker is, then

yell again. "Walker Wheeler! Your lattes are here!"

Walker acts like he doesn't hear me. Trina stomps over to me, red-faced. I look at her name tag. "Oh, good," I say. "You're the manager. Will you please give these to Mr. Wheeler? It's the order he called in a few minutes ago."

I hold the tray out to her but she doesn't take it. I leave it on the table next to where she's standing.

"Thank you so much," I say, and walk out the door.

I'm not happy to see Denton's pick-up truck in the driveway when I turn the corner to Carmen's house. Maybe he's okay but something about the guy annoys me. Carmen thinks he's the answer to her prayers. And I'll admit he's nice to Eddie. He took him to the fair twice, which made Eddie pretty happy. And he takes him swimming, and out for ice cream and to play miniature golf. And he's always buying him stuff.

Really, the stuff he buys for Eddie isn't all that great. Like he knows Eddie likes art, so he bought him a set of watercolor paints, but they were the kind in a little plastic box with about five colors, like you'd give to a three-year-old. Denton acted like they were something fit for Van Gogh.

"Look at these," he'd said, taking the paint set out of the Wal-Mart bag. He opened the box. "Blue. Yellow. Green . . . ," he'd said, like Eddie didn't know his colors?

Eddie was polite. He thanked Denton and put the paint box back in the bag – said he was saving them for later. Yeah, I thought, like when he grows up and gets married and has a little rugrat to give them to. Well, that's just what I thought. It seems like Eddie really likes the attention, even if the gifts aren't so special.

Anyway, Denton hella bugs me. He talks like he knows everything, and he acts like he owns the place, even though it's Carmen who pays the rent.

I go around to the back door. That cat with the screechy

meow is hanging around again. It steps in front of me, winding around, meowing.

"I don't have anything for you," I say, reaching down to set it aside. Its ribs are sharp against the palm of my hand. I can't exactly blame Eddie for feeding it.

I ease quietly through the door, trying to slip into our room unnoticed. It doesn't work. I'm halfway down the hall when Denton calls to me. "Hey, Mario, come out here and show your aunt a little respect why don't you?"

I know it'll be a big hassle if I try to ignore him, so I go into the living room where Denton and Carmen are sprawled in front of the TV. They make a funny looking couple. Carmen's five feet tall, at the most, and Denton's about six-six, at the least. I still haven't found anyone who's heard of him from his supposedly pro basketball days, but he's got the height and hands of a basketball player. I'll give him that.

Denton also says he was a Green Beret, and an undercover agent. As of now he claims he's got all of these landscaping contracts with millionaire clients but I don't know when he ever has time to work 'cause it seems like he's always hanging around here. I think his major talent is bullshitting.

"Hey, Carmen," I say.

Denton pauses the DVD. "I don't get you," Denton says. "Your aunt here's giving you and your brother a roof over your heads, putting food on the table, and you can't even bother to say hello when you come in."

I glance at the wastebasket – three empty beer cans. Two empties are on the table in front of Carmen, and Denton's got a beer in his hand. Considering that Carmen never has more than one beer in an evening, I'm guessing Denton's had enough to increase his already large capacity for talking shit.

Last week with about the same number of empty beer cans in view, old Denton was going on and on about how he was going to join the vigilantes patrolling the California border and he'd shoot to kill any dirty Mexican trying to sneak across – saying how they come to this country and take jobs away from hardworking citizens, and they have all these kids that people like him have to pay taxes to educate, and blah, blah, blah.

The funny thing is, everybody in this house is Mexican, or at least Mexican-American. Carmen was even born in Mexico. But she just sits and listens to his trash. The most she ever says is, "Now, Honey . . ." She totally caters to him, too. She's got this big job at the bank, loan officer or something, and lots of times she works late. Denton, the supposedly big shot landscaping contractor who hardly ever works, waits around for Carmen to come home and fix dinner and then complains if it's not exactly what he wants. I'm not around here very much, but when I am it looks to me like he's a total parasite.

Anyway, I don't want another rant from him tonight.

"What's up?" I ask Carmen.

"The Dow Jones," Denton says, and starts laughing.

As Eddie would say, that's so funny I forgot to laugh.

"School okay?" Carmen asks.

"Fine."

Denton gets up off the couch and goes to the back door. "Shut up! Scat!" he yells to the still meowing cat.

Another meow.

He steps out onto the porch, stomps his foot, and comes back inside. "That goddamned cat's back again," he says.

"Honey, why don't you take it to the humane society tomorrow?"

"Why don't you?" he says.

Carmen looks surprised, or hurt, or something.

"You know I can't handle a cat! I'm so allergic I'd probably just stop breathing!"

Denton opens another can of beer.

"Yeah, well somebody around here's probably feeding it," Denton says.

"Mario! You'd better not be feeding that cat!" Carmen

says. "You know I'm allergic to cats!"

"I'm not feeding the cat!"

"It's not hanging around for the scenery," Denton says, laughing like he's just made the funniest joke of the century.

"I've got homework," I say.

"Well, you'd better get it done!" Carmen says. Like it was my idea to come out there for a chit-chat in the first place?

"What is it?" Denton asks me.

"Huh?"

"Your homework. Did I stutter?"

"Government, English. Math."

"I mean specifically."

"A current events thing, compare and contrast characters in a novel, and some exercise with prime numbers," I say, giving him the bare minimum.

"What's the current events thing?"

"Something about Iraq," I say.

He does what I know he'll do – starts spouting off about the "rag-heads" and the terrorists, and the Muslims and Osama and how we're really kickin' some butt now.

Right, I think. That's why Max isn't home yet. That's why twenty-three American soldiers were killed by insurgents yesterday, that's why Osama's still on the loose. I don't say anything, though, because it's always stupid to try to talk to a know-it-all like Denton, and it's way stupid when he's more than half drunk.

"Get to your homework," Carmen says. "And tell Eddie he'd better get to bed pretty soon."

"Yeah. See you tomorrow," I say, and escape back to our room.

Eddie's sitting on his bed, leaned back against the wall, drawing on his sketchpad.

"What's this?" I say, looking down at the drawing. "Darth Vader?"

"It's Mr. Nice," Eddie says.

"He looks more like Mr. Mean."

"Maybe he's nice and mean," Eddie says.

I think it's supposed to be a joke, but he doesn't crack a smile.

I watch him drawing for a few more minutes, then ask, "Do you have homework?"

"Done."

"I wish mine were," I say, taking my stuff out of my backpack and spreading it out on the other bed.

Max used to sit with us at the kitchen table while we did our homework. She'd check stuff over now and then, and after we'd been at it for a while she'd make a big batch of popcorn with melted butter. Real butter, not that stuff you get at the movies. Here, it would be weird to do our homework in the kitchen – Carmen's kitchen. We mostly stay in our room whenever we're home. At least I do. I guess Eddie hangs out with Carmen and Denton some. I'm not around that much to know.

"Hey, Eddie. What'd you have for dinner tonight?"

"Pizza," Eddie says, not looking up from his drawing.

"Where'd you eat?"

"Here," he says, pointing toward the foot of the bed where a paper plate with a piece of pizza crust on it sits on top of his math book.

"Didn't you eat with Carmen?"

"Carmen ate with Denton," he says.

Between Jenna, and work, and school, and keeping in shape for soccer, I guess I haven't been thinking much about how things are for Eddie. I watch him working away on his drawing, with what's left of his dinner at the foot of his bed, and I wonder if maybe he's kind of lonely these days.

"Hey, Buddy," I say, "are you having fun at school?"

He shrugs his shoulders.

"Ms. Sumner's pretty cool, isn't she?"

Another shrug of his shoulders. So be that way, I think. I

shuffle through my math notebook, looking for the assignment. Eddie reaches for the paper plate and tears the pizza crust into tiny pieces. He stands on his bed and opens the small, narrow window above it, tosses the crumbs outside, and goes back to his drawing.

"Damn it, Eddie! Carmen's all psycho over that cat hanging around. Quit feeding it!"

It's nearly midnight by the time I turn off the light and crawl into bed. Eddie's already been in bed for a long time. I thought he was asleep, but a few minutes after I crawl under the covers he says in this really quiet voice,

"Mario?"

"Yeah?"

"Don't work late tomorrow night."

"I have to," I tell him.

"Please."

"Why?"

"I hate Thurday nights," he whispers.

"Why?"

"Because you're not here."

"But, Eddie, I can't just tell Sammy I won't work late because my little brother hates Thursday nights."

Way early in the morning I'm awakened by Eddie crying. "Mommy. Mommy. Mommy," he's saying in a sort of baby voice. I reach across and tap him on his shoulder.

"You're having a nightmare," I say.

"Mommy . . ."

I give him a light shake.

"Turn over."

He moves a bit, then he's quiet. Sometimes all it takes to stop a nightmare is a change of position. At least that's what I thought then. What I didn't know was that the really bad times had already started.

9

Second period Walker starts laughing as soon as he sees me walk in the door. That gets me laughing, too, even though I don't want to look uncool in front of Jenna.

"Man, you nearly got my butt fired last night," he says, laughing even harder. That's the way with Walker. He never takes anything seriously.

"I thought Trina was going to explode! She kept getting bigger and bigger, like she was filling up with angry gas – like some Willy Wonka kid."

"Or like when Bugs Bunny sucks helium and floats like a balloon over Porky Pig. Remember? And he's sputtering around trying to get down?"

The thought of Trina, floating red-faced and angry over the Golden Arches gets us laughing so hard we're both gasping and wiping away tears. Woodsy stands in front of the class, which is her signal for us to quiet down. I'd like to, but I can't. Just as I'm about to gain control, Walker puffs out his cheeks, like a balloon, and I start all over again. Jenna is looking at me like I'm some out of control giggle-freak, which I am right now, but I can't help it.

Woodsy says, "Would you boys care to share the joke with the rest of us?"

I take a deep breath and try to hold it, then another laugh bursts forth, louder still.

Between laughs, Walker manages to croak out to Woodsy, "You had to be there," which also sounds like about the funniest thing I've ever heard.

Woodsy walks down the aisle to where we're sitting and stands between our desks. She leans in, close to me, then turns and leans in close to Walker.

"It's the old sniff test," Austin calls from across the room. "Suspend 'em, Woodsy. They've been smokin' . . . "

"Austin . . . " Woodsy says, drilling him with "the look." He stops, mid-sentence. She's already put Austin on a kind of class probation, telling him if he can't commit to PC rules he'll have to find another class. He starts to say something, then apparently thinks better of it, which is a first for Austin. The good news for me and Walker is that we've managed to stop laughing. It really wasn't even that funny, it's just that Walker can crack me up like nobody else. Kind of like how I can crack Eddie up – except maybe not so much lately.

We break into groups to get started on our projects. I don't even want to look Jenna in the eye because I'm all embarrassed about my laughing fit, but then she passes me a note.

"Hello, Shy Guy," it says, with xoxoxoxo all along the bottom of the paper. Okay. I feel better.

There are five of us in the teen pregnancy group. Me, Jenna, Courtney, this girl named Barbara, and Norman. I feel sort of sorry for Barbara. She's way fat – like her butt's hanging over the chair on both sides, and she's got about five chins where most people only have one. It's kind of disgusting. I wonder why she doesn't go on a diet? But maybe she can't help it. Maybe it's some kind of glandular thing like you hear about sometimes. But then why doesn't she go to a doctor?

You may wonder why I'm paying so much attention to Barbara, when the love of my life is in the same group, sitting right next to me. I'll tell you why. Jenna is so close to me, I can smell her hair. And the way it smells, all clean, and fresh, reminds me of how it smelled when we were alone in her house, stretched out on the sofa, and she was kissing my neck and chest and I was breathing deeply of that same smell and . . . and if I don't look at Barbara, like right now, I'll get such a boner that my laughing fit will seem like the height of cool in comparison.

Barbara notices me watching her and gives me a shy smile. I look away. Of course, I've heard nothing anyone's saying, and now Norman is asking me what I think.

"About what?" I say.

"About what we were just talking about," he says.

"Give me a hint," I say.

"Statistics," Jenna says, smiling.

Norman sighs and leans forward in a way that lets me know he thinks he's a lot smarter than I am. Maybe he is. I know he gets good grades, and I heard he's already got a scholarship for a big university in the east.

"I'm thinking we should gather some statistics regarding teen pregnancy," he says.

"I read that France and Italy have really low teen pregnancy rates," Jenna says.

"Really?" Courtney says. "But I thought the French and Italians were supposed to be so hot?"

"Where'd you read that?" Barbara asks Jenna.

"I don't remember. I think I read it, but it may have been on TV."

"We need better references than that," Norman says.

I sneak a look at Jenna, who's passing a note to Courtney.

I hope it's a note about how she's totally, madly in love with me.

"How about if before we meet on Friday, we all find factual information on the subject of teen pregnancy, complete with references," Norman says. "That might help us organize things."

"Won't that be kind of repetitious?" Barbara says. "We'll probably all go to Google, or Yahoo, and come up with the same information."

"Maybe," Norman says. "But it's at least a start."

"And even if we all see a lot of the same stuff, we'll probably choose different things to bring in," Jenna says.

"I Googled teen pregnancy yesterday, just to see what would come up. There are over three million items. Let's say none of us will take more than one item from the same page. And we'll each bring in ten items," Norman says.

"I don't even have a computer," Courtney says.

"You can come over to my house tonight," Jenna says. "We can work on it together."

"I can't use the Internet where I live," I say, fishing for the same invitation. It works.

"Why don't you come to my house, too," Jenna says, smiling.

"Sure. Thanks."

"Or you could just go to the library," Norman says, all sarcastic. "You've heard of a library?"

I give him my high, squeaky, Barney-show voice with the wide-eyed look.

"Lliiii-berry? What's a liii-berry? Like a blueberry? Or a raspberry?"

I'm pretty good at the innocent little kid thing and Barbara and Jenna both laugh. Norman sighs as if he's oh, so, tired – of me.

I stay with the high squeaky voice and wide eyes.

"Mr. Norman! Mr. Norman! What's a liberry? Tell me!"

That gets another laugh. I know it's totally immature, but can I just point out that he's the one who got all sarcastic in the first place?

After class, Jenna and I walk out together.

"When you come over tonight to work on our project we just have to pretend like we're only friends if my mom's home."

Jenna says her mom totally freaks if she thinks Jenna has the slightest interest in a boy. Whenever Jenna picks me up from work her mom thinks she's with Courtney or some other girlfriend.

"I work late tonight, but I could come over around ten. Is that too late?"

"I'm supposed to be in bed by eleven on school nights, but you could come for a little while. My mom sometimes lets me stay up later for homework."

"Okay. Or we could be in bed by eleven if she insists," I say, giving her what I hope is a sexy look.

"Not exactly shy-guy talk," she says, laughing.

We walk down the hall together, holding hands.

"Come earlier if you can," she says. "So we can have more time."

I still can hardly believe Jenna likes me. I mean, really likes me. She's wicked cute, and popular, and she could have any guy she wants, and she wants me!

Except for Sammy, leaning in the doorway to the back room reading the Hamilton Heights Herald, Java Jive is totally empty when I get there after school.

"Hey," I say.

He nods.

"Did you walk past Starbucks on your way here?"

"Yeah."

"Busy?"

"Packed."

"Damn!" Sammy says.

I stash my backpack, heavy with unused books and note-book, on a shelf in the back room, then put on my apron and that funky little Java Jive cap and take my place at the coffee station. A few people wander in every now and then, but not nearly as many as before Starbucks. I rearrange the shelves, restock the condiments station, wipe off the tables, and mostly stand watching my fingernails grow. Around seven o'clock Sammy tells me to go home, even though I'm scheduled to work until ten.

"Maybe things'll pick up again tomorrow," he says.

"So, you want me at 4:30 in the morning?"

"No, just come in after school and we'll see how it goes."

CHAPTER

10

I hurry off to Carmen's – it's still "Carmen's house" to me. It'll never feel like home. A fifteen minute walk, ten minute shower, another twenty minutes to Jenna's – I'll be there by eight. I worry some about not working as many hours as I planned. I really want to get the insurance money together so I can drive Max's car. And I think about the pre-firefighting class I've signed up for next semester. But mostly I think about Jenna, and the smell of her hair. I think about how soft it is, how it feels to run my fingers through it, to feel it brush against my face as I lean in to kiss her. I think about the feel of her body close to mine, and start hoping that Courtney won't be there, and that her parents will be out, and that I'll have Jenna all to myself.

We've only been at her house alone, once, and I'd really like that to happen again. I reach into the inside pocket of my jacket and feel the foil wrapped condom . . .

I'm so caught up in my hopes for tonight, I nearly walk past the corner where I have to turn to go to Carmen's.

Denton's truck is in the driveway, but I don't see Carmen's car. Then I remember something about Carmen taking a class on Thursday nights. Some kind of style make-over thing. If you ask me, which nobody did, she can use it.

I walk to the back door and enter as quietly as I can. The TV is blaring away in the living room. Good. That means Denton won't hear me come in. I don't have time to listen to him spouting off about whatever his topic of the day is. If I wanted to hear a lecture I'd pay attention in government.

I open the door to our room, quietly, expecting to see Eddie at the table, drawing cartoons or doing his homework. Instead there's Denton sitting on the edge of Eddie's bed, with Eddie's face pushed down onto his lap. Denton's pants are open. His briefs are pulled down. He's holding Eddie's mouth down on his dick. I freeze, not believing what I see – Denton's arched back, his mouth half open, his eyes nearly closed, his big, basketball player hands surrounding Eddie's head . . .

I grab my backpack strap and swing with all my might, smashing Denton's head backward, knocking him against the wall. Eddie jumps away, throwing himself face down on the other bed. I leap at Denton, pulling my arm around his neck in a tight stranglehold. He grabs my arm. I hang on with all my strength. He struggles to his feet, breaking my hold, shoving me onto the bed. I jump up, lunge at him. He grabs my wrists and holds me at arms' length. I pull and twist, struggling to get loose, bellowing my anger in loud, incomprehensible roars.

He stands with his pants around his ankles, smirking, while I pull and kick and twist. Finally, words get mixed in with the roars.

"Dirty pervert! . . . Fuckin' bastard!"

I kick furiously at his balls, not connecting. He holds me away with his long arms.

"Calm down!" he says. "What's the matter with you, anyway?"

"Asshole pervert!" I shout. "Let me go!"

"Not until you stop acting like a crazy maniac!"

"Maniac! You're the maniac pervert!"

"Shut up!" he shouts, tightening his grip on my wrists. "I wasn't hurting your little brother! Tell him, Kid. I've never hurt you, have I?"

Eddie's still face down on the bed, a corner of the spread bunched into his mouth. He doesn't move.

"Call 911!" I yell at Eddie. "Get the cops over here!"

"Your brother's not going to do that," Denton says. "He and I have an understanding, don't we, Kid?"

Eddie doesn't respond to that, either.

I twist and squirm and kick, powerless to connect with anything but air.

"Here's what Eddie understands, and you will, too, if you know what's good for you." Denton says. His voice is low and steady – menacing. "You'll understand this before your auntie comes home."

He glances at his watch.

"You've got about twenty minutes to smarten up."

I try to jerk away. He holds on.

"You wanna call 911? Get me in trouble with the law?"

I kick at him again. This time I connect, but only to his shin. He pulls me in, spits in my face, and pushes me back out of reach again. I feel his filthy slobber running down my cheek. I butt him in the stomach with my head. He falls backward, losing his grip on one of my arms. I swing at him, hard, hitting his cheekbone with my tight fist. He punches me in the jaw. I fall back onto the bed, barely missing Eddie. I sit wiping spit and blood from my face and rubbing my jaw. Denton stands over me. Slowly he pulls up his shorts, then his pants. He fumbles with his zipper, never taking his eyes off me.

"Now. You're going to shut up, and stay shut up. Just like smart Eddie here. He knows how to shut up. You go to the cops, you know what's going to happen?"

"They'll lock your filthy ass up."

"Maybe," he says, smiling his nasty little half smile. "But first they'll want to protect you nice little boys. Which means they'll take you away and put you in foster homes. Probably a group home for you, Mister Mario. No nice family wants to take in a smart-ass seventeen-year old loser-boy like you."

He pauses to finish zipping his pants and buckling his belt. His cheekbone is red and swelling where my backpack connected.

"Eddie Boy here, they'll take him away and put him in a different foster home. You'll both change schools. One of you may be in Cucamonga and the other in Northridge. Who knows? Protective services go a long way to find foster homes. Maybe you'll get to see each other once or twice a month, if you're lucky. You get my drift?"

I don't get anything right now. I turn to look at Eddie, who still hasn't moved. I put my hand on his back to see if he's even breathing. He flinches at my touch, then shoves more of the corner of the spread into his mouth.

"You're making a big deal over nothing. Eddie and I were just having a little fun, weren't we, Kid? No harm done."

Denton moves back and sits down on the empty bed.

"No harm done," he repeats. "Think about it."

I am thinking – all kinds of thoughts spin around in my head. Like what else has he been doing with Eddie? And for how long? What about all the times he took him places, and "watched out" for him when Carmen and I were both working? And . . .

Over the din of the TV we hear the slam of the back door.

"Denton, Honey? I'm home," Carmen calls.

Denton stands up, puts my backpack on our study table and smooths the bedspread.

"Denton?"

"In here, Babe, helping the boys with their homework."

He checks to be sure he's all zipped up, runs his fingers through his hair, and walks out the door into the hallway. I sit stunned, trying to make sense of things. Eddie doesn't stir.

"Eddie?"

I pull gently at the edge of the spread, taking it from his mouth. He turns over on his side, facing the wall.

"What was Denton doing to you?"

"Something," he whispers.

"I know, something, but what?"

"Just something he likes to do."

I lean closer to him, to hear better.

"Has he ever done anything like that before?" I ask.

"I can't tell you."

"Yes, you can."

"No. I have to shut up."

"Not to me."

"Specially to you. Or he'll hurt us."

"He's already been hurting you," I tell him.

"It doesn't really hurt."

His whispers are getting even softer.

"I'm sleepy," he says.

"I'm asking you, has Denton ever done anything like that before?"

Eddie gets up from the bed, goes to the chest of drawers and gets his pajamas. He stands beside the closet, in the corner, back where I can't see him. When did he start hiding when he gets undressed? He comes out from his makeshift alcove with his pajamas on.

"Eddie, tell me about Denton."

He goes into the bathroom. I hear the water running and the noise of his racecar toothbrush for what seems like a long time. Then I hear Carmen pounding on the bathroom door.

"You're not the only one needs to use the bathroom!" she yells.

The buzz of the toothbrush stops. I hear the door open.

"Oh, Eddie, Sweetheart. I'm sorry. I didn't know it was you."

Eddie comes into our room, closing the door behind him.

"Tell me what's going on!" I say.

"I'm sleepy," he says, crawling into his bed. He turns over facing the wall and pulls the covers over his head.

When I hear Carmen leave the bathroom I go in and lock the door behind me. I wash my face with lots of soap and hot water, scrubbing hard where Denton's gob of spit landed. Suddenly I feel it running down my cheek again. I see Denton's giant hands pushing Eddie's mouth onto his slimy dick and I barely get the toilet lid up in time to puke my guts out. Right now, kneeling on the cold tile floor, shaking with anger at Denton, I really miss Max.

I wash up, again, and brush my teeth and rinse with Scope. I hold a cold wash cloth against my jaw, wondering if it's going to be all swollen tomorrow.

Back in our room I sit on the side of my bed, watching Eddie sleep, remembering this video they showed us back in the fourth grade. It was about what to do if anyone ever touched us where we didn't want to be touched. "Like on our noses?" Walker had said, which got a laugh from everyone but the teacher. Anyway, the video said if anyone touched you where you didn't want to be touched, or forced you to touch them in a way you didn't want, you should scream and run away. And you should tell someone, like your mom or dad. Unless they were the ones touching you like that. Then you should tell some other trusted adult. I wonder if Eddie ever saw that video?

I'm remembering how he begged me not to go to work tonight. Thursday. The night Carmen's not around. Why didn't he just tell me he didn't want to be alone with Denton?

I move over to Eddie's bed and give him a shake.

"Wake up, Eddie. We've got to talk."

He pulls the covers tighter over his head.

"I'm sleeping."

"Yeah? Well I'm not," I say, pulling the covers away. "You're not going to sleep until you tell me what's going on with Denton!"

Silence.

"Has he ever done anything like that before?"

More silence.

"Damn it, Eddie, tell me what's going on!"

He tries to pull the covers back over his head but I won't let him.

"I can't tell you."

"Yes, you can!" I yell.

"No! I can't!" he yells back.

He turns to face me, eyes now wide open.

"Denton'll kill us! He knows how! He learned it in the Green Berets. He showed me!"

"He showed you?"

"Yeah. It's a place on your neck. He made me pass out, and then he brought me back, but he could kill us just like that. He said he wouldn't want to kill me because he likes me, but he would if he had to. He said he wouldn't mind killing you because you're a smart ass."

Eddie's crying now, full out.

"I don't want him to kill us!"

"He's not going to kill us."

"He could if he wanted to," Eddie says. "He's way strong. Lots stronger than you are."

"I know," I say, flashing on the easy way he held me back as I tried to get at him.

"Listen. You've got to tell me everything. Like you've always done. You trust me. Right?"

He nods his head but his face is all scrunched up and worried looking.

"I can keep a secret. Remember how you kept Simba-Kitty hidden in our closet, and I helped you get food for him? Remember how long we kept that secret?"

He nods.

"When's the first time Denton messed with you? You know, like tonight?"

"Tonight?" Eddie asks, like he has no idea what I'm talking about.

"Yeah. Like with his pants down, and his dick out, like, you know, doing anything that was . . . weird."

I wait for a long time, then Eddie finally says, "After the fair. It was weird after the fair."

The fair? I count back. The fair ends just after school starts, so that had to be about two months ago.

"What happened?"

"Well . . . he took me to see the animals, and he got me all kinds of stuff to eat. We played lots of games and we rode whatever rides I wanted to ride. He told me he'd always wanted a son like me. He'd even want his son to have a hand like mine, because it makes me special. And . . . well . . . he was really nice."

Eddie stares at the ceiling. I wait. And wait.

"And . . . ? He was really nice, and . . . ?"

"And he said . . ."

More staring at the ceiling.

"Come on. He said what?"

"Well, he said he'd done so many nice things for me that day, wouldn't I like to do something nice for him? And I said sure."

"So what was the something nice he wanted you to do?"

Eddie starts crying again, and shivering, too, like it's cold, except it's about eighty-two degrees in here and he's under two blankets.

"You can't tell the cops," he sobs. "I don't want to be sent away from you."

"I won't let that happen."

"You can't tell!"

"Okay! I won't tell!"

"Swear?"

"I swear. Cross my heart and hope to die. Stick a needle in my eye."

"That's a baby swear. You have to swear to God!"

"Okay! I swear to God!"

Another long silence.

"So what nice thing did he want you to do?"

"Well, he wanted me to touch him . . . you know . . . in his pants. And he wanted to touch me, too."

"So you did?"

"Well . . . he was really nice to me."

"God, Eddie. He's a creep! And threatening to kill us doesn't sound very nice."

"That wasn't 'til later."

"So were you nice to Denton at the fair?"

"Not at the fair. After. He drove me up a windy road and then we turned off behind a house made of rocks."

"Sounds like Breeson Canyon. Was it there? Near where we skipped rocks with Max?"

"I don't know. It was a really windy road, though."

"There's an old deserted house up there," I say.

Eddie shrugs.

"So you parked there, and then what?"

"Then . . . well, he'd been really nice to me, and I liked him a lot, so . . . I was . . . nice to him. The way he asked me to be."

"What a pervert!"

Eddie turns his face back toward the wall.

"Well, he is, Eddie. Don't you know he's a pervert?"

In a voice so soft I can barely hear he says, "I thought you meant I'm a pervert. But I was just being nice."

11

So I'm going to tell you about what Denton's been doing, but I want to shorten Eddie's story some – just to get through the nasty parts as fast as I can.

It started with the touching stuff, and then it moved to, you know, oral sex. Denton told Eddie it was good to practice all kinds of sex stuff for when he got a little older and would be with a girl. It was best to practice with someone more experienced because then he'd know what he was doing once he got a girlfriend.

Sometimes Denton'd take Eddie to get ice cream, and then to the place on the windy road. Or, if no one else was at Carmen's place, Denton'd take Eddie into our room, like when I found them last night.

Once, just after the fair, he took Eddie to a place where he said he had a job. He told Eddie there was a boy there who got lonely when he had to stay by himself after school, and it would be nice to stop and see him. He said there was a big swimming pool there and told Eddie to take his trunks.

They bought a bunch of red jellybeans, which Denton said were the kid's favorites. Eddie chose yellow jellybeans. They parked in front of a big house that had a statue like the one in *Tía* Josie's front yard. They walked down the driveway and Denton checked the garage to see that no cars were there.

"See. I told you. No one's ever home here with this guy until late at night. He'll be happy for company."

They walked around to a door at the back of the house and Denton knocked.

"Who's there?" a voice answered.

"It's me, your old friend, Denton. I've brought a kid over to play with you."

He told Eddie, "Say hi to Jimmy."

"Hi, Jimmy," Eddie said.

"What's your name?"

"Eddie."

"Open the door," Denton said, "and you can talk in person."

"I'm not supposed to open the door," Jimmy said, then asked how old Eddie was.

"Nine," Eddie said.

"I'm only eight, but I like guys who are nine."

"Come on, Jimmy, let us in," Denton said. "We've got lots of red jellybeans."

Jimmy opened the door, but he seemed kind of scared.

"I'm not supposed to let you in anymore," he said.

"We won't tell," Denton said.

They went upstairs to Jimmy's bedroom.

Denton put the jellybeans down on the kid's dresser and told the boys to help themselves whenever they wanted. He pulled his pants down and showed them his penis. He said if they were lucky theirs would grow as big as his someday. Then he wanted to check their penis sizes and he had them pull their pants down, too. He took some pictures of them touching each other. He touched them, and had them touch him, too. He told them to watch what happened and he grabbed his penis and moved his hand on it in a way that made stuff come out. He told them to see if they could make their penises do what his did but then they heard a car in the driveway and Denton rushed Eddie out the front door before whoever it was got out of the garage. When they got back to Carmen's, Denton told her what a great time Eddie'd had swimming and playing with Jimmy, even though they never even got in the pool.

Eddie went along with it all at first. The blow jobs weirded him out, but Denton really liked that stuff. Eddie said it seemed fair to be nice to him because Denton always bought him things, and practiced basketball with him, and helped him practice telling jokes. Then, when Denton tried to . . . God, it's so hard to even think about this! I can feel this morning's doughnut climbing up from my stomach. I'll say it as fast as I can and get it over with.

It was back in our room, a couple of weeks ago, when Denton tried to do the dirtiest thing of all – you know, go into Eddie's butt hole. Eddie freaked out. He told Denton he didn't want to do any of that stuff anymore. He tried to get away but, of course, he was no match for Denton. When Eddie threatened to tell me and Carmen what Denton had been doing, Denton turned mean. He said he'd kill us both if Eddie blabbed, and that Eddie'd better just shut up and keep being nice to him if he knew what was good for him. The only thing that kept the nastiest thing from happening that time was that Carmen got home earlier than expected. Just like I did last night.

The morning after Eddie threatened to tell, Denton caught Eddie alone in the kitchen. He told Eddie he'd only been kidding about doing him in the butt, and they could just keep being nice to each other without getting mad – that way no one would have to die. Eddie's been trying to stay away from Denton, but it doesn't really work. And when he first started with Eddie in our room last night, he told Eddie that his birthday was coming up next week, and the early gift he wanted from Eddie was . . . the nastiest thing.

It's about two in the morning by the time Eddie's told me the whole story.

"We've got to make a plan," I tell him. "You can't go any-where with Denton anymore."

"But what if he makes me?"

"Well . . . we can't let that happen."

"Sometimes he waits for me after school and then he takes me up the windy road."

"Does he ever buy you stuff anymore?"

"No."

"Take you swimming, or for ice cream?"

"No. Now he only takes me up the windy road, or here to Carmen's when nobody's home."

I'm doing the math in my head. If I meet Eddie after school every day, that means one less hour of work at Java Jive. And even if I meet him and walk him back to Carmen's, then what? I go off to work, Denton goes to Carmen's, and Eddie's screwed. Literally. But where else can he go after school? How can I keep him away from Denton?

I'm all lost in my thoughts when Eddie asks, "Mario? Are you mad at me?"

"Not at you. I'm hella mad, though."

"You can't tell anyone!"

"Hey. I swore to God, didn't I?"

He nods.

"I'll get you after school tomorrow. You can go to Java Jive with me. You can sit there and do your homework, or draw, or read, or something. That way you won't have to be at Carmen's 'til I can be there with you."

"Okay," he says, pulling the covers back over his head.

I crawl into my own bed. Now it's my turn to stare at the ceiling.

Everything's quiet. No traffic sounds. No TV. Only the crickets. I lay awake going over and over what Eddie's told me. I'd like to kill that bastard! That'd teach him to mess with my brother! Just thinking about it gets my adrenaline pumping. I go into the bathroom to look out the window. His truck's still there in the driveway. I go back to bed – back to staring at the ceiling. I picture the knife block sitting on Carmen's kitchen counter. The butcher knife in the largest slot. If he's on his back I'd go directly to his heart. Plunge deep through his ribcage. No. Better still, the throat. The jugulars. Back. Side. Stomach. Whatever position he's in I can get to his throat. Easy. No more worries for Eddie about being killed by Denton. No more worries about Denton's giant hands, Denton's filthy games.

I ease out of bed and walk softly, silently, to the kitchen. The light from Carmen's kitchen clock guides my way. I take the largest knife from the wood block. Feel the fit of the handle, the weight in my hand. The blade, long and strong and sharp – sharp enough to put my brother's worries to rest.

"Mommy! Mommy!"

I rush back to our room to quiet Eddie, the knife still in my hand. He's thrashing around, covers tangled all around him.

"You're okay," I say, giving him a gentle nudge.

Footsteps down the hall.

I slide the knife under Eddie's bed just as Carmen comes through the door.

"What's wrong?" Carmen says.

"Just a nightmare," I tell her, straightening Eddie's covers.

She watches sleepily for a minute or two, then pads back to bed. I crawl back into my own bed, waiting for things to get quiet again. Eddie stirs around, mumbling something I can't understand. I reach across the narrow space between our beds and put my hand on his shoulder.

"It's okay," I tell him. "Everything's gonna be okay."

When he's finally quiet, and there's no other stirring in the house, I get the butcher knife out from under his bed and take it back to the kitchen. It slides easily into the designated slot and I go back to bed.

The thing is, if I killed Denton, then where would I be? Not watching out for Eddie anymore. Not feeling Jenna's arms around me, her soft lips on mine. Not playing soccer, or taking the firefighting course, not mixing mocha drinks or laughing at Walker. There's got to be a better way.

12

I get Eddie up earlier than usual hoping to get out of here before Denton's up. But there he is, sitting at the kitchen table reading the newspaper and drinking coffee like he's a normal person. We have to walk past him to get to the back door. He glances up at us.

"How's it goin'?" he says, like last night didn't even happen.

"Fuck you," I say, moving Eddie quickly ahead of me and out the door.

The cat's there.

"Hey, Blue," Eddie says, reaching down to scratch its head.

It starts with the leg-weaving, meowing routine.

"Shut up!" Denton yells from inside.

As if in answer, the cat meows even louder. Denton rushes out the back door and lunges for the cat.

"Shut up, goddamn you!"

Another meow.

In one quick, downward swoop, Denton grabs the cat, pulling it out from between Eddie's ankles. He holds it at arm's length, his giant hand gripping its neck.

"Don't hurt Blue!" Eddie yells.

Looking right at Eddie, Denton slowly closes his fist around the cat's neck. One more desperate meow and then – silence.

"IT-WOULDN'T-SHUT-UP," Denton says, dangling the lifeless cat in front of Eddie. Then he walks over to his truck and drops the body down onto a pile of trash bags between his lawnmower and weed-eater.

"I'll take care of that piece o' shit later," Denton says, going back into the house.

Eddie rushes to the truck and climbs up into the bed.

"Blue," he calls, tears streaming down his cheeks. "Blue. Come on, Blue."

He cradles the cat to his chest. Its head drops to the side at a weird, unnatural angle.

"Come on, Eddie," I say climbing in next to him and easing the cat from his arms.

I lift Eddie out of the truck and climb down beside him.

"We can't help Blue," I say.

"He didn't shut up," Eddie says.

I want to say something to make things better, but there's nothing to say.

We walk slowly, in silence, to Eddie's school. Here's what I can't get out of my head. The image of Denton's giant hand closed on the cat's crushed neck. The image of Denton's sick, creepy grin. The cat dangled in front of Eddie's wide, frightened eyes.

The bell rings just as we get to the playground gate.

"I'll pick you up after school."

Eddie nods. Head down, shoulders slumped, he walks toward Ms. Sumner's room.

I rushed us out of the house so fast this morning I didn't get to do my usual email routine, so I stop by the library to use a school computer. Grabbing the one available computer out of the bank of about twenty computers that line one wall of the library, I open Internet Explorer and go to Web Mail. After about five tries I still can't get where I want to go. Ms. Coulter, the librarian, must see that I'm frustrated because she leaves the checkout counter and comes over to where I'm sitting.

"Need help?" she asks.

"I can't get to my email account."

"Nope. Email sites are all blocked on school computers. They're set up for school use, not for personal use."

"All of them are blocked?"

"As far as I know. You might try the public library, after school."

It shouldn't be a disaster, missing one morning of email to Max. And it's nothing compared to other stuff that's gone wrong since last night, but . . . I just sit staring at the "this site not available" message on the screen . . .

"Are you okay, Mario? It is Mario, isn't it?"

I nod.

"Right. I remember you from your sophomore career project. Firefighting, wasn't it?"

I nod again, surprised that she remembers me. It's not like I hang out much in the library.

"So, are you?"

"What?"

"Are you okay?"

"Yeah. It's just . . . I wanted to email my mom. In Iraq."

"I'm sure you'll have better luck at the public library."

"I always email her in the morning. That's all."

Ms. Coulter glances toward her office, then turns her attention back to me.

"Maybe we can work something out," she says, motioning for me to follow her.

In her office, sitting at a small desk, is a kid about Eddie's age doing some kind of PowerPoint thing on a little laptop.

"This is my daughter, Rosie," Ms. C. says. "Rosie – Mario."

"Hi," I say.

"Hi," Rosie says, not looking up from what she's doing.

"Eye contact, Rosie," Ms. C. says. "Try it again."

Rosie looks up.

"Hi, Mario."

"Listen, Rosie, Mario needs to borrow your computer. Just for a few minutes."

"But Mom . . ."

Ms. C. gives Rosie a look that totally reminds me of Max – like she's about to do one of those "let's get this straight" talks.

"Mario's mom's a long way away, and the only way he can communicate with her is through email . . . that would be kind of hard, don't you think?"

Rosie looks at her mom, then at me.

"How far away is your mom?"

"7,650 miles," I tell her.

"Okay," she says, closing the PowerPoint program and sliding her laptop over to me.

"Thanks."

"Rosie comes in really early with me in the mornings. We got special access for her computer."

"Sometimes I email my Uncle David," Rosie says. "He moved away."

"How far?" I ask.

Rosie looks at her mom.

"About eighty miles," she says. "Not so far as Mario's mom."

Web Mail asks for my password.

"I send smiley faces to my Uncle David. Do you want me to show you how?" Rosie asks.

"It's okay," I say, opening a message from Max.

"Here, Rosie. You can help me put these library announcements out on the bulletin boards," Ms. C. says, handing her daughter a stack of papers and ushering her out of the office. I focus on Max's message.

From: Maria_27@hitmail.net
Date: October 30 7:42 AM
To: Mario Barajas <mario3@yoohoo.com>
Subject: Hey My Men

Hey guys. I'm so proud of you both! It sounds like you're doing great in school, even without me around to nag, nag, nag you about your homework. And Mario, to think you're being so responsible about saving money for car insurance! I guess my guys are growing up. Are you taking your vitamins? Don't forget! I want you to stay strong, and healthy. And Eddie, have you heard any good jokes lately? Animal jokes, doctor jokes, anything, 'cause I'm missing your jokes.

I loved the mac-n-cheese, and so did my sergeant who ordered me to share with him. He's cool, so I didn't mind. I don't want you to spend your insurance money on cases of the stuff, but anytime you want to send more mac-n-cheese you'll make at least two people happy.

This may be the last email I can get off to you for a few days. We're being moved to a different post. But don't worry, I'll still be in a pretty safe place.

I miss you guys to the moon and back. I love you to the moon and back. Take care of each other. Say hi to Carmen for me. – Megatons of love to you both – Max/Mom

I hate that Max is moving from one place to another! That means she'll be on the road. Which, I can't help noticing, is where car bombs happen. So telling me not to worry doesn't exactly keep me from worrying.

I hit "reply" and sit wondering where to start. In my head I'm saying:

"Hey Max. We're in a mess here. We need you to come home and help get things straight. Like now! Carmen's sex-pervert, cat-killing boyfriend is messing with Eddie big time. Sex stuff! You wouldn't believe it! And here's the reason you've not been getting any jokes from Eddie these days. Nothing's funny anymore. He doesn't even laugh at my farts anymore. So please, please, please, come home right now. We need you bad."

That's what I write in my head. Here's what I write for real.

From: Mario Barajas <mario3@yoohoo.com>
Date: October 30 8:17 AM
To: Maria_27@hitmail.net
Subject: what's up?

hey, max, glad the mac-n-cheese was a hit. i'll send more after I pay the car insurance. we're taking our vitamins, doing our homework, washing our hands after we go to the bathroom and before we eat and all the other stuff you'd be nagging us about if you were here. the racecar toothbrush you got for eddie is a big success. he's constantly brushing his teeth with it. you don't have to worry about us. eddie's at school, but next email he'll send you a joke. stay safe. megatons of love back at you, mario.

I reread my message, wishing I could say more, then click "send."

Instead of the usual swishing sound that lets me know my message has been sent, the screen first goes blank, then displays a box that says: "Web Mail has encountered a problem and needs to close. We are sorry for the inconvenience."

I'm trying again when Rosie comes back into the office. I get the same display.

"Damn!"

"You're not supposed to say bad words," she says, looking over my shoulder at the computer screen. "Oh . . . that happens all the time."

"So what do you do?"

"I just wait 'til we get home, where there's a better connection."

The warning bell rings. Ms. Coulter's shooing everyone out of the library. I give it one more quick try before she gets to me. Same display.

CHAPTER

13

Jenna and Courtney are talking outside the door to PC.
Jenna turns her back when she sees me.

"Hey," I say, walking up close to her.

She gives me a look that's not exactly loving.

"I thought you were coming over last night."

"I know. I couldn't make it."

"Ever hear of a telephone?"

"Yeah," I say. "But do you think . . . could I talk to you
alone?"

"I can take a hint," Courtney says, walking into the classroom.

"Something really bad happened last night . . ."

"Really?"

"Yeah. Really. With my little brother."

"Like what?"

"Like . . ."

"Hey, Dude!" Walker calls from halfway down the hall.
"Have you got the signs for tonight?"

I just stand there.

"Remember?" Walker says. "Courtney's birthday? We're surprising her? You, me, Jenna, Meredith, Trevor . . . We've been talking about it for weeks? You're on?"

"I'll be there," I say, barely remembering some talk about a party.

"Like you were going to be at my house last night?" Jenna says.

"Listen, Jenna . . ."

"Are the signs even ready?" Jenna says.

"Signs?"

Jenna just looks at me, disgusted.

"You know!" Walker says. "You said Eddie'd make a cool happy birthday banner?"

"Yeah. Right." I say.

Jenna walks into the classroom, not looking back.

"What's with you, anyway? Courtney says you totally stood Jenna up last night, and now it's like you've never even heard of the party? Or the signs you were supposed to get?"

"Sorry," I say. "I didn't sleep much last night."

"You better get your act together with Jenna or somebody else will," Walker says, walking into the classroom.

I follow behind, bits of memory coming back to me about party plans. Madison and Trevor are bringing silver and black Mylar balloons, Jenna's bringing the cake, I'm bringing a giant banner . . . Did I even talk to Eddie about the banner?

Today is a group-work day in PC and everyone in the teen pregnancy group has their ten teen pregnancy Internet items listed for discussion. Everyone except me, that is.

"I didn't have time," I say.

Jenna rolls her eyes in Courtney's direction. Norman gives a stupid snort of a laugh.

I ignore him. I know I gave a lame excuse, but what was I going to say? I couldn't do the job because I was busy trying to save my little brother from a sex pervert? I don't think so. Besides, we've got plenty to talk about with everyone else's list.

Since I didn't do my part in collecting information, everyone agrees that I have to take notes for the group. That's okay. It keeps my mind off Jenna, and a lot of other things.

There's an outburst of loud laughter from the "binge drinking" group across the room, and I look over to see Walker doing his imitation of a drunk trying to brush his teeth. I know that doesn't sound so funny, but if you could see him I'm pretty sure you'd have to laugh.

I turn my attention back to our group, where Norman is reading a quote he got from his Google search: "In the United States, between 1990 and 2000, the pregnancy rate for teens aged 15-19 decreased 28 percent."

I write: 1990-2000, prg. 15-19 minus 28%.

Courtney reads: "In one study of unplanned pregnancies in fourteen- to twenty-one-year-olds, one third of the girls who had gotten pregnant had been drinking alcohol when they had sex."

I write: 1/3 14-21 drinking with sex.

Norman cranes his neck, trying to see what I've written. I lean on the desk, shielding my paper with my forearm.

"I found the information I mentioned the other day," Jenna says. Jenna reads from her paper: "In the United States, the teen pregnancy rate is more than nine times higher than that in the Netherlands, nearly four times higher than the rate in France, and nearly five times higher than that in Germany."

"Even though there's been a big decline in our rates?" Norman says.

"Yeah, and not only that, our syphilis rate is about six times higher than the Netherlands, and our gonorrhea rate is over 74 times higher than theirs is."

"That's gross!" Norman says. "What's that got to do with teen pregnancy, anyway?"

"I don't know," Jenna says. "It just had that information on the same site as the teen pregnancy comparisons by country."

"I don't even know what gonorrhea is," Courtney says.

"Trust me, you don't want to know," Norman says.

"And how do you know?" I ask.

"I read books," he says. "At the library."

Barbara reads the items from her list, one of which states that sixty-two percent of pregnant and parenting teens had been sexually molested or raped prior to their first pregnancy.

"That's more than half!" Courtney says.

"Bright girl," Norman says.

I wonder, does that mean the guys too? The baby daddies? Will Eddie be a baby daddy? "Parenting teens." That's got to mean girls and guys, doesn't it?

More laughter from across the room. Woodsy walks over to the "binge drinking" group to check their progress and the laughter dies down. A few minutes later, she checks with us.

"How's 'teen pregnancy' coming?" she asks, smiling.

Norman explains that we're gathering statistics and then we'll decide how to organize our project. Woodsy looks over my shoulder, reading my notes.

"Interesting," she says, pointing to the item about sexual molestation and teen pregnancy.

"Yeah," Courtney says. "I don't think I'd ever want to have sex again if I'd been molested. Like wouldn't you just hate men?"

"It might make a girl want more, though," Norman says.

"That's ridiculous!" Barbara says, loud enough for the whole room to hear.

Everyone stares at Barbara, including Woodsy. I mean that was like rock concert volume. From Barbara?

Woodsy pulls a chair over and joins our group. She is very strict about not allowing any put downs in PC and I expect her to get on Barbara's case for telling Norman he's ridiculous. Instead she turns to Norman.

"Maybe that seems a little far-fetched, that molestation would cause girls to want more."

"But it could happen, couldn't it?" Norman says.

"Well, Norman, do you think if you'd been molested you'd want more?"

"That's different! I'm a guy!"

"What do the rest of you think?" Woodsy asks, looking away from Norman and including the whole group in her question. "Do guys ever get molested?"

I see it all again – Denton's hands. Eddie's mouth. Denton's dick. Blue's neck. I will myself not to puke. Struggle to shift focus. Courtney's talking. Listen to Courtney.

"I watched this thing on TV, about all of those guys who were molested by priests," she says.

"I'm not Catholic," Norman says.

Woodsy tells us that she was at a meeting with other PC teachers last month where some famous psychologist spoke. "He said one out of three girls and one out of six boys will have had an unwanted sexual experience with an adult by the time they reach the age of eighteen."

"That's so wrong, for people to mess with little kids like that," Barbara says.

I trace over my notes, darkening every word.

"The statistics might even be a little low for boys, because they're a lot less willing to report anything," Woodsy says. "But we're way off your teen pregnancy topic. See if you can come up with some ideas on how to put your presentation together before the bell rings."

Woodsy moves over to the drug abuse group. Jenna suggests we break the topic into two segments, problems and prevention. I hear her say it, because it's Jenna, but I don't hear anything else these last ten minutes of class because I'm thinking about molestation, and Eddie, and how I've got to keep him away from Denton.

Walker's waiting outside the classroom door when I leave PC.

"What took you so long? It wasn't Jenna, because she came out a long time ago."

"I needed to talk with Woodsy for a minute," I tell him.

He groans. "Being in the same group with Nerdy Norman hasn't turned you into a kiss ass, has it?"

"Sure, that's it," I tell him. "How many blog hits yesterday?"

"Man, it's so cool," he says, and launches into how he's getting hits all the way from Florida and New York.

Sometimes I appreciate that Walker's so easily distracted. Like right now. I was late coming out of class because I was making an appointment to talk with Woodsy. Walker doesn't need to know that, though.

I find Jenna at lunchtime.

"Can we please just talk?" I say.

"Okay," she says. She doesn't smile and she doesn't take my hand. We go to a table way in the back of the cafeteria, away from anyone we know. There are a couple of boys there, probably ninth graders, but they're busy with their PSPs and not paying any attention to us.

"So what was so bad that you couldn't even call me last night?" Jenna says.

I take a deep breath, wanting to tell her everything and not wanting to tell her anything, all at the same time.

"Well, it's about Eddie. I had to stay with him . . ."

"But weren't your aunt and that guy there? He wouldn't have been alone."

"Well, I mean, it's not safe for him there anymore."

"Not safe?"

She looks puzzled for a moment, then outraged.

"Oh my god! Do they beat up on him? Your aunt's so rude I bet she's just the kind of person to beat up on a little kid. Oh my god! Is that what happened to your brother's hand? Did she . . . "

"Shhh. Not so loud," I tell her.

The two guys at our table have lost interest in their PSPs and are staring at Jenna.

"But is that it? They beat up on your little brother?" she says, lowering her voice a little. "That's what you couldn't tell me?"

"Not exactly," I say. "Come on, I need some chips or something."

We walk over toward the vending machines.

"I thought you didn't like chips," she said.

"I don't. But we had to move away from that table. Those guys were practically taking notes."

"So?"

"So you've got to be really quiet about this stuff. It can't be like some noisy talk show thing."

We sit down on a bench near the vending machines. I reach for her hand and am happy she doesn't pull away.

"Anyway, why couldn't you leave Eddie last night?" she asks.

"Well, it's not like my aunt ever hits him or anything. And it's got nothing to do with his hand. He was born like that . . . It's just . . ."

I turn away, unable to get the words out.

Jenna slides closer to me and leans into my shoulder.

"You've got to promise me you won't tell anyone."

"I promise," she says, looking worried.

"Absolutely no one!"

"Promise."

"My aunt's boyfriend has been messing with Eddie, like . . . forcing him to do sex stuff."

"Oh my god!" Jenna screams. "That's horrible!"

"Shhh! You can't tell anyone."

Jenna puts her hand over her mouth and nods her head. We

don't have a chance to say any more about it because Trevor comes over and sits down on the bench next to Jenna. And then Walker comes over.

On the way to class Jenna wants to know if Eddie can still make the banner.

"Probably. Maybe it'll be good to get his mind off stuff. He can work on it at Java Jive, before we come to the party."

"We? You mean Eddie's coming to the party?"

"I can't really leave him alone. He'll probably just go to sleep there, anyway."

She nods.

"I'm sorry I got mad at you. I just didn't know . . ."

I give her a big, long hug. She hangs on tight, and I know that things are all right between us, that she understands.

Fifth period is English with Mr. Harvey. It's not a class I can afford to miss, but it's Woodsy's conference period and I need to talk to her. She's in her office with three kids crowded around her desk. She motions me in.

"You guys can work on this in the art room," she says, scooping up some papers and handing them to the girl next to her.

"Look," she says to me, holding up a poster. "This is much better than the old one, don't you think?"

It's the list of things we sign in our contract when we first start PC:

>*No put downs.*
>
>*Whatever is said in class is confidential.*
>
>*Respect yourself and others.*
>
>*No interruptions.*
>
>*Use "I" statements.*
>
>*Accept other viewpoints without judgment.*

"Looks good," I say.

The poster that's on the wall now is all faded, like maybe it's been up there since Woodsy started teaching at Hamilton, probably about ten years ago. This new one has bright colors, and little cartoon characters in the margins that emphasize each statement.

"You guys did a great job on this," Woodsy says. "Thank you all, soooo much!"

I'll be glad when the congratulations are over. The new poster isn't exactly my main concern right now.

As if she's read my mind, Woodsy tells the others to take the poster down to the art room and put a finishing spray on it. One of them starts to talk about various ways to hang it, and the best place to put it in the classroom, and blah, blah, blah.

Woodsy says, "Go on, now. Take the poster down to the art room for the finishing spray. Mario here has an appointment."

Finally, they leave. Woodsy motions for me to have a seat beside her desk.

"What can I do for you, Mario?"

In spite of having practiced over and over in my head exactly what I want to say to Woodsy, no words come out. So we just sit there at first. This would be way awkward with any other teacher, but Woodsy has this way of making you feel like . . . I can't exactly explain it, but maybe like she can understand where you're coming from, or she's on your side . . . something like that.

She's the one to break the silence.

"I hear your mom's over in Iraq."

I nod.

"It must be hard."

I nod again.

"Do you hear from her very often?"

"Email, mostly," I say. "We'll hear everyday for a while, and then there'll be a break."

"When did you hear from her last?"

"Today."

"Are you worried about her?"

"A little. But she says she's in a pretty safe place."

There's another short silence while I gather my nerve.

"What I wanted to talk to you about . . . well . . . remember how you said how many kids get molested?"

"When we were talking in your group today?"

"Yeah. I was wondering, like if you knew some kid who you thought was being molested, what would you do?"

She gives me this long look, like she's wondering if it's me.

"Like a little kid, who maybe can't watch out for himself. What would you do?"

She takes a deep breath.

"What would I do? I would report my suspicions to some-one who would do something to protect the child. As a teach-er, I'm legally bound to report suspicion or knowledge of abuse."

"Then what would happen?"

"Well, it would depend on the circumstances. Probably a social worker or a psychologist would interview the child and decide what steps should be taken."

"And then what?"

"Mario . . . " She pauses, as if carefully considering what to say next.

"Do you know a child who's being molested or abused in some way?"

If I say "yes," then what? I have to be careful. Besides, I promised Eddie I wouldn't tell and I've already broken that promise once. But I know I can trust Jenna not to tell anyone else, so I don't really count that as a broken promise . . .

"Mario? Do you know someone in a bad situation?"

"Maybe I know someone," I say.

"Maybe?"

"What if I do? And what if I tell you the kid's name, and where he lives, and everything. And then you report it, and he gets interviewed or whatever, and then what?"

"Something will be done to protect him."

"Like what?"

"It just depends. Sometimes the accused person is arrested on the spot. Sometimes he (usually it's 'he') has to leave the home and a restraining order is issued against him. Sometimes the child is taken from the home and placed in temporary foster care until things can be sorted out."

"I don't think this kid would do very well in foster care."

"Is he doing very well right now?"

The poster kids come back in, wanting to hang the poster.

"Not now," Woodsy calls to them.

"It'll just take a sec."

"Not now," Woodsy repeats.

They leave as quickly as they entered.

Woodsy glances at the clock.

"Mario. Listen. I don't know exactly what you're up against, or what this mystery child is up against. But we all have a responsibility to protect those who can't protect themselves. I'm legally bound to report such things, though you've been careful not to give me any reportable information. But you're also bound to take action. If you know a child is being molested, and I'm pretty sure you know that, you've got to get help for that child."

She shuffles through a bunch of papers in a file basket and comes up with a paper that lists several hot lines and agencies.

"Here's the number for the L.A. County child abuse hotline," she says, writing the number on an index card. "And here's another number for a national child abuse hotline."

She hands me the card and I shove it into my pocket.

"I know you're concerned, Mario. I can't tell you what to do, but you might at least call those numbers to get more information. You don't have to give your name if you don't want to."

"Thanks," I say.

Kids start coming into the classroom and I stand up to leave. Woodsy stands, too.

"Oh, wait," she says. "Here, give me the numbers back."

I take the card from my pocket and hand it to her. She copies something from the child abuse hotline paper that's still sitting on her desk.

"This is their website. Check it out," she says, handing the card back to me.

I nod.

Woodsy stands and follows me from her office into the classroom.

"Mario?"

I turn to face her. She opens her arms to me and I step forward into her broad hug.

"Come talk to me anytime you want."

"Thanks," I say.

"Good luck. I know you'll do what's right."

She turns and walks to the front of her classroom. I check the time and know that if I go to sixth period, math, I'll be about ten minutes late to get Eddie. A lot can happen in ten minutes.

15

Usually when I get to Eddie's school in the afternoon, cars are lined up down the block waiting for kids to get out. But today nobody's out there, even though there's only about five minutes left before school gets out. Only Ms. Sumner's in the classroom, sitting at one of the big tables looking over a bunch of drawings.

"Where is everyone?" I ask.

She looks up, smiling.

"Oh, hi, Mario. It's a minimum day today. I'm getting caught up on student projects."

"I came for Eddie," I tell her.

"We got out at noon. I think he went with his *tío* or whoever it is that picks him up sometimes."

"In the blue truck?" I ask.

"Yes, that's the one."

I run out of the classroom. Ms. Sumner calls something after me, but I'm already too far away to hear what she says. I run the eight blocks to Carmen's house. There's no truck in the driveway. I rush inside, calling for Eddie, but the house is empty. I get the car keys from under my jeans in the bottom drawer of our chest and run back outside to Max's car. I jack up the back bumper and kick the blocks out, then do the same in front. I toss the jack back in the car and get in.

After a few weak tries – start damn you! – it catches. I do a Y turn into the driveway and speed away. Maybe everything's okay. Maybe Carmen took the day off and the three of them went somewhere together. Yeah, and maybe Eddie sprouted wings and flew away. My mind is spinning. I turn left on Canyon Drive, heading toward Breeson Canyon on a windy road that I'm hoping is the windy road.

Even as fast as I'm driving it seems like it's taking forever to get to the place where the old rock house is. Eddie's school was out at noon and it's now almost three. A lot of bad stuff can happen in three hours and all of it's running through my head. I'm picturing all of the stuff Eddie's told me, like right now is Denton forcing Eddie's mouth down onto his . . . ? Or is he forcing his . . . into Eddie's . . . you know. Or is he holding Eddie by the neck, his big hand . . . like with Blue . . . is he . . . I can't even think the words, but that doesn't keep the pictures from flashing through my mind. Shit! I should have killed the dirty creep when I had the chance!

I step hard on the gas, going so fast the tires screech on the curves. I'm sweating buckets and thinking I should have told Woodsy the whole story and had her file a report. Or I should have done the Internet report, or checked Eddie's schedule or . . .

There it is – the rock house. I follow the dirt driveway to the back and get out, taking the jack handle with me. No blue truck. I rush back behind a dilapidated shed, choking the jack handle like a baseball bat. I look through a dirty window. Nothing. I push the door open with my foot, ready to swing. Still nothing.

Maybe this wasn't the right windy road. I look around in the shed then peer into the windows of the deserted house. I was so sure I'd find them here! Now what? They could be anywhere.

I drive back down the hill. Think like Denton, I tell myself. If you were Denton, where would you take Eddie? But I can't think like Denton because I'm not a friggin' sex pervert.

I go back to Palm Avenue School and find Ms. Sumner still alone in her classroom.

"Did Eddie say anything about where he was going after school?" I ask.

She looks up from her grade book.

"Is everything all right, Mario? Eddie seemed very withdrawn today."

"I just really need to find him and he's not where I thought he would be."

"He's not been home?"

I shake my head.

"Did you notice what direction the blue truck went when they drove off?" I ask.

"No. I wasn't really paying that much attention."

Ms. Sumner leans back and closes her eyes, which I remember from being in her class is a sign that she's thinking.

"You know, Mario," she says, opening her eyes, "now that I think back on it, I guess I didn't actually see Eddie leave in the truck. I just assumed he did because that's often the case."

"So he may have left by himself?"

"Or he might have gone home with a friend. Why don't you see if he's at Brent's? That's who he's with most of the time."

"I'll check it out," I say, turning to leave.

"Wait, Mario."

I pause.

"You seem very worried. Is there something you're not

telling me?"

"I'm just looking for Eddie is all."

"Well . . . " Ms. Sumner fumbles around in her purse.
"Here's my school phone number and my cell phone number. Call me when you find Eddie. If I don't hear from you by
four-thirty, I'll start calling around."

"Yeah, thanks," I say, shoving her card into my pocket next
to the child abuse reporting information.

I check at Brent's house but Eddie's not there. I swing by
Carmen's and this time both her car and Denton's truck are in
the driveway. I park around the corner on the next block, so
they won't notice that I've taken Max's car, then I jog back
to the house. I take a quick look in the bed of Denton's truck
– no cat.

In the house, Carmen and Denton are glued to her computer screen. I rush past them to our room.

"Where's Eddie?" Carmen calls after me. I look in our
room, already knowing from Carmen's question that I won't
see Eddie there.

"He's at Brent's," I lie, hurrying back toward the door.

"Hey. Not so fast!" Carmen says.

"I'm late for work," I say, not stopping.

Denton is up in an instant, blocking my way out the door.

"Your aunt said 'not so fast'," he says.

"Your behavior is totally unacceptable!" Carmen says.
"Denton waited for Eddie for over an hour after school today,
and he never showed up. No one bothered to tell us he was
going to Brent's!"

I stand there, trying to figure out what I can say that will get
me out of here in the fastest possible time.

"Well?" Carmen says.

"I'm late for work," I repeat.

"You just don't get it, do you? Your aunt here's trying to
give you boys a home, and watch out for you, and you, Mr.
Big Shot Mario, can't even bother to let her know where you

and your brother are going to be!"

Carmen jumps in, getting louder and louder with each word.

"Denton picks Eddie up from school, and takes him to all kinds of places he's never even been before . . ."

Yeah, right, I think. Like the windy road to perversion.

". . . Denton's the closest thing to a father poor little Eddie's ever known . . ."

Here Carmen breaks off, crying, then starts again, quieter.

"All I've ever asked is that you follow the most basic rules. Eddie'd be okay if it weren't for your influence," Carmen says, still sniffling, "but you can't even meet me halfway."

"Look. I'm sorry," I tell Carmen. "But can we talk later? I've really got to get to work."

"You better let your aunt finish this now," Denton says. Then he turns to Carmen, all sweet, and says, "You better just get it over with, Sweetheart."

Carmen takes a deep breath.

"Yeah, okay," she says to Denton.

"Sit down, Mario. We've got to have a serious talk."

I sit across from Carmen at the table, trapped, when I want more than anything to run out the door.

Carmen looks from Denton to me and back at Denton again. It's weird, like he's her boss or something.

"See. I thought I could do this, for your mother," she says, "but I can't deal with it anymore. Eddie's a good kid. He can stay here with us. But you . . ." she takes another deep breath. Denton puts his arm around her.

I sit still as a rock but inside I'm churning. I've got to get out of here. Find Eddie. Figure out what's next. I'm barely tracking what Carmen's saying. She continues, ". . . on top of everything else I find out you're sneaking around on sex sites on the Internet!"

The tears are gone now, and she's back to her loudest voice.

I don't exactly get what's going on here. Sex sites on the Internet?

"Denton showed me the record from last night. After I went to bed, when I thought you were emailing your mother, you were looking at horrible, disgusting pornography!"

"I didn't even use your computer last night!"

"Oh, don't lie to me!"

"If anybody was looking at porn it's your pervert of a boyfriend."

"You shut your filthy mouth!" Denton says.

"I've known from the beginning I couldn't trust you but I kept trying to give you the benefit of the doubt, for Maria's sake, but this is the last straw! I can't deal with you any longer!"

I'm trying to make sense of what's happening here, but nothing makes sense. Carmen thinks I'm the pervert?

"You can stay for another three days – time to pack up your stuff and find another place and then I want you out of here! I won't have this nasty filth in my house," she says, gesturing toward her computer.

"The nasty filth in your house is sitting right next to you!"

"Oh! You get out of my house!"

I stand so fast I knock the chair over behind me.

"I don't want you hanging around Eddie, either. Don't even think about coming back here!"

With this the tears start again. Denton puts his arms around her and she sobs into his shoulder.

"You don't know shit," I say, going back to the room.

In our room I get the car insurance money and the envelope with the important papers from my bottom drawer. I shove some clothes into my backpack, and hurry out the front door, with Carmen right behind me.

"Where does Brent live?" Carmen demands. "We'll get Eddie."

"Brent's mom took them bowling. She'll bring him back here about eight," I say, amazed at how fast a lie can come when you need it.

I'm already halfway down the block when Carmen yells after me, "What's Brent's mom's name?"

"Don't know," I yell back, still walking.

At the end of the block I turn and look back, relieved to see that Carmen's no longer standing outside. Turning the corner, I rush to Max's car. It starts right up. I guess the Breeson Canyon trip was enough to charge the battery.

Sometime between Carmen's accusations and my rush to fill my backpack, the cartoon-style light bulb went off over my head and I know exactly where to go.

16

Eddie's sitting in his white plastic chair with his sketch-book spread out on his lap, drawing. He looks up when he hears me round the corner behind the storage shed.

"I've been looking for you for hours!"

"I knew you'd find me," he says.

"How long you been here?"

"Since after school. Denton was there and you weren't, so I snuck out the back way and came here."

I glance down at the sketchpad and see that he's drawn a picture of the dangling cat.

"I want to bury Blue," he says.

"Denton's already done something with him."

"What?"

"I don't know. I looked in the truck and Blue's gone."

Eddie fills in some more details in his drawing, then in big letters at the bottom writes "R.I.P. Blue."

I sit down in the green chair, wishing we still lived in the apartment up front, with Max, and our biggest worries would be hiding from Leah's nieces.

Eddie's going over and over the "R.I.P." with black crayon.

"Denton could break your neck, too. And mine. Like he did to Blue," he says,

"Not a chance," I say. "C'mon. Let's get going."

"I don't want to see Denton."

"Me, either."

Eddie folds up his sketchpad and follows me out to the driveway. His face totally lights up when he sees Max's car.

"Cool! You got the insurance money!"

I've got it all right, I think. Stuffed down in the bottom of my backpack. I'll save that detail for later, though.

We stop at a gas station just outside of town. I use the pay phone to call Ms. Sumner while Eddie washes the windshield.

"I found Eddie," I tell her.

"Oh, I'm so relieved. Was he with Brent?"

"Yes," I lie. "Thanks for your help."

I don't give a flying fig about lying to people like Denton and Carmen, but I feel bad lying to Ms. Sumner. Still, it's not exactly the time to be telling the whole truth.

Next I call Jenna. She doesn't pick up, so I'm stuck with voice mail.

"Hey, Jenna. I'll be gone for a few days, with Eddie. But . . . what you said earlier today, like maybe I don't like you anymore . . . that's so not true! You're the best thing that's ever happened to me. I've never cared about any girl the way I care about you, and . . . so . . . I'll call you tomorrow. Hey, I'm really sorry about missing the party tonight. I want so much to be with you, but this thing with Eddie . . . We've just got to get away for a few days. I . . . I really, really care . . . I'll call."

Why didn't I just say it? I love you, Jenna. What's so hard about that? Not on voice mail though. But she must know how I feel about her. I mean, I want to be with her every chance I get, to hold her, and kiss her, and . . .

Eddie's finished with the windshield and waiting for me in the car by the time I'm off the phone. I fill the gas tank and then we take off for the freeway. I've had my license for over a year now, but I haven't had much practice driving on freeways. It's pretty easy though. You just get in a lane and follow the car in front of you until you want to get off.

"Where're we going?" Eddie says.

"Well . . . I thought maybe we'd go see *Tío* Hector and *Tía* Josie."

"And Simba?"

"Yeah. Simba, too."

"Do you think he's still alive?"

"Sure. Why wouldn't he be?"

Eddie gives me a look like how dumb can I be.

"Do you know how to get there?" he asks.

"Sort of."

"Tomorrow's the Halloween Harvest Festival," Eddie reminds me.

The Harvest Festival is the big Hamilton Heights event of the year, with a parade, and games, and a huge haunted house, and all kinds of other stuff.

"We're gonna miss it this year," I say.

We're at this place near downtown L.A. where all of the freeways come together and then spread out again and I've got to figure out how to get from the 110, where we are now, to Highway 101, which will take us up almost to Redville. I'm concentrating on the signs, and the traffic, and now I see I've got to cross over three lanes to the right to merge onto 101 and nobody wants to let me in.

"I'm supposed to be the master of ceremonies for our class show tomorrow."

"Can't happen," I say, managing one more lane to the right.

When I finally get out onto Highway 101, I look over at

Eddie. His face is all scrunched up again. He turns on the radio but the only reception we can get is some church guy talking about how we're all sinners. I reach over and turn it off.

"Listen, Eddie. I'm sorry you're gonna miss the festival tomorrow, but we're kind of in a bind here."

I tell him about this afternoon at Carmen's, and how she's kicking me out.

"But where will we go?" Eddie says.

"Not we," I say. "She wants you to stay."

"Without you?"

"Yep. Just you and Carmen and Denton – a little family of three."

"But where will you be?"

"According to Carmen, I can be anywhere you're not. I'm not even supposed to see you, or talk to you anymore, because I'm such a bad influence."

"So I'm supposed to be there by myself, with Carmen and Denton?"

"That's what Carmen says."

Eddie stares out the window, like he's all fascinated with the gas stations and fast food places that look like every other gas station and fast food place he's ever seen.

After about ten miles of silence, Eddie says, "I don't really have to go to the festival tomorrow. Candice wanted to be the MC anyway, but everyone voted for me. Everyone but one person, anyway."

"Candice?" I ask.

"Yeah."

Another ten miles of silence, then, "She was dying to be the MC."

It's dark now, and I'm not sure how much farther I should stay on this highway. I'm pretty sure there's a turnoff to Redville coming up soon, but I never paid much attention before, when Max was driving. I turn off at a rest stop to check the map.

Knowing what you already know about Max, you've probably guessed she's got emergency supplies in her car. Which is true. The car itself isn't great, but she's got road maps of California and Los Angeles County, a flashlight, extra batteries, flares, a first aid kit, a big bottle of water, and a ratty old blanket. "Preparedness" is one of the let's-get-this-straight themes she likes to harp on. I wish she were with us right now, getting us straight. I'm not sure if I can get us straight or not.

I pull in next to a van with a vicious looking dog that keeps lunging at the windows, banging his head against the glass. I take the California map and flashlight from the glove compartment.

"Are we lost?" Eddie says.

"I'm just checking," I tell him.

"It seems like we're lost," he says.

"No. Look. We're right here." I point to a spot on the wide, red, Highway 101 line, then to the town we just passed.

"And up here is where we turn off to get to Redville. See? It's maybe another two hours."

Eddie looks at the map and nods.

So okay. I know where we are, and how to get to Hector and Josie's from here. But Eddie's right in a way, too. It does seem like we're lost.

Eddie follows the red Highway 101 line on the map, doing his own version of math problems.

"Are we going sixty-five miles an hour?" he asks, just after a sign that says "San Luis Obispo, Seventy-four Miles."

I glance at the speedometer.

"Yep."

"All the time?"

"Well, it's not like *La Bamba* has cruise control, you know?"

"But almost all the time are we going sixty-five?"

"I guess."

"So, if we're going sixty-five miles an hour and it's seventy-four miles to San Luis Obispo, we'll be in San Luis Obispo in one and 9/65 hours."

His eyes shift right, like that helps him think.

"That's one hour and eight minutes."

"Minus the three minutes it took you to figure it out," I say.

"Okay, so in one hour and five minutes. But you've got to keep it at sixty-five miles an hour," Eddie says.

He sets the timer on his watch and tries to keep his eye on the speedometer. When we get stuck behind a slow-moving truck he starts fidgeting.

"Pass him!" he demands.

"I can't see far enough ahead."

"But there's hardly ever any cars coming the other way," he says.

"Yeah, well. We're not exactly on a good luck streak right now. I think I'll wait 'til I can see what's ahead."

Eddie sighs, like I'm taking all the fun out of the trip. At the next sign, I can tell he's refiguring how many more minutes to San Luis Obispo, but he keeps it to himself, which is fine with me. I've never really liked those kinds of math problems anyway.

It takes us one hour and seventeen minutes to get to San Luis Obispo from when Eddie made his first time estimate.

"You shouldn't have stayed behind that truck so long," Eddie says.

We're getting better radio reception now and I find a classic rock station, which gets Eddie off the speed-into-distance-equals-time kick. We've only got music for about fifteen minutes, though, and then it fades out again.

Man, I'm getting tired of driving. My butt's numb from sitting so long, and my shoulders are all stiff. Usually, when Max drives us up here, we pack a picnic and stop halfway at a park and fool around for a while. I guess we could pull into the next rest stop and get out, but I just want to push on through.

"What're we going to do tomorrow?" Eddie asks.

"I don't know," I say.

"How long are we going to stay at *Tío* Hector's?"

"I don't know."

The truth is, I've been wondering the same things myself.

Eddie watches the scenery for a while, green hills and oak trees, with houses every now and then.

"You promised you wouldn't tell," he says.

"I know."

"You can't tell!"

"I know, Eddie. We might have to sometime, though."

"No!" he screams. "Denton'll find us and kill us. I know he will!"

"Okay! I promised, didn't I?"

"You swore to God!"

"Okay!"

It's like Eddie gets all involved in the math stuff, or how he's missing the Harvest Festival, and he forgets all about Denton. Then, all of a sudden, Denton's back.

It's nearly midnight when I turn onto the highway that leads to Redville. Eddie's sound asleep and I've been worrying about Jenna for miles. Like did she get my message? Will she be mad if she stops by Java Jive and I'm not there? I bet Sammy's mad that I just didn't show up. I can live with that, but Jenna? I don't even want to think about it. I'm all anxious that my email didn't go through to Max today. I've never missed even one day before, and I'm afraid she'll think something bad has happened. Well, something bad has happened, but I don't want her worrying about us.

I turn the radio on again, but now the only radio station that comes in is in Spanish with lots of mariachi music. I listen for a few minutes, then turn it off. I know it's part of my heritage and all, but I'm not wild about mariachi bands, except if they're playing "*La Bamba.*" And I hardly know any Spanish – *abuelo* and *abuela*, for my grandparents, and *tía* and *tío*, meaning aunt and uncle. I can count to twenty in Spanish, but who can't? *Tamales*? I like *tamales* – the real kind, not the phony Casa Panchito kind. I can't stand *menudo*, though. According to my *Tío* Hector, I must be adopted because all Mexicans love *menudo*. Eddie? He's authentic Mexican because he has to have *menudo* every Sunday morning. So am I off the subject here, or what?

I shut off the radio and try again to make sense of my spinning thoughts.

What's the deal with Carmen, anyway? I was so worried about finding Eddie that I wasn't exactly focused on what she was saying. I try to replay that whole scene from earlier today, in her kitchen. What was going on? She was hella mad, but why?

And the whole Internet thing – like I'm the pervert in that house? She oughta open her eyes and take a good look at Denton . . .

As soon as I think "Denton," it comes to me. I'll bet Denton was over-the-top pissed when he missed out on his perverted thrills 'cause he couldn't find Eddie after school. Then he got Carmen going. And he must've added some of his favorite porn sights to Carmen's computer and blamed me. Carmen's totally blind where Denton's concerned. I guess that's how desperate she is to keep a man in her life.

But now what?

17

I turn onto Valley Road, which takes us through the town of Redville. Max got on my case last Christmas for calling the place a dump. I only said it to her and Eddie, not around *Tío* Hector or the rest of the people who live here.

"Let's get this straight," she'd started. She went on to say that these were decent people who worked hard for a living and they deserved my respect. I do respect them, and I'll keep my Redville opinions to myself, but the place is a dump! Rundown buildings, thrift stores, skinny dogs wandering around. I mean, Hamilton Heights isn't exactly Beverly Hills, but it's a whole lot nicer than this. There's not even a decent coffee place here. Not even a Starbucks and practically every town in the world has a Starbucks. McDonald's is here, but even though they've started advertising specialty coffees, I bet you still can't get a hand-crafted mint mocha chip frappuccino powered up with a vitamin enhaced doubleshot anywhere underneath the Golden Arches.

What am I doing here, anyway? Eddie and I both probably could have stayed at Walker's for a few days, until we figured something else out. Or Leah might have taken us in for a day or two. Eddie could have been the MC tomorrow. I could have seen Jenna. I'm about to drift off into Jenna-land when I remember how scared I was for Eddie, and how I can't be with him all the time. And how determined Denton is to get Eddie off by himself. And I think well duh, I had to get Eddie out of there. So here we are now, only about a mile from *Tío* Hector and *Tía* Josie's place. It's close to midnight and we're going to knock on their door and tell them . . . tell them . . . What will we tell them?

I reach over and poke Eddie.

"Wake up!"

"I've got to pee," he says, not opening his eyes.

"We're almost there."

"What if I can't hold it?"

"You can. Look, there's their house."

I turn into the driveway and shut off the engine. There's not a light on anywhere. They're probably sound asleep. Eddie starts to get out of the car.

"Wait. I don't think we should wake them up."

"But I've got to go!" he whines.

"Go in the bushes," I tell him.

"That's disgusting," he says, but he gets out of the car, unzipping on the way. I'm sitting there trying to decide whether or not to ring the doorbell when *Tío* Hector opens the back door and peers out.

"Hey, *Tío*," I call to him.

He rubs his eyes, like he can't believe what he's seeing.

"It's me. Mario," I say.

"Mario! *Ay, Mijo*! What're you doing here?"

He comes walking out and I get out of the car to greet him. He's barefoot, wearing a tee shirt and baggy boxers, with a smile that lets me know I'm welcome. He throws a big bear hug on me.

"What brings you here at this time of the night?" he asks,

laughing.

He stops suddenly and motions to me to be quiet. I hear what he hears.

"It's just Eddie," I say.

He laughs again.

"We have indoor plumbing even up here in Redville," he says.

"We didn't want to wake you," I tell him.

Eddie comes out from behind the bushes and Hector gives him the bear hug treatment, too.

"*Ay*, how much you've grown since last Christmas!" he says.

Eddie squirms out of his hug and goes running off toward the barn.

Tío Hector looks after him, puzzled.

"Where's he off to already?"

"I think he's looking for Simba."

"Everything okay? Maria's okay?"

"Yeah. We heard from her a couple of days ago," I tell him. "Her unit's being moved, but she says it's just from one safe place to another."

"And you drove here by yourselves?"

"Yeah."

"Car's still holding up okay?"

"It's got this knocking sound sometimes, in second gear, other than that . . ."

Eddie comes out of the barn. He's carrying Simba, who's now a very big cat, though still not a lion. He's got both arms around Simba, holding him close to his chest.

"Simba's alive!" he announces.

"Told you," I say.

"Josefina!" *Tío* Hector calls out loudly. "Guess who's here?"

"The angel Gabriel?" she asks, belting out her window-shaking laugh.

"Close. It's Mario and little Eddie!"

Tía Josie comes shuffling out, still laughing. She's wearing red satiny pajamas and her long grey hair sticks out all over, like maybe she just stuck her finger in a light socket. She rushes out the door and down the steps, throwing her arms around me, hugging me tight. We're about the same height but she must weigh twice as much as I do. Her hugs are the softest hugs I've ever known. She hugs Eddie, who's still hanging on to Simba, then stands back and looks us over.

"Ay, hijos, you must be hungry, aren't you?"

She leads the way into the kitchen and takes food from the refrigerator without waiting for an answer.

"Sit down," Hector says, motioning toward the table.

The three of us sit at the big round table where we've eaten so many Christmas dinners. Simba slides out of Eddie's arms and onto the floor. *Tía* Josie stands at the stove, heating beans and tortillas.

I didn't even know I was hungry until I got a whiff of the warming beans but now my mouth is all watery and my stomach is sending "feed me" messages to my brain.

"What brings you guys here in the middle of the night?" Hector asks again.

Josie puts a plate of beans and tortillas in front of us and pours us each a glass of lemonade.

"Let them eat first. Then we'll talk," Josie says.

Hector goes to the refrigerator and gets a can of beer, then sits down again. Josie heaps more beans onto our plates and then she pulls up a chair, too. They both sit smiling at us, like they couldn't be happier that we got them out of bed at midnight and now we're eating their food.

When we've eaten our fill, Hector says, "So tell me now. What brings you here tonight?"

Eddie's face gets that scrunchy, closed-up look. He gets down on the floor, next to Simba.

Josie puts the leftover food back in the refrigerator.

"You boys want more lemonade?" she asks.

"No thanks," I tell her.

"Another beer, *Papi*?"

"Just sit with us, Josie," Hector says.

He glances down at Eddie who's totally engrossed in scratching Simba's head, then turns his attention to me.

"So, let's see. It's Friday night. There's a football game, parties. Another Kung Fu movie's just out. It's a busy night at the skating rink. And you two decide to get into the car and drive all night to come to our house? And it's not even Christmas?"

I can't think of what to tell them, so I just sit there, like a lump. Hector and Josie wait, like they've got all night. Well, or all morning. Finally, the silence is worse than trying to talk.

"We're sort of in trouble," I say.

Eddie darts a look at me that says "no!" just as loudly as if he'd screamed it.

"What kind of trouble?" Hector says. Now he's got a scrunched up worried face and so does *Tía* Josie.

"Well . . . just . . ."

"Tell us what kind of trouble," Hector says. "School? Fighting? Stealing? What? Are the police about to come after you here, with their guns and bullhorns and battering rams? That kind of trouble?"

Josie gets up and locks the back door, then goes to the front window and looks out, as if Hector's idea about the cops coming for us is about to become a reality. I guess living in fear of *la migra* before they were citizens left its mark.

"Not trouble with the law," I say. "Nothing like that."

"What trouble, then?"

"Well . . . we're just not getting along very well with Carmen."

Hector's face does a kind of slow-motion shift, like from scrunched and frowning, to relaxed, to lips stretched up with crinkles at his eyes to a full-out laugh.

"That's your trouble? That's all? No one can get along with Carmen. She's *loca* in the *cabeza!*"

This sets him off laughing again.

"What happened?" Josie asks.

"Well . . ." Eddie gives me another of those "no" looks.

"She says I don't follow her rules. She's sick of having me around and I can't live there anymore."

"Carmen and her *pinche* rules," Hector says, shaking his head.

Did I say earlier that *Tío* Hector doesn't get along with Carmen? Something about how Carmen borrowed money from Hector and Josie a long time ago, and never paid it back. And how when their father was dying, Carmen didn't go visit him in Mexico. They sort of tolerate each other at Christmas time, but that's about it.

I tell Hector, "Carmen says I'm a bad influence on Eddie and I've got to stay away from him. That's what Denton says, too."

"Denton?" Hector says.

"Her boyfriend. He sort of lives there."

"*Ay!* Another one? That slut!"

"Hector!" Josie says, gently touching her fingers to his mouth. "Don't say that! *Ella es su hermana!*"

"It's the truth," he says.

"I don't care. You shouldn't say it."

She looks first at Eddie, then at me. "Stay with us until Maria gets home," she says. "We've got room. We'll take good care of you."

"That's what you should've done in the first place," Hector says. "I told Maria . . ."

"It's just . . . well, I want to graduate with my class," I say. "And Eddie wants to stay at his school, too, with his friends and all."

"It's not worth putting up with Carmen!"

"What's Maria say? Did she tell you to come to us?" Josie

asks.

"She doesn't know yet," I tell her.

"You didn't tell her you were driving up here?" Hector asks.

"Well . . . we left in kind of a hurry. And it's not like we can just pick up the phone and call. I really need to email her though. Do you have a computer yet?"

Josie throws back her head and lets out another bellowing laugh. Hector joins in.

"We haven't felt the need," Josie says, wiping her eyes. "We don't even need one of those automatic coffee makers. What do we need with a computer?"

I join in the laughter, but Eddie just sits on the floor, petting Simba, as if no one else is even in the room.

Josie turns her attention to Eddie.

"You know, Simba always sleeps in the barn, next to the goat. But he'd probably like to sleep on your bed tonight. If that's okay for you?"

Eddie gives a hint of a smile, then coaxes Simba down the hall to the room where we always stay.

After he leaves, Josie asks, "Is Eddie all right?"

I don't know what to say.

"You know, how he always comes in full of jokes? He seems a little sad to me."

I shrug.

"He's tired," Hector says. "It's a long ride."

"He must miss Maria."

Hector pushes back from the table.

"C'mon, *mi señora*. I'm tired, too."

"I'll be in soon," Josie says, rising to give Hector a kiss.

"I'll get our stuff from the car," I say.

"Mario, you know you and Eddie are welcome to stay with us for as long as you want."

"Thanks, *Tío*."

Josie follows me to the door and hands me a flashlight.

"The sheets are clean in Vincent's bedroom," she says. "And you know where to find fresh towels."

I get our backpacks from *La Bamba* and lock her up, then take our stuff into Vincent's old room. Eddie's on the floor, playing with Simba. Or I should say trying to play with Simba. For his part, Simba just lays there looking bored. Eddie's dangling a shoestring in front of Simba's face, which drove him crazy when he was a kitten, but now he doesn't even lift a paw to bat at it.

Vincent's baseball trophies are all shined and polished, still sitting on top of the chest of drawers. I used to wonder why Vincent didn't play pro baseball if he was so good, but Max said he knew from the time he was twelve that he wanted to be a lawyer. Baseball was just for fun. Law was for real.

Josie peeks through the doorway, then comes in.

"*El gato gordo*'s getting too lazy to play," she says to Eddie. "Simba and I should go to Weight Watchers, but we don't want to," she laughs.

She opens the windows halfway and fluffs our pillows.

"Sleep well," she says, kissing each of us on the forehead.

It's around noon by the time I wake up on Saturday. I probably would have slept all day, but people are talking kind of loud, right outside the window by my bed. My first thought is I've got to call Jenna. Then I remember that my email to Max didn't go through yesterday.

I sit on the edge of the bed, rubbing my eyes, only half-listening to the voices outside. When I hear my name mentioned, I start listening with both ears.

"She says Mario's incorrigible!"

"I don't even know what that means, but I know it's a lie!"

I recognize Hector's voice. I get up and take a quick peek out the window. Hector, Vincent, and Josie are sitting at the table, under the big eucalyptus tree, eating lunch. I don't know where Eddie is, probably off trying to retrain Simba to fetch.

"It means he's out of control. He refuses to follow any rules, he's got a bad attitude, and . . . "

I sit back down on the bed, close to the window, so I can

hear everything they're saying.

". . . she wants them back down there tonight. She wants me to ride with them, so they'll be sure to get there. I told her I couldn't do it today, but I could maybe make it work tomorrow."

I'd like to get dressed, but I don't want to leave the window.

"They're not going back unless they want to," Hector says.

"That's not how it is, Papa. Carmen's their legal guardian. It's the same as if Maria said the boys had to come home. You'd see to it that they got home."

"It's not the same. *No es igual!*"

"Legally it is. Right now, the boys are runaways, and, according to Carmen, it's all because of Mario."

"They're not runaways! They're with us. Have her call me, I'll tell her!"

"Carmen called me because she didn't want to talk to you. She figured the boys might be here, and she asked me to check it out."

"Why did she think they'd be here?" Josie asks.

"Well, they'd looked all over for them at the usual places, and when they noticed the car was gone . . ."

"They? Who's they?" Hector asks.

"Carmen and her boyfriend. She says they're planning to get married. She says this guy treats Eddie like a son. They're both nuts about Eddie, but she says Mario's turned into a real troublemaker."

Hector says something in Spanish. I don't know what it is, but I don't think it's nice.

What I'm thinking right now isn't nice, either.

There's some shuffling around – probably Josie is up filling everybody's plates.

"I've got to get back home. Elena's got a book group meeting at three, and I told Hannah I'd take her to a movie, but I wanted to see what was going on over here. Where is Mario, anyway? I saw Eddie out in the yard with the cat, but . . ."

"Mario's still sleeping," Josie says. "That's a long drive, and we stayed up for a while after they got here."

"I'll look in on him. See if I can at least say hello before I leave," Vincent says.

I quick crawl under the covers and put the pillow over my head. In a short time, I hear the bedroom door open.

"Mario?" Vincent says, softly.

I don't move.

"Mario?" He's a bit louder now.

I still don't move.

There's a pause, then I feel Vincent's weight on the edge of the bed. He jostles my arm.

"Wake up, Mario. We should talk."

I move the pillow off my head and turn over.

"Sorry to wake you, but I need to talk to you."

I sit up, resting my back against the wall.

"From what Carmen told me on the phone this morning, you're not only a runaway, but you've kidnapped your little brother. If you're not back there by tomorrow night, she's going to file a police report. Me, I've never thought of you as a troublemaker, and I figure maybe you left there for a reason. So I'd like to hear your side of things before I deliver you back to Carmen."

Vincent looks at me with such sincerity and concern that I'm tempted to just start talking and see what happens.

"I've got to leave pretty soon," he says. "Tell me why you decided to come up here all of a sudden."

I'm trying to figure out what to say when Eddie comes rushing in.

"Hi, Eddie," Vincent says, standing to give him a hug. "Mario and I were just talking about why you boys decided to come see us."

Eddie goes all stiff and Vincent steps back.

"You promised to God!" Eddie screams.

He runs down the hall and into the bathroom, slamming the door behind him. I hear the click of the bolt as it jams into a locked position.

"What's wrong with Eddie?" Vincent asks.

I get up, grab my pants from the chair, and slip them on. I stand outside the bathroom door.

"Hey, Eddie. Open up. It's okay."

He doesn't open the door. He doesn't answer. All I hear is the vroom-vroom of his racecar toothbrush.

Vincent comes to the door and knocks loudly. Still nothing but vroom-vroom.

"Come on, Eddie!" I shout. No change.

Vincent pulls a chair over and sits in front of the bathroom door.

"He can't stay in there all day," he says.

I sit on the floor and lean my back against the wall. Vincent looks at his watch.

"What's with your brother?"

I shrug.

Josie walks into the hallway, looking worried.

"Eddie won't come out of the bathroom," Vincent says.

"Is he sick?" Josie asks.

She puts her ear to the bathroom door. "What's that noise?"

"Toothbrush," I say.

Vincent checks his watch again.

"I've got to go, Mama," he says, standing and kissing her on the cheek. "I'll call you when I get home."

Turning to me, he says, "Whatever the problem is here, we need to know what's going on."

On his way out the back door, I hear Vincent call to Hector, "You better go in there and see if you can get Eddie to open the bathroom door."

Eddie doesn't respond to *Tío* Hector either. When the noise of the toothbrush stops I'm not sure if Eddie has turned it off, or if the batteries have just run out.

"Little Eddie? *Ven mijo*," Josie calls. "I'm baking cookies. Come lick the bowl for me."

That doesn't work, either.

Finally, after he's been in there for over an hour, I decide to crawl in through the window and get him. Hector brings the ladder from the garage, and I climb up level with the window. Eddie's sitting on the floor by the bathtub, his head resting against his knees, his toothbrush gripped between his thumb and index finger stubs. I tap on the window. He looks up. I motion for him to unlock the door. He gives an angry shake of his head and turns his back to me. The window is one of those double-hung old-fashioned kind. It's already open by a couple of inches, but when I try to open it further, it won't budge.

I get down from the ladder and Hector climbs up to give it a try. No luck. I step up again and tap on the window.

"You might as well open the door, Eddie, and save us all some trouble."

It's as if he hasn't even heard me.

"Damn it, Eddie! Cut the crap and open the friggin' door!"

Still no response. I fold up the ladder and carry it to the garage. Hector gets his toolbox and we go back to take the door off its hinges.

In the kitchen, Josie sits at the table, talking on the phone. She gives us a worried look as we walk past.

"I'll call you back in a few minutes, *Mijo*, after we get him out," she says, then hangs up and follows us down the hallway. I try one more time to convince Eddie to come out. Hector demands. Josie pleads. Nothing.

I hold the door in place while Hector taps the pin from first the bottom hinge and then the top. We slip the door off and lean it against the wall. I go to Eddie where he still sits on the floor and take him by the arm to pull him up. He jerks away from me.

"You swore to God!" he shouts.

"Damn it, Eddie, stop being such a punk!"

"Liar!"

I grab him by both arms now and pull him to his feet.

"You little shit! I've just . . . "

Josie comes in behind me and pulls me away. I rush past Hector out the bathroom door, down the hall, out the back door and into the driveway. I yank at *La Bamba*'s door handle, forgetting I locked her up last night. I bang my fist, hard, against the door. Why does everything have to get so screwed up? I've probably totally lost it with Jenna by doing the great disappearing act last night. Sammy'll probably fire me for not showing up at work. I've taken Max's car without keeping up my end of the insurance bargain and I'm being accused of kidnapping! Every damned last one of these problems is all because I'm trying to protect my little shit of a brother from that asshole Denton and then Eddie pulls this shit!

I kick the tire, flash on the image of Denton forcing Eddie's head down on his dick, turn the tire into Denton's face and kick it harder and harder until his face is pounded to a pulp. I limp over to the porch steps and sit rubbing my bruised hand. I take off my shoe and massage my toes the way Max taught me to do when they got all stiff and sore when I first started playing soccer.

Jenna. I've got to call Jenna, but not from the phone here, where everyone can hear everything. And Max. I've got to email Max. If she's in a place to check email, I know she'll be worried about us, not hearing from us for going on two days now. And why does Eddie have to go and get all crazy on me?

I'm still mindlessly rubbing my toes and thinking the same thoughts over and over again when Hector comes out and sits down beside me on the step. We sit for a long time without saying anything. I put my shoe back on and tie the laces, then retie the laces on the other shoe.

"Why's Little Eddie so mad at you?" Tío Hector asks.

"He thinks I broke a promise."

"Did you?"

"No."

"What was the promise?"

"If I told you I'd be breaking the promise," I say.

Hector reaches for a twig that's on the ground beside the bottom step. He uses it to clean the dirt from under his fingernails, then flicks it back onto the ground when he's finished.

"Well, I guess you better go try to make things right with your brother. We can't do anything with him. He won't even eat one of Josefina's cookies. That's not like Eddie," he says, shaking his head sadly.

"Where is he?" I ask.

"Curled up on the bed in Vincent's room when I left."

I go back in and find Eddie stretched out on the bed with Simba stretched out beside him. Eddie's rubbing Simba's ears while Simba purrs a constant thank you. I sit on the edge of the bed, careful not to disturb the contented cat. Eddie doesn't look at me, but he doesn't turn his back on me either.

"I'm in a lot of shit because of you, and it pisses me off that you say I'm a liar when I'm not."

"Yeah, well I bet God's pissed off at you, too. You swore to God you wouldn't break your promise and you did! I know you did because I saw you, and now Denton's going to find us and kill us!"

Eddie flops over on his side, again showing me his back. Simba jumps off the bed and hurries out of the room as fast as his fat body can move.

"What do you mean, you saw me break my promise?" I ask.

"I saw you telling Vincent."

"But you didn't hear me!"

"Vincent said you were telling him why we left Carmen's!"

"Well I didn't! I was trying to think up some lie to tell for you, because of that stupid promise I made to you! And my life's all messed up because I care about you and I'm never going to let that pervert Denton get his hands on you again, and all of a sudden it's like you don't even trust me and I've never ever been anything but the best brother I can be and . . ."

My throat closes, blocking my words. I walk across the room to the other bed and sit with my head in my hands, fighting tears. Eddie comes over and sits down next to me. I don't look at him. I can play that old turn-away-and-shut-up game, too.

"Sorry," Eddie whispers.

I stay still.

"Sorry," he says, turning up the volume.

He moves in close and puts his arms around my waist, holding on with what must be all of his strength.

"I'm just so scared Denton will kill you. That's all."

I put my arm around his shoulder and pull him closer.

"We've got to stick together, Buddy," I tell him. "We can't be afraid of Denton."

After a while we go out to the kitchen for cookies. I expect to see the usual damned chocolate chip cookies, and I see from Eddie's look of pure pleasure with his first taste that I'm right. But I'm wrong, too. Josie motions to a smaller plate of cookies.

"For you, Mario," she says, showing me the cookies she baked from dough kept separate and unspoiled by chocolate chips.

"**D**o you think I can use Vincent's computer to email Max?"

"I don't see why not, *Mijo*," Josie says. "I'll call him for you though, just to be on the safe side."

I go into the bedroom and get the car keys and my money from my backpack. Josie's on the phone when I come back to the kitchen and I stand waiting for the okay to go use Vincent's computer. Josie hands me the phone.

"Hey, Vincent. I really need to email Max. She expects to hear from us every day."

"No problem. I'm on my way out with Hannah but I'll leave a key for you under the big blue rock, just to the right of the back door."

"Thanks," I say. "See you later."

"Hey, not so fast," Vincent says.

"What?"

"We've all got to talk. That thing with Eddie was crazy this morning. My parents may not be showing it because they always want things to be calm and happy, but I can tell they're terribly worried about Eddie's self-imposed stint in solitary confinement."

"He won't do it again," I say.

"Okay, but there's more going on with you guys than just you're having a hard time getting along with Carmen. Am I right?"

"Yeah. I guess."

"So listen, Mario. I've promised Hannah I'll take her to this movie, and if we don't get out of here soon we'll miss the beginning and she'll be all disappointed and what should be a fun time won't be. But after the movie, and after Elena and I take Hannah trick or treating, we're coming over there for dinner. Will you be there?"

"Probably."

"No. Not probably. I want you and Eddie to be there for sure. We need to have a family meeting about what's going on with you two. I need you to give me an alternate perspective, otherwise all I have to go on is Carmen's view, which is that you're an incorrigible trouble maker who is leading Eddie astray . . ."

In the background Hannah's demands that they leave now are getting louder and louder.

"I'm coming, Hannah! Go get in the car and buckle up. I'll be right there . . ."

"So Mario, like I said, I don't see you as a troublemaker, but you've got to help me out some. We'll see you about seven. Okay?"

"Yeah, okay," I say.

T he key is under a blue rock, just like Vincent said. A big bright blue rock. With a yellow sun painted on top – Hannah's work, I'm sure. Not exactly an inconspicuous hiding place, but it's there. That's what matters.

When I get within ten feet or so of the back door, their dog,

Rovie, starts in with this booming loud bark-growl combination that'd be enough to scare anyone away. Rovie cracks me up. She's not much bigger than Simba, but she's got a super deep, intense bark that sounds more like it's coming from a ferocious pit bull than from this little wimp of a mutt. So I guess they don't have to worry about hiding their key in an obvious place.

I open the door and Rovie gives one last half-bark, then starts running in big, wide circles around me. I get down on the floor and crawl toward her, hissing and meowing. She jumps at me and runs away, comes back again and runs away. She stretches flat on her belly and crawls toward me and now I'm laughing so hard I can't meow anymore. When she gets within arm's reach of me she rolls over on her back, spreads all four legs wide, and looks straight at me, inviting me to rub her belly. I swear she'd wink at me if she could. I give her a few soft knuckle rubs, then go to the computer in Vincent's office.

Three of the walls are lined with books – mostly law books, with a few history books here and there, plus three full shelves of books about Cesar Chavez, the guy who started the Farmworkers Union. He's like some kind of hero to Vincent. Max said it was Cesar Chavez's work that got Vincent interested in law. Most people think lawyers are scum bags, but Vincent studied law so he could help poor people. At least that's what Max told me.

The fourth wall is taken up mainly with big French doors that lead out onto the patio and pool area. Maybe I'll go for a swim after I call Jenna and email Max – take my mind off things. I dread the coming "family meeting," but I don't know how to get out of it.

I sit in Vincent's swivel chair, pick up the phone and dial Jenna's number. I know it's a long distance call. I don't think Vincent will care, but if he does I'll just pay him back for it.

"Hey, it's me," I say as soon as Jenna picks up. "I miss

you."

"Mario . . ."

Something in Jenna's voice scares me.

"Do you miss me, too?" I ask.

"Mario, I don't think I can do this anymore."

"What do you mean?" I ask, afraid to hear the answer.

"Pretend that we're together. Pretend that I'm important to you."

"No. Don't say that. We are together. You are important to me."

"I feel sorry for your little brother, but . . ."

"Jenna. Listen. I love you."

Long pause.

"If you love me, then why've you always got some excuse about why you can't see me, or call me, and . . ."

"Don't cry, Jenna. Please, whatever it is . . ."

"Do you know how I felt when you didn't show up last night?"

"I called. Didn't you get my message?"

"I don't want messages! I want you in person! Courtney had a real person with her last night! Meredith had a real person with her, too."

She's crying full out now, and I don't know what to say.

"All I had last night was a message! Me and my message! What a great time we had at the party! It's my senior year, and I'll probably be going to the prom and all the rest of the parties with a message! Why don't you just say you don't want to be with me and get it over with?"

"God, Jenna, I want to be with you more than anything! You've got to believe that. Right now, except for you, my life is a total mess. You are absolutely the only thing in my life that's right for me."

Another long pause.

"And you are the only thing in my life that's wrong for me."

"Please, give me a chance. You'll see. As soon as I get back, I'll make it all up to you."

Pause.

"I don't even know where you are, Mario. Or when you're coming back. Maybe you have a secret girlfriend."

"There's no one but you, Jenna. I'm in Redville, with my aunt and uncle. Things were bad for Eddie and I had to get him out of there."

"When will you be back?"

"Soon as possible. Maybe Monday."

"You'll get things worked out by Monday?"

"Hopefully."

Another long silence.

"I really am sorry for your brother, but . . . I just want to have a great senior year, and I want to do it with more than a message."

"Jenna . . ."

The phone goes dead. I press redial and get Jenna's voice-mail. What can I do to make things right again? I put my head down on the desk feeling all hollow inside. Rovie comes over and rests her chin against my leg, as if she senses my sadness. I pet her head while I try to convince myself that things aren't as bad as they seem.

I call Walker.

"Where the fuck were you last night?"

"I'm in Redville. I had to get Eddie out of there."

"Redville? With the wetbacks?"

"Don't be an asshole."

"Just kidding. But what're you doing up there anyway?"

"Wishing things weren't so messed up."

"Yeah, well you really blew it with Jenna. Trevor took both Meredith and Jenna home last night, and guess who he dropped off last?"

"Shit!"

"I warned you, didn't I? I warned you, and you still ran off to Redville."

"But do you think Jenna and Trevor . . .?"

"Courtney says Jenna doesn't really like Trevor, but she likes the attention. You just better get your butt down here and take care of business."

"I know. But I've got to get things worked out with Eddie first."

"Why not just call the cops? Let them take care of it."

"The cops?"

"Well, yeah! If the guy's molesting Eddie, just turn him in."

My brain is moving in slow motion . . . why is Walker talking about molestation . . . how could he know . . .

"Or tell your aunt the guy's getting his rocks off . . . "

"What makes you think that?"

"Courtney said that guy's getting his jollies with Eddie. That so sucks!"

Courtney told Walker? Which means Jenna told Courtney?

"You still there? Mario?"

"Yeah. It's just, nobody's supposed to know any of this. I promised Eddie that I wouldn't tell anyone and now . . ."

"Hey, don't worry about it, Dude. I won't tell Eddie I know anything. I hardly ever see him anyway."

I hear a horn blasting in the background.

"Hey, sorry, gotta go. My mom's dragging me over to visit my grandma and she's waiting in the car for me. Later, Dude."

The phone goes dead and I sit staring out the window. I'm thinking little kid thoughts. NO FAIR! JENNA LIED!

I try Jenna's number again, and again I get her voice mail. I'm angry, and numb, and empty, and wishing I could somehow get Jenna off my mind. If only I could just stop thinking about her.

I turn my attention to the computer to get the email task

over with. There's a message from Max sent earlier this morning.

From: Maria_27@hitmail.net
Date: October 31 8:42 AM
To: Mario Barajas <mario3@yoohoo.com>
Subject: Leveling with you

My dearest sons,
First let me tell you that my wounds are not serious, and I'll be back in the field within two weeks. That's the first thing I want you to know. I'm okay. Please hang on to that awareness, because what I'm going to tell you next is very difficult for me to write, and probably will be just as difficult for you to read.

I came close to death yesterday. We were on the road, only about six miles from our destination. There were eight of us in the vehicle. I was in the middle seat, in the back, and our sergeant, the mac-n-cheese guy I mentioned earlier, starts showing the guy on the other side of me a batch of pictures his wife had sent him. Pictures of their new baby. I'd already seen all the pictures, so I slid over to the outside and let the sergeant take my middle seat, so they wouldn't have to keep passing the pictures across me.

So not more than five minutes after we change places, this IED goes off under our Humvee. I'm blown off to the side, a piece of shrapnel embedded in my upper thigh. The sergeant and the guy who was looking at his pictures were blown apart. The other five, including my friend Becky, got a few bruises--no worse than you would get in a regular soccer game, Mario.

Here's a sight that will haunt me for the rest of my life. Most of my sergeant's body landed back behind the Humvee. But his severed right arm landed just a few feet away from me. His hand was clutching a totally undamaged picture of his three-month-old son, bright eyed and smiling, as if the world were a good and happy place to be. And I can't help thinking that if the sergeant and I hadn't traded places, his son would still have a father. And you boys would no longer have a mother. And the only communication I've had with you since I left home has been so shallow. About macaroni and cheese, and being in safe places, and blah, blah, blah. It's true that I love the mac-n-cheese you send, and it's true that the places I've been in have been relatively safe in comparison to a lot of other places in Iraq. But the bigger truth is, there's no safe place. And there's a lot more to talk about than macaroni and cheese. I've been trying to reassure you, and just write the good stuff. But in trying to protect you we've lost that connection we've always had, where we talk about it all, no matter how bad. And now more than ever is a time for us to stay connected and to keep our bonds strong. So if something terrible happens to any one of us, we'll still have the fullness of that person to hold in our hearts.

There's another image that haunts me. This was just a few days after I arrived in Iraq. We were driving through a little village, on our way to our assigned post. A woman, the mother I guessed, was cradling a boy in her arms, rocking back and forth, wailing the most heart-wrenching sound I've ever heard. The boy, about your size, Eddie, had been killed in the crossfire between some insurgents and our troops. That mother and son sometimes show up in my dreams, but sometimes I am the mother, and one of you is the son, and I wake shaking and drenched in sweat.

Maybe I shouldn't tell you these things, but it's the only way I know to keep my heart open to you, without restraint.

And what about you? Your messages too, give only pleasant details. I want more. I want the whole of your lives. I know you don't want to worry me about anything, but I much prefer worrying to losing touch with what's really going on with you.

I miss you guys to the moon and back. I love you to the moon and back. Take care of each other. Let me in on the whole of your lives.

Max/Mom

I read the message over and over again, picturing the unattached arm. The smiling baby picture. The dead boy who looked like Eddie. My chest tightens at the thought of Max nearly getting killed. I reread the parts about how she wants us to know everything, not just the good stuff, so we can stay as connected as we've always been. And I read that sentence about how she wants to know the whole of our lives. I know she's right. It's time to stop hiding the bad stuff. I take a deep breath and press reply. Here goes.

From: Mario Barajas <mario3@yoohoo.com>
Date: October 31, 4:07 PM
To: Maria_27@hitmail.net
Subject: Leveling

Dear Max,
hope your leg gets better real soon, and that you won't have such a scar that you'll have to wear one of those old fashioned bathing suits that comes down to your knees. lol. thanks for leveling with us (well, eddie hasn't seen your message yet, but he will, soon) about your horrible experiences. i swear, i couldn't even breathe the first time I read about how you were almost killed. and the things that haunt you now--i just wish we could have kept things like they were, and we'd all still be back in our apartment, living our safe lives. but we're not, and since you want to know the whole of our lives, i'll fill you in on things I've been leaving out.

it helped that I knew you were okay from the very beginning of your message, so I want to start by telling you that eddie and I are okay, too. but things have been hard for us lately. i'm just going to try to tell this straight out.

denton's been messing with eddie since we moved in over there. i didn't know anything about it until Thursday night, when i caught him forcing eddie to give him a blow job. fucking pervert! i know you don't like it when i use the f-word, but I bet you're with me on this one. talk about haunting images -- seeing denton's giant hands forcing eddie's head down onto his disgusting dick is mine. denton was wanting to butt fuck eddie, too. that part didn't happen, but it would have if we hadn't run away to redville. probably the reason you haven't been getting any jokes from eddie lately is because of that fucking pervert. so anyway, i fired up la bamba and drove to redville yesterday, to tío hector's and tía josie's. i didn't get the extra car insurance yet, but i had to get eddie out of there. carmen's totally fucked up--accusing me of stuff I've never even thought of. she wants eddie back right now, so she and denton and eddie can be a perfect little family. she's kicking me out and telling me I can't even see eddie any more. that can't happen.

when i first found out, eddie got me to promise i wouldn't tell anyone because he's so scared. denton threatened to kill us both if eddie ever told, and eddie believes him. he's been telling eddie to shut up about everything, and then he broke a cat's neck, right in front of eddie, because the cat wouldn't shut up. eddie had a total meltdown this morning because he thought i'd told vincent what's been going on. he locked himself in the bathroom and wouldn't come out. tío hector and I had to take the door down to get him out.

i've missed some school so i could watch out for eddie, also screwed up at work for the same reason. jenna just broke up with me because i haven't been able to see as much of her lately and i totally stood her up for a party last night because we were on our way up here. i know i haven't told you a lot about jenna, but i love her and now she's gone. so now you know the short version of the other side of our lives. i'm not sure what's next for us, but you can trust me that denton's never going to get his filthy hands on eddie again.

i'm soooo glad you're alive. i miss you to the moon and back. i love you to the moon and back. i'm sorry about your sergeant and the other guy, and i hope your leg is better soon. – mario

I press send, then turn on the printer and wait for it to warm up. I want Eddie to read Max's story for himself, and my reponse, too. He may not like that I told Max about Denton, but I'm glad I did. I had to.

I pull up my sent message and select print. There's a bunch of whirring and clicking but nothing happens. Same thing when I try to print Max's message. I check the printer. Well duh. It might help if I put a couple of sheets of paper in the tray.

Driving back to Hector and Josie's I realize that one of my wishes came true today. When I read how Max almost died it got Jenna off my mind. Not a good trade, though.

20

When I get back from Vincent's, I find Eddie in the back-yard with Hector, helping him carve a huge pumpkin.

"Look!" Eddie says, smiling. "I drew it."

"It looks like you drew it," I say, laughing at the silly pump-kin smile and the winking eye.

"Eddie's good at drawing, and I'm good with the knife," Hector says. *"Somos buenos cómplices.* We're a team."

"We're going to do two more," Eddie says, pointing in the direction of two more pumpkins. They're as big as those exer-cise ball things you always see advertised on TV. I reach into my back pocket for the printed email messages.

"Look at his ears," Eddie says. "You haven't even noticed his ears."

Hector laughs. "First time I ever carved ears on a pumpkin, but it's a pretty good idea."

I take my hand from my pocket and run my fingers around the pumpkin's carved ears.

"I bet this'll look cool when the candle's lit," I say, noticing how only a small hole is carved away for the ear canal, or whatever you call it, and then how the outline of the outer ear is scraped away in layers.

Eddie gives Hector a high two, and I decide to keep Max's email to myself for a little while longer – at least until after dark, after the pumpkins are all lit up on the front porch. Why interrupt Eddie's fun right now with news that Max practically got killed?

It's not until we sit down to dinner and I see the spread of food on the table that I suddenly realize I'm starving. Except for those two chocolate chipless cookies, all I've had today is drama.

I take a big mound of chicken with rice and dig in. I'm embarrassed when I look up to see that I'm the only one eating. Even seven-year-old Hannah's waiting until everyone else is served. Josie just laughs, though, and tells me to go ahead, growing boys need their strength. I hope I'm still growing, 'cause I'd like to end up taller than I am right now.

Hannah's dressed up in a Cinderella costume, and even though she's all through trick or treating, she wants to leave it on. They invited Eddie to go out with them, but he was having too much fun with the pumpkins. Hannah sort of hero-worships Eddie because he's such a good artist. She's brought a giant sketch pad over with her and Eddie's promised to draw a picture of Cinderella for her after dinner. It's like she's obsessed with Cinderella. She's even got Cinderella stickers all over the front of her sketch pad.

"Did you manage to email Maria today?" Vincent asks.

With a mouth full of food, I can only nod yes and keep chewing.

"Any news from her?" Elena asks.

Again I nod yes.

"How's she doing?"

I chew and swallow the last of my big bite of chicken.

"She's doing okay. She'll be in the same place for a while now, so that's good."

It's not exactly a lie, it just feels like a lie. But I don't want to go into details until I've had a chance to talk through stuff with Eddie.

Elena starts talking about her book group meeting, and this book that retells the story of creation from Eve's point of view. Elena taught English before Hannah was born, so she's big on books and she always wants to know what we're reading.

"*Harry Potter*," Eddie says.

"*To Kill a Mockingbird*," I say.

Elena seems impressed with that – great American novel and all – but she probably wouldn't be too impressed if she knew I'd been at it for three weeks and I'm still only on page four.

"You ought to try *The Parrot in the Oven*," Vincent says.

"I'm pretty full just with the chicken," I tell him.

That gets a big laugh, and then Vincent explains that *The Parrot in the Oven* is a book written by a guy who grew up in a place sort of like Redville, which gets Hector talking about some book about a peach. I don't think I've ever seen Hector read anything but farm magazines and *Popular Mechanics*, but he says he can relate to the peach book.

Eddie does a parrot joke riff starting with "What's smarter than a talking parrot? A spelling bee," and ending with "What do you get when you cross a parrot with a shark? A bird that will talk your ear off." There are another bunch of corny jokes in the middle, but you don't need to hear them all. Hannah cracked up over them, though. I have to admit I'm happy to hear Eddie telling jokes again.

Looking around the table, I see that everyone but me has stopped eating. I take a small bite of the little bit of food I have left on my plate. I hope the book talk keeps going, not because of the books, but because that and my very last bite of food are all that's keeping us from the dreaded family meeting.

"What about you, Hannah, what are you reading?" I ask, desperate to keep the conversation going.

"*A Series of Unfortunate Events*," she says, launching into a long story about these orphan kids with an evil *tío* and all the bad stuff that happens to them. I'm not really listening to the details of the story, though. I'm stuck on the title. *A Series of Unfortunate Events* sounds more like my life than a book.

"*Ama*'s reading *Cinderella* to me, too," Hannah says.

"Over and over again," Josie adds, smiling.

She stacks some plates and carries them to the kitchen and Hannah follows after her.

"Can I stay over tonight, *Ama*?" she says.

"Sure. We'll set you up on the sofa."

The doorbell rings and Eddie races to answer it, grabbing the bag of Trick or Treat candy to dole out. So far, everyone who's come to the door tonight has commented on how great the pumpkins are, the best they've seen, and I guess Eddie doesn't want to miss a chance for a compliment.

What's at the door is way scarier than any witch or monster costume, though. It's Carmen. She throws her arms around Eddie, clutching him in something that looks more like a wrestling move than a hug.

"We've been worried sick about you. Are you all right?" she says, all teary-eyed.

Vincent and Elena stand to greet Carmen, and Josie and Hannah come from the kitchen to see what's going on.

Hector goes over to them, putting his hand on Eddie's shoulder.

"No need to worry about Eddie. We're doing just fine, aren't we?"

"Look at our pumpkins, Aunt Carmen. I designed, and Hector carved," he says, pointing through the still open door to the pumpkins on the porch.

"Nice," she says, not bothering to look.

"One of the candles is out," Eddie says, rushing to the garage for a replacement.

"Sit down, Carmen, you must be hungry from that long drive," Josie says.

"Hannah, *Mija*, get your *Tía* Carmen a clean plate and some silverware."

Carmen gives me her nastiest look.

"You've gone way too far this time, Mario!"

"Come on, sit down," Josie says, putting some food on the plate Hannah's brought out for her. Carmen sits down at the table and Elena pulls a chair up beside her. I move to the sofa and start flipping through one of Hector's farm magazines. Carmen's cell phone rings and she picks up.

"Hi, Honey," she says, her voice turned all sweet and syrupy. "I just now got here . . . Yes, they're both here . . . I know, Sweetheart . . . He's definitely coming home with me . . . No, of course not! . . . Just Eddie . . . Yes, I'll call you when we leave . . . Love you, too."

"That was Denton, my fiancée," Carmen says, flashing a diamond ring in Elena's direction.

"Congratulations! When did this happen?" Elena asks.

"Just this morning."

"He proposed to you this morning, and gave you this beautiful ring, and you got in your car and drove up here without him?"

Carmen laughs. "He started a big landscaping job today, so he couldn't get away. But I won't be gone long."

I continue flipping pages, looking at the magazine, listening.

"Tell me about him, do you have a picture?"

"No. He's got this thing about not having his picture taken," she laughs again. "But he's handsome, and he's very nice."

Tía Josie sits down at the table across from Carmen and admires her new ring.

"Denton and I were up all last night, talking. You know, it was such a shock to us when we realized Mario had kidnapped Eddie – we were both so worried . . ."

I feel like puking up my dinner, but I want to hear the rest of Carmen's fairy tale so I stay below the radar, listening.

"All I've ever wanted was to be married and share my life with someone I love, and that's what Denton wants, too. We think the reason we never found the right person is that we were meant for each other. And Denton's always wanted a son, and he loves Eddie so much . . . he's always taking him places and doing things for him . . ."

I'd like to throw the lamp at her! How can she be so stupid?

" . . . Once we heard from Vincent last night that Eddie was safe, well . . . we just decided to commit to each other, and to be a real family. So this morning, right after breakfast, Denton went out for a little while, like on a mysterious errand. And he came back with this ring. It was so sweet."

"I thought he was starting a big job today," Elena says.

"Well, he went in around noon. He wanted me to have this, to seal our decision. He told me he's been saving his money for a ring since the first day we met. He just knew in his heart I was the one."

I go out onto the front porch. Eddie's talking to some little kids from across the road, showing them the details of the pumpkin ears, and the dimple in one pumpkin's cheek. Hector's sitting on the steps.

"Eddie can't go back there with Carmen and Denton," I tell Hector. I'm about to say more when I hear my name from inside.

"Where's Mario?" Carmen says, sounding frantic. The next second she's barreling out through the front door.

"Damn you, Mario, don't even think about pulling another trick like the one you did yesterday! Give me your car keys!"

Eddie jumps off the porch and disappears and the little kids go back across the road. I walk past Carmen to go after Eddie, but she's right behind me, telling me I'm crazy, I must be on drugs to pull such a stupid trick as stealing a car and kidnapping Eddie and blah, blah, blah. I keep walking, shutting out her noisy bullshit, looking for Eddie. Maybe he went back inside. I go in through the back door, with Carmen right behind me, and Hector behind her.

"I WANT THOSE GODDAMNED KEYS!" she screams again, grabbing my arm and hanging on with both hands. Every muscle in my body tightens. My fists are clenched in anger. It's all I can do to keep from smashing her bullshitting mouth shut. Hector moves in, inches away from Carmen.

"Let go of Mario," he says. *"¡Suelte a mi sobrino!"*

Hannah stands in the kitchen, next to Josie, looking wide-eyed at the commotion. Elena comes in and leads her past us, out the door.

"Come on, let's see what Eddie's doing," she says.

Josie's saying over and over again, "Calm down. *¡Cálmense por favor!"* but it's like elevator music for all the good it does.

"I told you! Let go of Mario," Hector says.

"Leave me alone, Hector, this is my business, not yours!"

I jerk away. She grabs at me and misses. I move toward the door.

"You sneaky bastard!"

"Get out of my house!" Hector yells. *"¡Lárgate mi casa!"*

Now Vincent's next to his dad, echoing Josie's "calm down" chant.

"I said get out! This is my house and you don't talk to people like that in my house."

"I'm not leaving 'til I get those keys! I'm not giving this sneaky bastard one more chance. You think I'd let him kidnap little Eddie again?"

"Come on, Carmen, let's go talk this through," Vincent says, taking her by the arm to guide her into the kitchen. She doesn't budge.

"I'm not letting him out of my sight until I've got those

keys," Carmen says.

I start through the back door and Carmen takes a step to follow.

"Mario," Vincent says, "Come back in and sit down."

"After I find Eddie," I say.

Vincent steps in front of me.

"Elena and Hannah and Mama will find Eddie. You go back in the house and help us sort things out."

"Take his keys," Carmen says.

"Go sit down," Vincent says. "C'mon Papa, sit down."

Finally, after a lot of jockeying around and a few more traded insults, Vincent gets us all herded into the living room. Carmen starts in again – how I stole the car, how I kidnapped Eddie, how I'm a sneaky trouble-maker.

"So okay, let's hear the other side," Vincent says. "Why did you run off with Eddie?"

"Because Carmen's kicking me out and she says she won't even let me see Eddie anymore. And I told Max I'd watch out for him, no matter what."

I'm sitting on the sofa, next to Josie, who looks ready to cry. Hector's sitting in his recliner next to the sofa, but he's not reclining. He's sitting forward, on the edge of the chair, like he's about to pounce.

"Why would you want to separate these two boys, Carmen?" Josie says. "That's not right. *No está bien.*"

"Wake up and smell the coffee, Josie! Things aren't always so nicey, nicey! You don't have a clue about what Mario's really like! He's a terrible influence on little Eddie!"

"We know what you're like!" Hector says. "You've got to be the worst influence of all! Why Maria ever agreed to let you keep . . ."

"I was doing her a favor! So they could stay in Hamilton Heights! But Mario! I can't stand a sneak. I let him use my computer to email Maria and he's sneaking around on sex sites. He was even sneaking around on Denton's computer!"

"That's bullshit!" I say.

"Denton showed me last night, after you left!"

She turns to Vincent. "Denton didn't say anything earlier because he said he didn't want to get Mario in even more trouble with me. But when Mario took Eddie like that, Denton said he wanted me to know everything. So he showed me his Internet history. He leaves his laptop sitting around the house sometimes and he just noticed a week or so ago that Mario's been sneaking around with pornography. It's so disgusting, I can't even . . ."

"That lying pervert!" I say, jumping up from the sofa. "I've never even touched his computer! I couldn't, even if I wanted to. He never lets it out of his sight and you know it, too!"

"And my computer, too! Pornography!"

"Don't be stupid! Denton's the guy looking at 'tender young bod' sites!"

"I won't put up with this! I'm taking Eddie home right now!"

"Eddie's staying with us until we talk to Maria," Hector says, standing up.

"You don't have any say in the matter," Carmen screams.

She fishes around in her purse, pulls out an envelope and waves it in front of Hector.

"I'm their official guardian and I'm taking Eddie home with me!"

She hands the envelope to Vincent. "Check it out. You're the big lawyer."

Vincent shuffles through the papers, puts them back in the envelope and hands them back to Carmen.

"It's all legal, Papa. She's in charge of the boys."

Josie, Elena, and Hannah come in carrying their flashlights.

"Is Eddie here?" Josie asks.

"We thought you went to get him," Vincent says.

"We couldn't find him. We thought he came back inside."

21

Near the barn I start to call for Eddie, then stop before any sound hits the air. So . . . if I call him and he comes out, then what? Carmen takes him home with her and Denton gets a convenient sex toy? Not a good idea.

Others are outside now, calling to Eddie, flashing their lights around. As usual, Carmen's the loudest.

"Eddie, Honey . . . Eddie, Sweetheart . . ."

I don't get her. She keeps getting promotions at the bank, so she can't be that stupid. Does she really believe that I'm the bad guy?

Simba saunters out from behind the house and scratches at the back door, probably hoping for leftovers. I veer off in the opposite direction, knowing that if Simba's nearby, Eddie probably is, too.

Vincent calls to me from where he's leaning against *La Bamba* in the driveway.

"What's with your brother – locking himself in the bathroom, running away – what's going on?"

"He doesn't like Carmen's boyfriend."

"He doesn't like Carmen's boyfriend, so he locked himself in the bathroom? Sorry, but I don't get the connection here."

"It's hard to explain," I say.

"Try."

Vincent's always been nice to me, more like a *tío* than a cousin, because of the age difference. He's waiting patiently for me to tell my side of things. I'm so tired of dealing with the drama, I'd like to spill my guts, right here in the driveway. Just spill it all out and let what happens happen. But . . .

"Come on, Mario, give me a chance."

"First, I have to talk to Eddie," I tell him.

"Hard to do right now, isn't it?"

"Yeah, but . . ."

"This is hard on my parents. They had a very hard life when they were younger. Now, they mostly have a relaxed, happy life. They deserve it. But all of this yelling and screaming and swearing – it's too much for them."

In the distance we hear Carmen again, "Eddie! Sweetheart!"

Vincent shakes his head.

"Something happens to my father when Carmen's around. Like he's got to fight the forces of evil or something. He gets crazy, which gets my mother all nervous and upset."

I catch a glimpse of Simba going back behind the house again.

"What?" Vincent says, noticing my distraction.

"Nothing. Just Simba going back to the barn."

"Believe me, if Eddie were in the barn, I'd have found him. I know every little hiding place in there, from when I was a kid hiding out."

I laugh at the thought of Vincent hiding out. According to Max he always did everything right when they were kids.

Vincent gazes up at the sky, which is bright with stars and a half moon. It's pretty impressive, this sky. Where we live

near L.A. – where we used to live when we had a home that is
– city lights compete with the few stars that are bright enough
to shine through our smog-heavy air. We never see a sky this
bright at home. I wonder if Eddie's noticed the bright sky tonight. I wonder how bright the sky is over Max. Suddenly a
shooting star flies across the sky.

"Wow!" I say.

"Wow! is right. Hannah says if you make a wish when you
see a shooting star it'll come true." Vincent laughs. "I think
she'll give up on that idea pretty soon, though. She made a
wish on a shooting star a few nights ago, and I'm sure she
wished for a pony. No way," he laughs again, then turns serious.

"You know, thinking about Hannah, only three years
younger than Eddie, I wonder . . . She's so lighthearted and
secure. Her biggest worries have to do with whether or not
she'll get a pony, or find the right Cinderella costume for Halloween. How would that be if she thought she had to run away,
or lock herself up in the bathroom. What if she stopped being
lighthearted, the way Eddie's stopped being lighthearted? I
can hardly stand the thought of it."

What I know is, the reality's a whole lot harder than the
thought. I don't say that, though.

I like being out here with Vincent, watching the sky, listening to him talk. But right now I wish he and Carmen and
anyone else still looking around out here would go inside, so I
could go back behind the house and find Eddie.

"I'm going to ask you a favor, Mario."

"What?"

"I'm going to ask you to let me hang on to your keys for
you."

"Why?"

"Because I want to get Carmen to spend the rest of the
night at our house, and she's so paranoid about you boys running away again I don't think she'll leave while you have ac-

cess to a car."

"I don't think so."

"Mario, come on. She's driving my parents crazy. I won't give her the keys, I'll just keep them for you."

I mull it over.

"If I don't get her to leave with me, Papa will demand that she get out of his house, and then things will get physical, and that wouldn't be good. So, what do you say?"

"Yeah, okay."

What difference does it make? It's not like I can't hotwire a car. I go into the bedroom, get the keys from my backpack and take them out to Vincent.

"Thanks," he says, then goes off to find Carmen.

Back inside, Hannah's whining to Elena.

"But Mommy, you said I could stay here tonight!"

"That's before things got crazy," Elena says.

"But Mommy, *Ama's* going to read *Cinderella* to me, and *Abuelito's* going to make *menudo* in the morning."

Elena laughs. "Since when did you like *menudo*?"

"But Mommy, I have to stay over!"

"No. That's enough now. Daddy can get us some *menudo* for in the morning."

"I hate *menudo*!" Hannah says, which gets a laugh from everyone but Hannah, who is so offended she stomps off to wait in the car.

Elena kisses Josie on the cheek.

"Take these for Hannah," she says, handing Elena a baggie of cookies. "Take Carmen, too."

"We're trying," Elena says. "Where's Hector, anyway?"

"Out scraping and polishing the rust off the old tractor. Scraping out his madness."

"If Carmen visited more often that tractor would be looking like new," Elena says. "Let us know when Eddie shows up."

As Elena opens the door I get a glimpse of Vincent and

Carmen in the driveway. Watching from the window, I'm relieved to see Carmen get into her car and follow Vincent and
his family down the road.

I go back outside, to where Simba'd been earlier in the evening. My flashlight beam lands on a partially screened over
crawl space. I pull the screen aside and shine the flashlight
under the house. There's Eddie, sitting on the ground, holding
Simba on his lap. He jumps as the light settles on him. I move
the light away and stick my head through the opening.

"Jeez, Eddie, there must be a million spiders in here."

"I haven't seen any," he says.

"Well, come on out, anyway. Carmen's gone."

"She'll be back."

"Not tonight. Come on, I've got to talk to you, but I'm not
coming in there. It's filthy! What've you been doing in there
all this time, anyway?"

"Building mountains and roads. Listening to people looking for me."

I shine the light around again. There are little mounds of
rocks here and there, and scraped dirt leading up to them. I've
got to hand it to Eddie. He knows how to entertain himself.

"Cool," I say.

He crawls toward the opening.

"Hannah said she wouldn't tell, but it's okay that she told
you."

"What do you mean? Hannah knew where you were?"

"She found me when Elena and Josie were looking in the
barn."

"Well, she didn't tell me anything. I saw Simba around
here and figured you were nearby."

"She said she'd bring me *menudo* in the morning, but she'd
pretend it was for her."

Aunt Josie makes a big fuss over Eddie when we come
inside.

"You need hot chocolate," she says to Eddie, but when he starts to follow her into the kitchen she tells him to stay right where he is, on the porch by the washing machine.

"Get your clothes off and leave them there. All of them," she tells him. "Then race to the shower. I won't look."

Josie goes back to making hot chocolate, while Eddie stands by the washing machine, not moving. At first I don't get it, and then I remember how he's been hiding lately, whenever he changes clothes. I go to the bathroom and bring out a big bath towel, which I hold up as a kind of screen. He strips down, wraps the towel around himself, and goes into the bathroom. I go back into the kitchen and sit down.

"He didn't lock the door, did he?" Josie asks.

"It's still off the hinges."

"*Ay*, that Hector! Out scrubbing rust off the old tractor for hours but he can't put the bathroom door back up? *Ay*," she sighs, stirring the milk. "Does he know you found Eddie?"

"I guess not. I'll go tell him."

"Tell him to come in, too. Fix the door before we go to bed."

I pick up the flashlight again and walk to the far back, where the old tractor sits. *Tío* Hector's at the front, bent low, working on the grill. Most of one side is bright and shiny, while the other side is red with rust. He stands when he sees me.

"I found Eddie," I say. "He's in taking a shower."

"I bet he needs one. It's nasty under there."

"You knew where he was?"

Hector concentrates on wiping his hands on the rag he keeps tucked into his belt.

"I saw Hannah talking to him through the crawl space, but I figured, let him be for a while."

"Well, Josie sent me to tell you he's inside now, and you should come inside, too."

"Where's Carmen?"

"She went home with Vincent and Elena."

He tucks the rag back under his belt and we walk together to the house. Eddie's sitting at the table in a tee shirt that comes down to his knees. He's sipping hot chocolate and nibbling a cookie. Hector gets a beer from the refrigerator and sits down.

"*Ay*, what a day," he says.

"You better call Vincent and tell him we found Eddie," Josie says.

"Then Carmen'll be right back over here."

"Well, you've got to call, anyway. They're worried."

He picks up the phone and dials.

"Vincent? Yeah, we found Eddie . . . Under the house . . . Yeah . . . Give her a sleeping pill, or get her drunk or something . . . No . . . She can't come over again tonight . . . She can't," he says, and hangs up.

"Don't worry," he says to Eddie. "She's not taking you anywhere until we hear from your mother. I don't care what her *pinche* papers say."

Before we go to sleep I get the printed email messages from my pants pocket and sit down on Eddie's bed, my back against the wall. He's stretched out on his side, his head propped up on two bunched up pillows.

"I want to read Max's message to you," I tell him.

"I can read it," he says, making a grab for it.

"I know, but it's really long, and I want to be sure you don't miss any parts."

"I don't skip stuff!" he says.

"Just listen," I say, and start reading. When I get to the part about how Max almost died, Eddie takes the pillows from under his head and hugs them closely against his chest. The sound of my own voice putting those words out into the room makes the message even more real than when I first read it. I kind of choke up at the part about how we could have been the ones without a mom, and again about keeping our bonds strong, but I swallow a lot and read on. When I finish reading, Eddie just lays there, hugging his pillows. After a while I ask him if he gets it.

"Get what? Her leg's messed up and she almost died and two other guys really did die!"

I wait for a while, wondering if maybe I should've just kept it all to myself.

"Do you get the part about how Max wants to keep her heart open to us, so she's got to tell us the good stuff and the bad stuff?"

He moves the pillows back behind his head.

"Yeah, I get it. 'Cause how can we still know her if we don't know the bad stuff, too."

"You get what's she's saying about how she wants to know the whole of our lives?"

He nods his head.

"Okay, so here's what I emailed back to her."

I hand Eddie my printed message and sit on the bed, waiting for him to read it. He barely glances at it when he throws it down on the bed and runs into the bathroom. The vroom-vroom of the toothbrush starts up again. Maybe it was the part about Denton forcing Eddie's head down on his disgusting dick that set him off.

When he finally comes out he sits next to me on the bed, reading the rest of the message, then hands it back to me without saying a word.

I really want to go take a shower, but what if he runs off again because I told Max what I swore I wouldn't ever tell?

"I needed to tell all of that to Max. I don't want us to lose that connection either. And I don't want to be all bottled up inside with keeping secrets."

"You didn't tell her everything," Eddie says.

"Like what?"

"Like you didn't tell her I'm not a pervert!" he says.

"She knows that!"

"She knows I give blow jobs! You told her I give blow jobs!"

"I told her Denton forced you! That's not your fault!"

"Then why didn't you tell her so!"

"Jeez, Eddie. I want to go take a shower now. You can email her yourself, first thing in the morning."

"You tell her, too."

"Okay!"

I stash the printed email messages in the bottom of my backpack, then take a long, hot shower. Eddie's asleep when I come back into the room. I turn out the light and crawl into bed, but as tired as I am, I can't get to sleep for all the stuff I've got circling around in my head. I fumble my way down the darkened hall to the phone in the kitchen. I reach for a flashlight so I can see the numbers, but the batteries are dead, I guess. I get the other flashlight by the door and call Jenna. I get her voice mail.

"I need to talk to you," I tell her, waiting a while, hoping she'll pick up. She doesn't.

When I go to set the dead flashlight back on the counter, I notice how light it feels. Unscrewing the end, I see that the batteries aren't dead. They're gone. New life for Eddie's toothbrush.

I use the working flashlight to guide my way back to the bedroom. It seems as if I've barely fallen asleep when I'm jolted awake by Vincent. He's waving copies of our recent email in front of my face.

"What's this about?"

I rub my eyes, trying to get oriented. My backpack still sits undisturbed beside my bed.

"Get up, and get to the kitchen!" Vincent says.

Eddie stirs at the noise.

"You, too, Eddie, come out to the kitchen!"

22

That expression about someone "wringing" their hands has never made sense to me. But that's exactly what Josie is doing right now. She's not bustling around preparing food, or bringing someone something to eat, she's sitting beside Hector, wringing her hands. I sit down next to her.

"What's this about, getting everybody up so early on a Sunday morning?" Hector asks.

"Something that can't wait," Vincent tells *Tío* Hector. Then he turns to Eddie. "Have a seat."

Eddie sits next to me, folds his arms on the table, and puts his head down, like on rainy days when we used to play "Seven-Up" at recess time.

Vincent pulls a chair up between Eddie and Elena.

"I'll put some coffee on," *Tía* Josie says, getting up.

"Just sit with us, Mama. You need to be in on this, too." Vincent says.

Aunt Josie hesitates, then sits back down.

"Where's Carmen?" I ask.

"She and Hannah were still sleeping when we left," he says. "We left a note for them."

It's like everyone's decided this is the time to do their deep breathing exercises or something because that's the only sound in the room right now, breathing. Hand wringing doesn't make any noise. They're all looking at me, and I'd like to follow Eddie's example and hide my head in my arms, but it wouldn't make anything go away.

Vincent sets the emails on the table in front of him.

"That's between me and Max and Eddie," I say, grabbing for the papers.

Vincent pulls them away.

"That sucks! You let me use your computer and then you snoop into our business!"

Eddie moves his head down from the table, resting it on his knees and covering his ears. Elena leans toward me.

"This is just the first thing that came out of the printer this morning when I tried to print a receipt."

"Well . . . you didn't have to read it. It's private!"

"I'm sorry, Mario, but all of Carmen's talk about the awful stuff you do on the Internet . . ."

"That's so wrong!" I say. "I'm not the one in that house who's the pervert porn guy!"

"Well, I didn't know what to think. Carmen can be pretty convincing. Anyway, when these messages turned up this morning . . ."

"Look at it our way," Vincent says. "You and Eddie show up out of the blue. Carmen says you've kidnapped Eddie. She says you're a trouble-maker, into nasty Internet stuff, and a very bad influence on your brother."

He nods his head in Eddie's direction.

"What we all see is that something's very wrong with Eddie and neither one of you is helping us understand anything."

"Eddie just needs more time with us," Hector says. "He was his old self yesterday, working on the pumpkins and telling parrot jokes."

"And then he ran off and hid under the house for hours," Elena says.

"Yeah, after Carmen came in screaming about how she was going to take him back with her!" I say.

"Carmen's enough to make anyone hide under the house," Hector says. "Get Carmen out of here and Eddie'll be fine."

"He misses Maria is all," Josie says.

"No, that's not all, Mama," Vincent says, glancing at the papers on the table. "I know you and Papa always want to think everything's okay, but it's not."

He picks up the emails."

"Mario's right that these messages are between the boys and their mother, but some of what's in here matters to us all. Just listen to this . . . the subject is leveling . . ."

"Let Mario tell them," Elena says.

Vincent nods and hands me the messages, like I don't already have them memorized.

"Well," I say, glancing at the papers, "Max is okay. She was wounded . . ."

"*Ay Dios!*" Josie says.

"How bad?" Hector asks.

"Not bad. A piece of shrapnel in her leg, but she'll be back . . ." I check her wording, " . . . back in the field in two weeks."

"*Ay*, they should send her home," Hector says, his face filled with sadness.

"Two guys in the same Humvee were killed," I tell them. "That's about it." I leave out the details of the severed arm with the photo, and the dead kid that reminded her of Eddie.

Josie gets the leftover Halloween candy, puts it all in a bowl and sets it on the table. She gently rubs Eddie's scrunched up shoulders.

"Have some candy, *mijo*."

Eddie shakes his head no without looking up.

The phone rings and Hector answers.

"*Bueno!*" he says, then listens while the soft sadness in his face turns to stony anger.

"No! You stay off my property!"

"I'm not talking to her!" Hector says, handing the phone to Vincent.

Hector paces around.

"She's not welcome here. She better not show her face around here," he says.

Vincent sighs.

"Okay, Carmen . . . We'll be over there in about thirty minutes or so . . . That's totally unnecessary . . . Give us thirty minutes . . . Don't do that. We'll work it out as a family . . ."

"Let me talk to Hannah before you hang up," Elena says, reaching for the phone.

"Thirty minutes, Carmen. It's 9:07 now." Vincent hands the phone to Elena.

"Carmen? Let me talk to Hannah . . . Oh . . . well, okay. When she wakes up, tell her I'll be right home . . . Thanks . . . Bye."

Elena hands the phone over to Josie to hang up. Hector is still pacing.

Vincent says, "Carmen's threatening to call the police if we don't have Eddie back over there in thirty minutes – says we're holding him hostage."

"*Cabrona!* Let her call!" Hector says.

"She does have legal rights as their guardian," Vincent says.

Josie's wringing her hands again.

"Sit down, Papa. Let Mario finish telling you about the emails."

Vincent turns to me. "Tell us about Denton."

Eddie slides out of his chair and sits scrunched up under the table, shaking his head, no, no, no.

"Well . . . "

That's as much as I can think of to say, so I don't say any

more.

"Come on, Mario. This is a very serious accusation, and if it's true . . ."

"Is it true, Mario?" Elena says. "Has Carmen's boyfriend been molesting Eddie?"

Eddie's gripping my ankle, and I can feel the fear in his grip, the plea in his heart, for me to shut up.

"Mario?" Vincent asks. "Is it true?"

I shake my head. "It's true."

I reach down and take Eddie's hand in mine and try to coax him out from under the table. He doesn't move.

"Sexually molesting him?" Elena says.

"*Ay, Diosito!*" Hector says, getting up from the table, pacing. Josie shakes her head back and forth, back and forth, as if she can't believe what she's hearing.

"Doing bad things to Little Eddie?" Josie says. "*Ay, Dios! Ay, Dios!*"

"Like I told Max in the email," I say.

"This is the guy who just gave Carmen a ring?" Elena asks, incredulous.

I nod.

"My God, Mario. Why didn't you tell her?"

"I promised Eddie I wouldn't tell. Denton told Eddie he'd kill us both if we ever told anyone and Eddie believes him."

"Eddie thinks this guy will kill him? And you?" Vincent asks.

"There was a stray cat . . ."

I tell the story of Blue, and how Denton said the cat wouldn't shut up as he dangled its body in front of Eddie.

Josie gasps. Hector sits back down, next to her. She turns to him and he puts his arms around her, pulling her close.

Elena is down on the floor now, level with Eddie.

"Come on out, Sweetheart. You're safe with us."

He stays put.

"Eddie, did Denton do bad things to you?"

No answer.

Elena stands up and I take her place, leaning down level with Eddie. "Come on, Buddy. It's going to be okay," I tell him. He still doesn't move. I'm really getting tired of this shit.

Vincent looks at the clock.

"We've got to get back over there before Carmen files a report."

"We should call the police, anyway," Elena says.

"Yes, but a kidnapping accusation against Mario wouldn't be a good place to start. Carmen's threatening to file a report against my parents, too," Vincent says. "Us, too, probably, if we don't get back over there with Eddie. She's acting a little crazy right now."

"It's not an act," I say. "She is crazy."

"Come on," Vincent says, looking under the table at Eddie, who's curled up in a tight little motionless ball.

Vincent checks his watch again.

"We've really got to go," he says to me. "And Eddie's got to go with us."

I get under the table and pull Eddie out, then pick him up and carry him to the car. Even if he's not very big for his age, he's still a load to carry. I wish he'd just act normal.

Josie and Hector start to follow us, but Vincent convinces them they should stay home.

"Carmen makes you crazy, Papa," he says. "And you make her crazy, too. Things are crazy enough as it is."

"Don't you let her take Eddie!" he shouts.

"Not until we know what's going on," Vincent says.

Backing out the driveway, I see Josie wringing her hands, watching after us, and Hector, pacing. How different this is from such a short time ago, when they stood in this driveway and greeted us with laughter.

When we pull up in front of Vincent and Elena's, we see Carmen leaning against the open front door, talking on her cell phone.

"Shit!" Vincent says, rushing from the car. "You were going to give us thirty minutes before you called!"

Carmen covers the bottom of the phone with her hand.

"I'm talking to Denton! Do you mind? . . . Denton, Honey, I'll call you right back."

She puts the phone into her skirt pocket and runs to greet Eddie. It's a repeat of last night – throwing her arms around Eddie, telling him how worried she's been, throwing hard looks my way.

When we go inside, Hannah and Rovie are watching a "Blues Clues" DVD in front of the giant TV. Eddie flops down beside them.

"I'm sorry I couldn't bring you any *menudo* this morning," Hannah says. "My mom wouldn't let me stay over last night."

"That's okay," Eddie says. Neither of them takes their eyes from the screen.

Carmen's now in the kitchen talking in whispered tones to Denton. Vincent takes a few steps in that direction when Elena takes his arm.

"Wait, Vincent. I don't want Hannah around any more yelling and screaming. Last night was awful for her."

"Well . . ."

"I'll take her and Eddie to the library for a while, and for an ice cream – give you a chance to get things worked out."

"You can't take Eddie. That's the whole point of our rushing back over here, so Carmen's got Eddie in her sights."

"Eddie needs a break. I'll clear it with Carmen."

I don't know what Elena says to Carmen, but pretty soon she's got a bunch of art supplies packed up and library books to return and she's leading Hannah and Eddie out the door. Hannah's got the big sketchpad with the Cinderella stickers tucked under her arm.

"Elena . . . don't let Eddie out of your sight," Carmen

yells.

"Have fun, kids," Vincent says, closing the door behind them. He takes the emails from his pocket and motions for me to follow him into the family room, where Carmen is again on the phone to Denton. Vincent waits for Carmen to hang up, then puts the emails on the bar in front of her.

CHAPTER

23

"**Y**ou lying shit!" Carmen says, ripping up my email message and shoving the shreds in my direction.

"See what I mean, Vincent? Why I can't have Mario around little Eddie, filling his mind full of filth?"

"It's that asshole pervert Denton who's filling Eddie with filth!"

Carmen swings her arm wide across the table and power-slaps me in the face before I even see it coming. Vincent jumps from his bar stool and grabs both of Carmen's hands. I'm too stunned to move. My cheek's totally numb, like it's been shot full of Novocain.

"Take it easy, Carmen. Calm down," Vincent says.

Carmen gives me another long, hateful look, then turns to Vincent with a sob and an onslaught of tears. He lets go of her hands and pats her awkwardly on her shoulder.

I touch my fingers to my hot and stinging cheek.

"Get some ice on that," Vincent says.

I guess the numbness must have moved from my face to

my brain or something, because all I can think to do is just sit there with my hand on my cheek.

Vincent gets a package of frozen peas from the freezer and hands it to me. I hold it to my cheek. He goes back over to the counter and gets a box of tissue, which he places in front of Carmen. He takes a seat on the barstool at the end of the bar.

"We've got to get to the bottom of this," Vincent says.

"He's at the bottom of this," Carmen says, wiping at her face with the tissue. "You have no idea what he's put me through. And now these horrible, filthy lies!" she says, gesturing to the shredded message, still crying.

"You've never suspected Denton was doing anything inappropriate with Eddie?"

"God, no! I told you, Denton loves Eddie like a son! Why don't you just ask Eddie?"

"We did."

"And what did he say?"

"Nothing. He didn't say anything," Vincent says.

"Because there's nothing to say," Carmen yells.

Vincent looks from Carmen to me and back to her. That oldies song, "You Were Meant for Me," rings out from her cell phone. She checks the display and answers.

"Hi, Honey . . . Eddie? Well, no, you can't talk to him right now because he's with Elena and Hannah . . . No, Sweetheart . . ."

She takes the phone into the living room, where we can't hear her.

Vincent gives me a searching look.

"You saw this thing, right? You actually saw this Denton guy forcing Eddie to . . ."

"Yes, I saw it!" I yell, slamming the frozen peas down on the table. "Why would I say I saw it if I didn't? It makes me want to puke just thinking about it!"

I put the peas back in the freezer and slam the door.

"You think I'd email something like that to Max, in fucking

Iraq, if it wasn't true?"

"I'm just trying to figure out what's going on, Mario. I'm getting two totally different stories, that's all."

Carmen comes back into the family room carrying her keys and her overnight bag.

"I've got to get home. Denton's very worried about us. Eddie's got school tomorrow. I've got to be at work. I've wasted enough time up here."

"Eddie's not going back with you," I tell her.

"Oh, yes he is, Mr. Mario! I'm his legal guardian and he's going with me!"

"Leave him with us for a few days," Vincent says. "Until we can get things sorted out."

"There's nothing to sort out! I'll call the police in a heartbeat if that's what it takes to get Eddie out of here."

She turns to me. "If I had my way you'd already be in juvenile hall, but Denton, the guy you're spreading filthy lies about, wanted to cut you some slack. He goes 'No, don't involve the police. It'll just make things worse for Mario.'"

She wipes new tears away.

"I couldn't bear to tell him what you said . . . "

Rovie starts up with her imitation of a pit bull. The back door opens with a rush and Hector bursts in, with Josie right behind. The dog drops the vicious bark and wags her tail, winding around Hector and Josie's legs. They don't even notice.

"Maria just called," Hector says, breathless.

"Max?" I ask. Like he'd be breathless over a call from some other Maria.

"She wanted to talk to you and Eddie. If you call back right now, you might be able to reach her. Here's the number," he says, handing me a slip of paper with about seventeen numbers on it.

"She's okay?" I ask.

"She says she's fine."

I go to the phone in Vincent's office and dial. It rings twice, then I get some strange noise, not a busy signal, or a ring, or a dial tone, something I've never heard before. I hold for a while to see what will happen, then hang up and dial again. And again. And again. Shit!

Even from the office I can hear Carmen and Hector going at it. Hector's telling Carmen that Max wants us to stay with them for a while and Carmen's acting like he's made the whole phone call up.

I try one more time. No luck. I go back out to the family room.

"You couldn't reach her?" Vincent asks.

I shake my head.

"She said if you couldn't get through today, she'll call our place again tomorrow – sometime between ten in the morning and three in the afternoon, our time."

"What else did she say?"

"They removed the shrapnel. No problem. And she wants you both to stay with us until she can at least talk to you . . ."

"I've had enough of this shit," Carmen says. "I'll pick up Eddie at the library. Just tell me how to get there."

She walks to the back door, and waits for instructions, then stomps back into the family room.

"God damn you, Hector! Move your car so I can get out!"

Hector doesn't even look at her.

"Now!" she demands.

Who knows what kind of scene would have come next, if Elena and Hannah hadn't come in right then, with Eddie tagging behind.

"Hey, Eddie," I say. "Max called. She'll call again tomorrow when she can talk to us."

He gives me the slightest glimmer of a smile.

Carmen goes over to Eddie and takes him by the hand. "Come on, Sweetheart. Go get in my car."

Carmen grabs Hector's keys, which he's left sitting on the

kitchen counter. He grabs them back in one, quick move.

You can imagine the racket that follows. Between me and Hector both shouting that Carmen's not taking Eddie anywhere, and Carmen screaming back at us, and Vincent and Josie doing their calm down chants – chaos doesn't begin to describe the scene.

The only one not saying anything is Eddie, who just stands watching. Well . . . Elena and Hannah aren't saying anything either, but they're not even in the room. Who knows how far Elena had to take Hannah to get her beyond the range of screaming and yelling? Pretty far, is my guess.

Carmen's voice is at top volume now, demanding to leave with Eddie, defending Denton.

"Mario's a filthy liar!" she screams. "You want the truth? Ask Eddie!"

She turns to Eddie.

"Tell them, Honey. Did Denton ever do anything bad to you, or anything to hurt you?"

The whole room goes quiet, all eyes on Eddie, waiting. He looks over at me, then at the floor. He says nothing.

"Satisfied?" Carmen says.

I go to Eddie and kneel down in front of him.

"Tell them, Buddy," I say. "Don't be afraid."

He looks at me, his eyes filling with tears.

"Denton won't hurt us. C'mon, back me up here."

I don't know if you play soccer or not, or if this happens in other sports, but I've felt it on the soccer field more than once. Your team is definitely winning, or losing, either way, and then you feel a shift, like it's in the air. Before anything really changes, you feel the shift. It may happen in seconds, or it may take half a game, but things shift.

That's how it is, right now in this room. Things shift. Nobody moves. Nobody says anything. But there's a shift in trust and it's away from me. I try one more time.

"Eddie?"

The tears are pouring down his cheeks now, but he says nothing.

Vincent is the first to break the heavy silence.

"Give me your keys, Papa, and I'll move your car so Carmen can get out."

"Maria wants them to stay with us," Hector says. But hands over his keys.

"Let me just go find Elena and Hannah, so they can say goodbye," Vincent says.

I go into the bathroom and wash my face. I examine the big red blotch on my cheek, taking my time, not wanting to be there when Eddie walks out the door with Carmen on his way back to hell.

Damn it! Why didn't he just say something? Or at least nod his head! Did he think Denton would magically appear with his lethal neck pressure move and kill us on the spot? What can I do? I can't let Denton get to him again.

I'll wait until everyone's asleep, hotwire *La Bamba*, get Eddie from Carmen's and take him . . . where? Or I'll call that abuse hotline and turn Denton in and then . . . what? If Eddie's still following Denton's "shut up" order, will anyone believe me? And when will I ever get my life back? Or will I always just have to be trying to watch out for Eddie? Trying and not doing such a great job of it?

I've stayed in the bathroom a long time – a lot longer than it should have taken Vincent to get Elena and Hannah so they can say their goodbyes. Carmen's still in the family room, though, with Eddie beside her, waiting. Hector and Josie have wandered into the other room and are watching TV.

One look at me and Carmen gets all fired up again.

"Vincent! Come on, we've got to get on the road!" she yells.

Vincent and Elena come into the room together. Vincent's carrying Hannah's big Cinderella sketch pad.

"Can you please move the car now?" Carmen says.

Vincent shakes his head.

"Look at these," he says, flipping through the sketch pad until he finds what he's looking for.

Carmen glances at the picture, frowning, then moves in for a closer look.

"And this one," Vincent says.

Elena stands next to Vincent.

"Show her the one that's got the red in it, farther back."

He turns a few more pages.

"There," Elena says.

Eddie sits down on the floor next to Rovie, who immediately turns over on her back and bares her stomach. Eddie reaches out and pets her, still watching the activity around the sketch pad. I sit down next to him.

"Your drawings?" I ask.

He nods.

"And look at this one," Elena says, turning another page and pointing to something toward the lower part of the drawing.

Carmen looks at the paper, then glances over at Eddie.

"We've got to go," Carmen says. "These are just a kid's drawings. They don't mean anything."

"I think they do," Elena says. "What I learned in my years of teaching is that kids don't draw these things unless they've had some kind of . . . experience."

CHAPTER

24

Monday morning. I should be in school. Eddie should be in school. But here we are in Redville. I look over at Eddie, still sleeping. For a minute I wonder what would have happened if he'd gone back with Carmen. What if he was waking up in the same house as Denton this morning? Don't even go there, I tell myself. I've already got enough of those haunting pictures stuck in my brain without imagining more.

The smell of bacon seeps into the room. That's usually better than an alarm clock as far as getting me out of bed goes. Not this morning, though. Real life heavy drama turns out to be pretty tiring.

I'm still staring at the ceiling, checking out the cracks left from the last earthquake, when I hear Eddie stirring around. Pretty soon he crawls in next to me. He's all shaky. I pull the extra blanket up around him.

"It's going to be okay," I tell him, hoping I'm telling the truth.

We stay like that for a while, me staring at the ceiling, Eddie with the shakes, and the smell of bacon growing stronger by the minute.

"Let's go eat some breakfast," I say.

Hector's already at work at the garage, but Josie doesn't go to her job in the school cafeteria until later.

By the time we finish breakfast and Josie leaves for work, it's nearly ten o'clock. Eddie and I settle in to wait for Max's phone call. I need to talk to Jenna, if I can just get her to pick up. I don't know which is worse, missing her so much, needing her so much, or feeling so pissed that she didn't keep her word to me. All I know is, I've got to talk to her. Also, I've got to call Sammy to see if he'll hold my job for me, or if maybe I'm already fired. I want to talk to Walker, too. Trouble is, I'm afraid to use the phone because that might be just the time Max would try to call.

We watch reruns of "Leave it to Beaver" and I wonder if anyone ever really lived like that, even fifty years ago, or a hundred years ago, or whenever. Eddie spreads his art stuff out on the coffee table and does more of those weird, dark drawings. Simba's stretched out, sleeping on top of Eddie's colored pencils. I guess that's okay, since Eddie's not using many colors these days anyway.

More out of boredom than interest, I dig *To Kill a Mockingbird* out of my backpack and start reading. It would be a good thing if I could at least be caught up with English when I get back to school.

I'm still kicked back in Hector's recliner, reading, when Elena comes in carrying a couple of grocery bags.

I get up and take one of the bags from her.

"Thanks . . . Hey, Eddie. How're you doing?" Elena says, flashing a big smile at him.

Eddie looks up, nods, and goes back to his drawing.

"Any news from Maria?"

"Not yet."

I follow Elena into the kitchen and put the bag on the counter next to the other things she's just brought in.

"Before I forget . . ." Elena says, tossing me the keys to *La Bamba.*

"Where's Carmen?" I ask.

"She stormed out right after you boys left with Hector and Josie – threatened legal action, said you'd turned everyone against her with your lies . . . "

"Same-o-same-o," I say.

"Well . . . she was in a rage when she left. But . . ." she glances toward the living room and lowers her voice. "Vincent and I couldn't let Eddie go back with her after we saw those drawings. Have you taken a close look at any of them?"

"Not really."

Elena finishes making sandwiches and I get out sodas and chips and put them on the table.

"I have noticed the pictures he's been drawing lately are a lot different than they used to be – darker and with big mean-looking characters," I say.

"Three of the drawings he did in the library yesterday clearly show . . . I mean, you don't notice it right off . . . but . . ."

She lowers her voice even more, barely whispering.

"If you look carefully you'll see that they show . . . oral sex."

I put plates and napkins on the table, not looking at Elena. It's pretty embarrassing to hear my cousin's wife talking about oral sex.

"When I saw, I mean really saw, what he was drawing . . . between that and what you'd already told us about Denton . . . we couldn't let Eddie go back with Carmen, no matter how official her guardianship rights are."

The phone rings and I jump for it. Wrong number.

"I mean, when I say the drawings clearly show . . . fellatio . . . it's more like in the style of Picasso. You know?"

I shake my head, hoping Elena will explain to me about

Picasso's style and stop talking about the long "f" word stuff. I guess she's ready to change the subject, too, because she calls to Eddie that lunch is ready and the three of us sit down to eat.

"I've got to get Hannah from school pretty soon, but I wanted to check in with you guys first," she says, taking a bite of the half-sandwich she's fixed for herself.

When Eddie finishes his sandwich he stands to leave.

"Wait. Look what I brought you," Elena says, taking a new package of colored pencils and a sketch pad from one of the bags. Eighty pencils. I didn't know there were that many colors.

Eddie smiles at Elena and takes his new stuff back to the coffee table. Elena sits frowning, watching Eddie leave the room, and I think maybe she's mad. He could at least have said thank you.

When he disappears from view she asks, "Has Eddie talked to you at all today?"

I think back over the morning, trying to remember.

"No, I guess he hasn't."

"Now that I think about it, I don't think he said anything at the library yesterday, either," Elena says. "When's the last time you heard him say anything?"

"I'm not sure," I say. "Maybe when he told Hannah it was okay that she hadn't brought *menudo* to him?"

Elena nods, thoughtfully. "Maybe," she says.

We sit nibbling at potato chips for a minute or so, then Elena takes a pencil and note pad from her purse and prints F-R-A-N-K D-E-N-T-O-N.

"Is that how Carmen's fiancée spells his name?"

"As far as I know," I say.

"Vincent had one of the law clerks in his office run a check on a Frank Denton. They didn't find anything. There was a car theft on a D-E-N-T-E-N, but that guy was fifty-seven years old, and five-nine. Carmen said her Denton was in his late thirties, right? And very tall?"

"I'm not sure how old he is, but he's definitely very tall. I wish they could find something on him – something to make Carmen face facts."

"If they had fingerprints, then even if he's been using a different name they could run an accurate check on him. You don't have anything he might have handled, do you? Anything with a hard surface?"

"I don't think so."

"How about in the car? Did he ever use any tools from the trunk, or anything like that?"

I do a mental inventory of everything in the car and in my backpack, but there's nothing.

Elena walks to the door, ready to leave, when Eddie comes in with something in a small Wal-Mart bag. On the outside, in heavy black marker, he's printed "DO NOT TOUCH CONTENTS – FINGERPRINTS."

He hands the bag to Elena. She opens it and looks inside, then holds the bag open for me to peer into. It's that kiddy-watercolor paint set.

"Denton gave those to Eddie. I don't think he ever used them."

"You never handled these?" Elena asks.

Eddie shakes his head.

"And Denton did?"

Eddie nods.

"He opened the lid and showed Eddie all the colors when he first gave it to him," I say.

Elena closes the bag, places it carefully in a separate compartment in her purse, and goes off to get Hannah from school.

The phone rings once, around three, but it's just Hector calling to ask if we've heard from Max. It's not until after seven that she finally calls.

"It's so good to hear your voice," Max says.

"How's your leg?"

"Better. It's going to be fine. Listen, I don't know how long this connection will last. I've already emailed you a long message and I want you to read it as soon as you can. But the short version is please, please, stay with Eddie at Hector and Josie's 'til we . . ."

There's a lot of static on the line and I just get hints of what she's saying with her voice cutting in and out. Then it clears again.

"Let me talk to Eddie," she says.

I hand the receiver to Eddie.

"Mommy," he says, so softly I doubt she even hears him.

He listens and nods, and listens and shakes his head, then hands the phone back to me.

"Max?"

"I don't have much time, Mario, and I've got to talk to Eddie. Will you please put him on the phone?"

"I did," I tell her. "It's just . . . he's not talking much these days."

"Not talking?"

"No. But he wants me to tell you he's not a pervert."

"Oh, God. Put him back on."

I hand the phone to him again. He holds it to his ear, nodding and listening, wiping at his eyes with his free hand. When he gives the phone back to me, all I get is static and then the steady buzz of a lost connection.

E ddie and I get into *La Bamba* and drive to Vincent's so we can read Max's new email. What used to be an occasional knocking sound in second gear is now a steady bang. I don't think Hector's had a chance to check it out yet, but I guess it's not getting better on its own.

No one's home at Vincent's, so we get the key from under the blue rock and let ourselves in. There are two emails from

Max. The first one is very long, and it's definitely about more than macaroni and cheese. Eddie stands beside me, following along over my shoulder while I read out loud. Max tells us how sorry she is for the trouble with Denton, and how we've done exactly the right thing by coming up to *Tío* Hector's, added car insurance or not. And she's way pissed that while she's off fighting for our country, some creep is messing with her kids. She reminds us that everyday, all the time, she's sending love our way. She tells Eddie he's a good boy, and that none of this is his fault. She says I'm a good brother for getting Eddie away from Denton, and she's proud of us both. She's applied for an emergency leave so she can help us get things worked out. At the end, she writes, "STAY WITH HECTOR AND JOSIE. DON'T TAKE A CHANCE OF GOING ANY-WHERE NEAR DENTON!!!"

The second message is addressed just to Eddie and must have been sent right after Max's phone call. I get up from the desk chair, so Eddie can get a better view of the computer screen.

"This one's just for you," I say.

He sits staring at the screen, and I can't tell if he's read-ing the message or not. I move over behind him and read out loud:

Dear Eddie, I know with all my heart that you are NOT a pervert. You've been very badly treated by a man you trusted. I'm so sorry this happened to you, but it was NOT your fault. I've put in for an emergency home leave, but whether I get one or not you're safe now, with Mario and Tío Hector and Tía Josie. I know this is not exactly a "hakuna matata" time for you, but everything's going to be okay.

Eddie sits in front of the computer for a while longer, then takes Rovie out back to play ball. I try again to reach Jenna. No luck. I leave a message with both phone numbers where

I can be reached up here, and ask "What was it about your promise to tell absolutely no one that you didn't mean?"

I call Walker. No luck there, either. I send an email back to Max. I don't make things seem better than they are. I tell her that *La Bamba*'s making funny noises, and Eddie's not talking at all, and that Jenna's not talking, either. At least not to me. When I'm finished with the email, I just stare at the wall for a while. It's strange. Back home, between work, and school, and Jenna, I had no free time at all. Here it seems like time is all I have.

Vincent, Elena, and Hannah come home just as Eddie and I are leaving.

"Can Eddie stay over, Mama? Please? Please?"

"You know the rules, Hannah. No sleepovers on school nights."

"But PLEASE! We won't talk late, or giggle, or anything!"

That's a really safe bet right now, with Eddie – no talking or giggling.

"Maybe Friday night," Elena says.

"Sure," Vincent says. "Then we can go to a movie, or maybe to play miniature golf. Would you like that, Eddie?"

Eddie nods his head yes, but he doesn't seem too enthused. Maybe he doesn't like miniature golf anymore, what with all the after-golf activities Denton forced on him.

We get back to Hector and Josie's around nine. Josie's watching the Home Shopping Network. Besides cooking shows, that's all she ever watches.

"Somebody called for you," *Tía* Josie says. "I wrote the number down by the phone."

I rush to the note pad with high hopes. It's Walker's number. Oh, well.

25

It's after ten when I finally get through to Walker.

"Hey, Dude. I thought you'd be back today."

"I thought so, too, but Max asked me to stay here with Eddie a little longer."

"I talked to your crazy aunt today."

"Why?"

"When you didn't show up at school today, I called to see if you were at her place. She's all 'Leave me alone. He doesn't live here anymore.' She sounded hella pissed . . . When are you coming back anyway?"

"I'm not sure."

"Who cares if the witch kicked you out? You can always stay at my place."

"Thanks," I say. "Hey, did you see Jenna today?"

"Yeah, I saw her. Like I told you, girls need lots of attention. She's hella pissed at you."

"Yeah, well I'm pissed at her, too."

"Why?"

"For blabbing Eddie's business all over when she promised not to tell anyone."

"Hey, man, what's the big deal? It's only Courtney and me. How pissed are you, anyway? Like breaking-up pissed?"

"No. I don't want that. I just want things to be right between us again."

"Courtney says Trevor and Meredith broke up."

"I don't care about Trevor and Meredith! I'm talking about Jenna!"

"So am I," Walker says. "Get a clue."

"Shit!"

"Hey, soccer practice starts Wednesday. Coach Reyes says if we wanna play we better turn out for the first day of practice. That means you better get your butt down here."

I groan.

"What? You'll be back in time for soccer. Right?"

"I don't know."

"So have you called the cops on that bastard yet?"

"No."

"No? Why not?"

"I think Eddie's too scared to testify."

"But you saw it, didn't you?"

"Yeah, once, but if Eddie won't back me up . . . my own family almost didn't believe me."

"I thought this stuff was only on TV."

"I wish."

Hector comes to the kitchen doorway for the second time, checking to see if I'm still on the phone.

"I should go," I tell Walker. "But talk to Jenna for me will you? See if she'll at least pick up my phone calls?"

"Okay, but listen, you better get back here in time for the weekend. My parents are going to some convention or something. Party time!"

"Just talk to Jenna for me," I tell him.

It's only ten-thirty and I'm not really tired, but there's nothing else to do so I go to bed. I could stay up and watch HSN with Josie, but I'll pass on that one.

I decide to read in bed for a while. That always puts me to sleep. The strange thing is, *To Kill a Mockingbird* doesn't put me to sleep like books usually do. Not only that, it keeps me from thinking about things I'm tired of having spinning around in my head – at least for a while. Then I come to a part where the girl, Scout, talks about how moody her brother is, and how her father advises her to try climbing into Jem's skin and walking around in it for a while. That gets me thinking about how it would be to walk around in Eddie's skin for a while. How would it be to believe Denton would come kill us? How would it be to feel like my mouth was never clean? If I can't forget the picture of Denton forcing Eddie's mouth down on him, how is that for Eddie? Once I try climbing into Eddie's skin for a while, I can sort of forgive him for not talking, and for not backing me up when I needed him to.

I turn my attention back to the book. With the steady clicking of the crickets in the background, I read about how Jem and Scout keep finding little presents in the knot-hole of a tree, and I remember how nice it was to come across the surprises from Max after she left for Iraq.

Before anyone else is awake, I put on sweats and my running shoes and quietly slip through the back door. I stretch out my calves and quads and start out jogging at an easy pace. Down a farm road, between a row of bare peach trees, I pick up speed. The air is cool. Damp, but not too damp. It's good running weather. My feet pound against the dirt road in a steady, hard, beat. I slow to a jog, then sprint again. Sweat drips down my forehead. My sweatshirt, now soaked, clings to my back. Making a wide turn, I lengthen my stride and run at a comfortable pace back to the house.

I'm sitting on the porch steps, catching my breath, when Vincent turns into the driveway. He slams to a stop and rushes from the car, waving a manila folder in my direction.

"Look at this. Is this the guy?"

He pulls a paper from the folder and hands it to me. It's a mug shot, full face and profile, of a guy named Denny Franks. He has a mustache, and longer hair, but it's Denton all right. I don't even have to read that "Denny Franks" is 6'5" tall to know it's Denton.

Vincent sits down beside me.

"What do you think?"

"Yeah. That's him. He doesn't have a mustache and his hair is real short, but that's him."

"You sure?"

I look again, studying the picture carefully.

"Yeah. I swear."

"You may have to," Vincent says.

"Huh?"

"In court, I mean. You may have to testify against him in court."

"What about Eddie?"

"I don't think Eddie will need to testify unless he wants to."

"Eddie doesn't even want to say anything to us these days. I doubt he'll want to say anything in court."

"Well, this guy won't be around to bother him anymore, anyway. He's a pedophile with a record a mile long. He's been in violation of parole for the last year or more for failure to register as a sex offender. Redville County sheriffs have already called the Hamilton Heights Police. He'll be in jail before the day is over."

I flip through the other papers in the folder. Lewd acts against a nine-year-old. Sodomy against a seven-year-old girl. Rape of three boys, two nine-year-olds and one eleven-year-old. Sales of child pornography.

"The prints from the paint set did it," Vincent says. "The county crime lab put a rush on processing for me and this information came in early this morning."

"If he's a pedophile, why does he want to marry Carmen?"

"Look," Vincent says, pointing to an entry at the bottom of the second page and another near the middle of the next page.

One of the entries says how "Denny Franks" consistently molested the eight-year-old son and seven-year-old daughter of a woman he was engaged to. The other entry says that he molested the ten-year-old son of a woman he was living with.

"It's a pattern with him," Vincent says. "He uses women to get to the children."

I sit there with Denton's records spread out in front of me, staring at the nasty smirk on his mug shot. I want to bury that face in the pile of horse manure outside the barn. I want to cut off his dick with the pruning saw. I want to rip out his guts with the pitchfork . . .

"Mario . . . Mario!"

Vincent has hold of both of my shoulders and is staring straight into my face.

"Mario? You all right?"

I shake my head, trying to emerge from my killing fantasy. My hands are trembling and my breath is coming fast. My heart is pounding so hard I wonder if it's going to jump right out of my chest like I saw in a movie once.

"Deep breaths," Vincent says, taking a deep breath himself and releasing it slowly.

"Come on. . . . In . . . Out . . ."

After a few tries at following Vincent's breathing patterns, I come back past my rage to the real world of *Tía* Josie and *Tío* Hector's back porch steps, with Vincent sitting beside me, and the promise of jail for Denton.

"You okay?"

I nod.

"Sure?"

"Yeah. I'm okay now. Thanks."

"It's the old deep breathing technique Elena and I learned in natural childbirth classes. It doesn't take the pain away, but it helps the mother not be overcome by it."

Maybe I'm still not thinking clearly, but what Vincent's just said makes no sense to me.

He laughs. "Not that you were giving birth to a baby! It's a way to get calm in other situations, too."

Vincent takes a twenty from his billfold and hands it to me.

"Take Eddie down to the Pancake Barn for breakfast. I know he likes that place, and I want to show this stuff to my parents without Eddie having to see it all."

"I don't think he's even up yet." I say this at the same time the back door opens and Eddie sticks his head out.

"Hey, Eddie. Finish getting dressed and I'll take you to the Pancake Barn," I tell him.

He nods and disappears back inside.

"He needs to know that Denton's going to jail," I say.

"Right. But he doesn't need to know all the filthy details," Vincent says, indicating the manila folder still sitting beside me on the porch.

I get a whiff of my now dried sweatshirt and know I can't walk into any restaurant, not even the Pancake Barn, reeking of stale sweat.

"First I need a shower," I tell Vincent.

"Make it quick. Dad's got to be at work pretty soon and I want to get this over with."

At the Pancake Barn, Eddie opens the menu and points to the picture of blueberry pancakes with whipped cream, and I order the Rancher's Special – three eggs over easy, six sausage links, fried potatoes, biscuits and gravy. I've got a side view of this old guy sitting at the counter, also eating what looks like the Rancher's Special. His bulging fat belly droops over his belt, and rests gelatin-like against his thighs. His butt hangs over the stool, completely enveloping it. I wonder if it's too late to change my order?

Eddie's fiddling with the cow salt and pepper shakers, making the pepper shaker chase the salt, then making the salt turn to chase the pepper. I'm not great at knowing the best way to bring up stuff that's hard to talk about, so I just blurt it out.

"Denton's going to be arrested today," I tell Eddie.

The cows stop playing chase. Eddie gives me that big-eyed scared look.

"He's done the same stuff to other kids that he's done to you."

It's like he's a statue now. He doesn't move a muscle or change his expression. I sit watching, relieved when he finally blinks, showing he's not really turned into a statue.

"Talk to me, Eddie."

He looks back at the cows. The waitress brings our food and asks Eddie, "Will this be enough syrup for you?"

He nods.

"Thanks," I tell her.

"This no-talking routine is getting boring, Eddie, and I'm really tired of it."

Eddie smears his pancakes with syrup, adds a thick layer of whipped cream, then shoves a huge bite into his mouth.

"Okay, fine then."

I turn my attention to my own breakfast. I've got other stuff to think about anyway. Except I don't think about other stuff. I keep thinking about how I wish I could be there to see the cuffs clamped on that scumbag sicko Denton. See him shoved into a cell and hear the clank of the iron bars slammed behind him. I wonder if it'll be on TV? Probably not up here. I wish I could see the expression on Carmen's face when she gets the news. Maybe they'll even pick him up at her place.

So I'm munching away, all happy with visions of Denton being hauled off to jail, and I look over at Eddie and he's just sitting there watching me, all scrunchy-faced and worried looking. Except for the first big bite of pancakes, it looks like he's hardly eaten any of his breakfast.

"Hey, come on, Eddie. Eat up."

He picks up his fork and pokes around at the pancakes.

I watch him, this kid who's so different from the little brother I knew just a couple of months ago, and all of a sudden I feel so sad I want to cry. He looks up at me with his bright blue eyes that don't sparkle anymore.

"You're safe now, Eddie. Denton's going to jail. Maybe they're locking him up right this minute. His ass is fried."

I raise my hand for a high two, but he just keeps poking around at his pancakes.

"Listen, Eddie, remember Max's email, where she said everything's gonna get worked out?"

He nods.

"Well, it is! This is the beginning. You don't have to worry about that pervert anymore!"

He nods again but he still looks worried.

"You won't have to testify in court or anything! Denton's hella violated his parole and he's going to jail whether you tell what he did to you or not."

I talk on and on, trying to reassure him. His face loses some of that scrunchy look, but he still doesn't say anything.

Vincent and Josie are sitting at the kitchen table drinking coffee when we get back. I guess Hector's already at work.

As soon as we walk through the door, Josie goes straight to Eddie and puts her arms around him.

"*Ay, mijo, mijo, mijo,*" she croons, in a soft, gentle voice. "*Mi mijo.*"

Eddie wiggles away and goes into the living room with his drawing stuff.

Vincent takes the folder with all of the information about Denton's nasty history and tucks it inside his briefcase.

"I'll let you know what we hear," he says.

Josie sits back down, shaking her head sadly.

"Eddie can go to work with me today," she says. "It might be good for him to be around other children."

"He say anything yet?" Vincent asks, nodding his head toward the living room.

"Not a thing."

"Any idea what that's about?" Vincent asks.

"I don't know. It sounds kind of crazy but . . . I wonder . . ."

"What?"

"Well . . . I guess Denton was pretty scary all those times he told Eddie to shut up and stay shut up. Like he'd find him and kill him if he didn't shut up – kill us both if either of us told."

"But Eddie was talking when you guys got up here," Vincent says.

"Yeah, but that was before I told everyone about what Denton'd been doing."

Eddie comes back out into the kitchen. Vincent puts his hand on Eddie's shoulder and looks down at him.

"It really is going to be okay," Vincent says. "That guy's going to be locked up for a long time."

Eddie nods.

Vincent kisses Josie on the cheek.

"Give me a call if you need anything, Mama," he says, then picks up his briefcase and leaves.

I wait until 3:10 to call Jenna because I know she always turns her cell phone on as soon as she gets out of school. She answers right away.

"Hey, Jenna."

"Mario?"

"Yeah. Why haven't you been answering my calls, or calling back?"

"I answered this call, didn't I?"

"Yeah, probably because you didn't recognize my new number. I hate that you don't pick up my calls."

"Yeah, well I hate that sarcastic message you left on my voice mail, too."

She quotes the message in a whiny voice, "What about your promise to tell absolutely no one didn't you mean?"

"Hey, that wasn't sarcastic. That was an honest question. You promise not to tell anyone and then I find out you've been blabbing everything around!"

"I didn't blab everything around!"

"So how did Walker find out? Did he read it in the paper?"

She pauses.

"Walker?"

"Yeah, Walker! He told me I should just turn my aunt's boyfriend in since he'd been molesting Eddie."

Long silence. I wait.

"I only told Courtney. I tell her everything. I know she can keep a secret."

"Yeah, like you did!"

"I'm sorry!"

Now it's my turn to stay silent.

"Really, Mario, I am sorry. I didn't think she'd tell anyone . . . But what difference can it make? Your little brother doesn't have to know."

I don't know what to say. I still feel sort of betrayed, but I also really want things to get back to being good with Jenna, and I hate arguing with her. So I change the subject.

"Hey, listen. I got my own cell phone now. You can call me any time, day or night. My number's 831-555-3713."

"831?"

"Well, yeah. It's a Redville area code. I just got it! I'm standing outside the phone place right now. You're the very first person I called. I really miss you, Jenna, and I . . ."

"I miss you, too. When are you coming back?"

"Pretty soon. Walker says I can stay with him."

"Pretty soon?" Jenna says, her voice going all scratchy.

"Well, yeah. Things are kind of complicated . . ."

"I already told you, Mario. I don't think I can do this. I want a boyfriend who can be there for me, not some kind of on and off guy . . ."

"Jenna! I'm not on and off! I've been . . . this thing with Eddie . . ."

So I took over a hundred dollars from my saved insurance money for a prepaid cell phone deal so I could talk to Jenna any time and she hangs up on me after one minute and twenty-seven seconds. I should have taken the deal with the least possible minutes.

Of course, I try again. Of course, she doesn't answer. That does it. I've got to see her in person. I'm no good on the phone. I've got to get down there. I know if I can just see her, hold her and talk to her in person, I can make things right. I can start making up the work I've missed in school, too, and I can show up for first soccer practice. I've got to get back to Hamilton Heights. I want my life back!

It's not quite four o'clock. If I'm lucky, I can get to Jenna's before eleven tonight, I'll give a light tap on her window. She'll ease it open, and . . . For the first time in weeks I feel like maybe everything's going to be okay.

I buy soda and trail mix for the trip and head toward the Interstate. I feel sort of guilty about leaving Eddie, but he's safe here. Besides, why should I let my life fall totally apart for him when he won't even talk to me? I'll call him as soon as I get on the highway. He'll understand.

I'm waiting at the last signal in town, itching to get on the interstate and start counting off the miles, when *La Bamba* bombs. Shit! No matter how hard I push the clutch in, or how hard I pull at the gearshift, nothing budges. It idles peacefully in neutral, but no way can I get it in gear. I get out, reach in through the open window so I can steer, and start pushing. Two guys from the convenience store run out to help, and we get *La Bamba* pushed over to the side of the road. I call Hector who says he'll come get me in just a few minutes. I start the engine and try the gears again. Nothing. Waiting, I wonder if I'm ever going to get my life back. Also, I wonder why I didn't take auto shop back in the tenth grade, when I had the chance.

When Hector arrives he gets behind the wheel of the car and tries everything I've already tried, with the same results. He fiddles around under the hood, tries again, shakes his head, then fiddles some more.

"I hope we can fix it without putting in a whole new transmission," he says.

He takes a heavy chain from his truck and chains *La Bamba* to its back bumper. My job is to sit in the car and put the brakes on whenever we come to a stop, so the car doesn't roll into the back of the truck. When we get back to Hector's, we unchain *La Bamba* and roll her into his garage.

"I probably can't get to this until the weekend, but we'll get her fixed up," he says.

Inside, Josie and Eddie are at the kitchen table. Josie is clipping and sorting coupons from the paper and Eddie is drawing. He looks up and smiles when I walk in. I show him my new cell phone. He checks out a few games, then hands it back.

"You can use it whenever you start talking again," I tell him.

He nods and goes back to his drawing. I lean over to take a look. It's a dull-red colored car, like *La Bamba*, and its grill is curved down, in a sad face. Tears are coming out of its headlights and it's got a big band aid on its hood. It cracks me up.

"Show it to Hector," I say.

Eddie picks up the drawing and holds it up so we can all see. Josie starts laughing, then Hector, then we're all laughing, even Eddie. Josie tacks the picture on the wall, above the hardware store calendar, and every time she looks at it she starts laughing again.

After dinner, Josie lets me borrow her old Dodge Neon to go over to Vincent's to see if we've got any email. We do.

From: Maria_27@hitmail.net
Date: November 3 5:24 AM

To: Mario Barajas <mario3@yoohoo.com>
Subject: Not macaroni and cheese

Dear Mario and Eddie – A very quick message to tell you I'm being moved to a different field hospital – seems I've picked up an infection – so you may not hear from me for a few days. I'm still hoping for the leave, but who knows? Take care of yourselves and each other. Eddie, I can't tell you enough that none of this was your fault. Mario, I'm so proud of you for staying with Eddie in Redville until we can all figure out the next step. I know it's not your favorite place to be, and that you're missing school and friends, but Eddie needs you so much right now, and you're absolutely doing the right thing. Countless megatons of love to you both – Max/Mom

So okay, maybe driving down to Hamilton Heights and leaving Eddie up here on his own wasn't such a good idea after all. Maybe *La Bamba* was smarter than I was about the decision to leave Redville.

I email Max back, telling her that Denton's in violation of probation and is going to be arrested soon, if it hasn't already happened. Then I print a copy of Max's message to take back for Eddie. On my way out, I stop in the kitchen where Elena sits helping Hannah with her math.

"Where's Vincent?" I ask.

"He had to make a quick business trip to L.A." Elena says. "He'll be back tomorrow night."

She says this in a kind of vague way, like maybe there's more to the trip than general "business."

"Do you think you understand this now?" she says to Hannah.

"Not really."

"Well, try the next two on your own, and I'll come check them," Elena says. "I'll walk Mario out to the car."

We go out the back door and stand in the driveway, talking.

"I don't really want to hide things from Hannah, but I don't necessarily want her to have to deal with all of the lurid details and the drama of what's going on right now," she says.

"I know."

"Vincent went down to talk with Carmen."

"That was the business?"

"She called. You know how upset she was when she left Sunday night?"

"You said she was in a rage."

"Well, that was nothing compared to today. Apparently Denton was arrested around eleven this morning. Carmen called Vincent at his office, asking for legal help and wanting to borrow money to bail him out."

"Can he get out on bail?" I ask.

"Vincent says there's no way they're going to let that guy go. But it sounds as if Carmen's totally losing it!"

"She always sounds like she's losing it," I say.

"I think this is beyond the usual. When Vincent got off the phone with her he dropped everything and came straight home. He threw a few things into his suitcase and was out of here in about ten minutes. He said she was talking so crazy, he didn't know what she might do. He thought she could be suicidal."

"Really?"

As much as I don't like Carmen, the thought that she might off herself shocks me.

"I know Hector doesn't have any use for Carmen . . . But she's been nice to us, and Vincent's always felt a little bit sorry for her."

"So . . . what'll he do?"

"I don't know. Just try to get her settled down I guess. Remember when she first got in here the other night, she was so happy, with her new ring, and big plans and all . . ."

"Yeah, big plans to take Eddie back so he could be Denton's sex slave," I say.

"No, Mario. That wasn't her plan. I know she wasn't looking at anything realistically, but that wasn't her plan. Her plan was to get married and live happily ever after. And in less than two days she went from that high of happiness to seeing it all crumble, and to seeing that the supposed man of her dreams was truly evil – the man of many kids' nightmares."

"I hate him," I say.

"Yes, but . . ."

"Mommy!" Hannah calls. "I don't get this!"

"I better get back to her. I don't know if Vincent's had a chance to call Hector and Josie about his trip south, but it's best if they hear it from him."

"Yeah, okay," like I want to spend time talking about Carmen anyway.

When Vincent returns from Carmen's, he's got the back seat of his car loaded up with our stuff.

I drag two big trash bags full of my clothes from the car. "I'm not really planning on staying much longer," I tell him.

"Yeah, well you're not planning on going back to stay at Carmen's, are you?"

The answer to that is so obvious I don't bother to say it out loud.

"You've got to keep your stuff somewhere," Vincent tells me. "Better here than there."

Vincent looks all worn out from his time with Carmen, plus all the driving. It turns out, he spent three days down south with Carmen, not just one day as he'd originally expected. When he got down there she was in such a frenzy he had to take her to an emergency care place where they gave her massive doses of some drug just to calm her down. Then he took her home and sat with her to be sure she didn't try anything crazy. So no wonder he looks worn out.

After the drugs wore off a little, he went through the whole folder of stuff from Denton's official records. Then he went through it again the next day, when she was on a much lighter dosage.

"This is not a guy you want to help get out of jail," he told her.

Vincent doesn't know if she actually got it or not, but he had to get back up here for his own business.

It's Saturday morning before Hector has time to even look at *La Bamba*. What he sees is not good news. It needs a new transmission. He can get a rebuilt one pretty cheap, but it's still more than I have money for. Or time for, either. I've got to get back to Hamilton Heights and Jenna. The few phone calls she picks up from me are cold, and we always end up arguing, and I've got to see her in person. Eddie'll be okay up here without me for a few days.

I call about bus tickets. It's $52 from Redville to Palms, which is about fifteen miles from Hamilton Heights. I call Walker.

"Can you pick me up at the Palms bus station tonight?"

Walker groans.

"I thought you'd be glad I'm coming back."

"It's not that. My dad somehow got wind of the party plans and now they're making me go with them to that lame convention."

"When will you be back?"

"Monday morning, just in time for school. And you know what else?"

"What?"

"They've even hired a security guy to be sure no one else parties here either. How paranoid is that?"

So now I've put my trip off until Monday, when Walker can pick me up, and when I'll have a place to stay. I hate to think of being away from Jenna one more weekend, when I know from Walker that Trevor's hanging around her all the time.

Late in the afternoon I finish reading *To Kill a Mocking-bird.* The study guide Mr. Harvey gave us said to focus our reading on themes of prejudice, sacrifice, courage, and some other things I can't remember now. I think there's a theme he missed, and that's how an older brother has to do everything he can to help the younger kid. Once Scout was in danger, Jem did everything in his power to protect her. As hard as he tried, though, he couldn't do it alone.

27

In my dream the bell is ringing. I'm late to class, but as much as I hurry, I keep getting farther and farther away from my classroom. I'm running at my top speed, but other students are passing me up as they go strolling by. And the bell keeps ringing and ringing and ringing . . .

"Mario! Wake up!"

Tía Josie jostles me.

"Telephone! It's Maria."

I pull myself out of the dream and into the kitchen, where *Tío* Hector hands me the phone.

"Max?"

"I'm arriving at the San Francisco Airport Sunday evening, 8:30."

"Where are you?"

"A military airport in Germany. With about a hundred people waiting for this phone. 8:30 Sunday evening. You got it?"

"Yeah. You okay?"

"The short version? Yes."

"How's Eddie?"

"Okay – in the short version."

"We'll get the long versions soon. Gotta go. Love you."

Max hangs up and I stand looking at the phone, wondering if I'm still dreaming.

Hector takes the phone from my hand and hangs it up.

"What'd she say? Is she all right?"

"Sunday evening, 8:30, the San Francisco Airport."

"She's coming home?" Josie says, rubbing her eyes.

"I guess she got the leave," I say.

"How long?"

"I don't know."

"How's her leg?"

"Okay, I guess."

"What else?"

"That's all I know. She had to hurry."

"Well . . . I guess we'll get the details when we see her tomorrow night," Hector says. "I'll borrow Vincent's van and we'll meet her at the airport."

Maybe I'm not dreaming.

"For now, I'm going back to bed," Hector says.

"Yeah. Me, too," I say.

Back in bed I count the hours between now and when I'll see Max. Twenty-one hours! Eddie squirms around in his bed, like he's having a nightmare. I get up and go sit on the edge of his bed.

"Hey, Eddie! Good news!" I say, rubbing his back, trying to wake him without startling him. He rolls over, away from me.

"Eddie! Max just called."

He rolls over on his back.

"You awake?"

He nods, still keeping his eyes closed.

"Did you hear what I said? Max just called. She's coming home. Tomorrow!"

He rolls over on his side, facing me, his eyes wide open now.

"Tomorrow. Only twenty-one hours from now. *Tío* Hector's going to take us to meet her in San Francisco."

Eddie keeps looking at me, like maybe he thinks he's having a dream, too.

"Eddie, get it? Tomorrow we'll see Max!"

He closes his eyes again and sinks back into his pillow. The corners of his mouth turn up in just the slightest hint of a smile. "Mommy," he whispers, turning on his other side and seeming to fall immediately back to sleep.

T he airport is filled with the sights and sounds of families and friends shouting names, greeting one another, laughing, crying, hugging, kissing.

Where's Max?

We watch in silence as one soldier after another comes into view at the top of the escalator. I'm beginning to think the phone call really was a dream when I get a glimpse of her easing her way onto the moving stairway. She's on crutches and her camouflage uniform hangs loosely from her shoulders. Eddie catches sight of her, too, and is jumping up and down, waving his arms.

"MAX!" I yell.

She sees us now, and breaks into a huge smile. She half-lifts an arm from one of her crutches in a quick wave, then grabs hold in time to swing off the escalator. We rush to her and surround her with hugs.

"You Mario?" a big, burly guy standing behind Max asks.

"Yeah."

"Here's your mom's stuff," he says, setting a big duffel bag down beside me.

"Hey, thanks, Paul," Max says.

"No problem," he says, touching her lightly on the shoulder and disappearing into the crowd.

"I'll get the car," Hector says.

We make our way out to the curb to wait for him.

Aunt Josie and I bombard Max with questions. Is she hungry? Does she need to sit down? How long is her leave? How long was the flight? How does she feel? Eddie stands as close to her as he can get without throwing her off balance.

"Did they arrest that guy yet?" Max asks.

"Tuesday. I emailed you about it."

"I haven't been able to check mail since I moved from the first field hospital."

"You've got a lot to catch up on," I say.

"But he's still in jail?"

"For a long time," I tell her.

When Hector pulls up to the curb, we help Max into the shotgun seat so she can ride with her leg straight out in front of her.

Aunt Josie hands Max a thermos of the *albóndigas* she made earlier in the day. Max unscrews the wide tip and breathes in the steam, then takes a sip.

"Ummm."

She takes several more sips, then pauses to breathe in the aromas again.

"You have no idea how wonderful this is, Josie," Max says.

Josie laughs. "There's plenty more at home."

Max laughs, too. We all laugh, even though it's not that funny. It's just good to laugh.

It's after midnight when we get back home and Max can barely keep her eyes open.

"There's so much to talk about . . ."

"Get rested," Hector says. "There's time."

I carry Max's duffel bag into the bedroom Eddie and I have been sharing and put it on top of the chest. *Tía* Josie's made a bed on the sofa for me, so Max can have the bed I've been sleeping in.

"You need anything?" I ask.

She shakes her head and motions for me to sit down next to her on the bed. She takes my face between her hands and looks deeply into my eyes, then holds her cheek against mine for a moment.

"I'm so glad to be here, Mario. To see you. We're going to be all right."

"I know," I say.

Eddie comes back from the bathroom and sits down next to Max, on her other side. She gives Eddie the same treatment, looking into his eyes, holding her cheek against his, telling him we're going to be all right. He smiles and nods.

"Now, I'm just so tired," she says.

"There's nothing you need?" I ask again, standing.

"Not a thing."

I go out to my bed on the sofa and fall asleep within minutes. Early in the morning, before dawn, I'm awakened by Hector stirring around, getting ready for work. Dragging the cushions and bedding from the sofa into the bedroom where Max and Eddie are still sleeping soundly, I arrange a makeshift bed on the floor between Max and Eddie's beds and go back to sleep. When I awaken again, it is to the sound of Max talking to Eddie, who is curled up next to her in bed. I lean up on my elbow.

"It's so great to wake up to you guys," Max says. "I want to get caught up on everything! First, though, I've got to change my bandages and do a little first aid. You guys may want to use the bathroom first, because this will take me a little while."

By the time I get back from my run, Max is all cleaned up in civilian clothes, sitting in the living room with Josie, drinking coffee.

I sit down next to Max.

"Phew!" she says, waving her hand in front of her face.

"Okay, I can take a hint," I say.

In the bathroom, Eddie is still brushing his teeth. I turn on the shower, strip down, and get in under the hot spray.

"Your teeth are clean, now," I tell Eddie, as I get out of the shower and dry off.

He's still brushing when I go back to the living room. *Tía* Josie's gone off to work now, and Max is flipping through the morning newspaper still sipping coffee. She looks up when I come into the room.

"You've no idea what a luxury a morning like this can be," she says.

"How's your leg?"

"Better. I just have to be careful to take care of it, to get rid of the infection . . . Where's Eddie?"

"Brushing his teeth."

"I guess that racecar toothbrush really changed his habits, huh?" she says, smiling.

"That and Denton," I tell her.

Her smile fades.

"What do you mean?"

"It's like maybe his mouth always feels dirty now, after what Denton did to him."

Max shakes her head sadly, then goes to get Eddie.

Here's how we spend the day. Trying to get lazy Simba to fetch, and talking. Eating leftover soup with lots of warm corn tortillas, and talking. Doing a load of laundry, and talking. Looking at *La Bamba*, and talking. Well . . . Max and I do the talking. Eddie nods and shakes his head, still not saying anything. By early afternoon I've told Max everything I know about Denton, and she's asked all the questions she can ask.

Over and over again she tells Eddie that none of what happened was his fault. That he is not a pervert. Then she gets an envelope from her duffel bag.

We sit on the front porch, in the sun, and she shows us her

pictures. There are several of friends she got to know in Iraq – some she shared quarters with and some she worked with in communications. She pauses before the last two pictures. Then she shows us a picture of herself and her sergeant, sitting side by side at a mess hall table, both holding big spoonfuls of macaroni and cheese in front of their faces, mugging for the camera.

"This is one of the guys who was killed in the IED explosion."

After a slow, deep breath, she shows us the next picture, of a little bald-headed, smiling baby.

"This is the sergeant's baby. The baby who doesn't have a dad anymore. The baby of the dad I traded places with, just before the explosion."

The three of us sit silently looking at the two pictures, the dad and the baby, and then Max puts her hands tightly over her face as if to hold back the onslaught of tears and sobs that can't be stopped. I put my arm around her, not knowing what to do. She shakes her head back and forth, gasping, tears rushing down her cheeks. Eddie stands and puts his arms around her.

"It wasn't your fault, either," he says. "Nothing that happened was your fault."

And then we are clutching one another, heaving great sobs of at least a 7.5 seismographic intensity. Then, slowly, the sobs die away, with intermittent after-shocks, until we are all breathing steadily and our cheeks are dry.

Max puts the pictures back in the envelope and tucks them into her jacket pocket. When Josie comes home Max asks if we can borrow the car to go to the store. She tells Josie to kick back and put her feet up, we're going to fix dinner tonight.

I drive, because of Max's bad leg, and Eddie sits in the back writing out a shopping list. First on his list is kitty treats, because he still has hopes that Simba will play fetch again.

We buy six boxes of mac 'n cheese, extra cheese to add

to it, salad stuff, and two cartons of ice cream – chocolate-chocolate chip for almost everyone else, and vanilla for me.

When Josie sees the packages of mac 'n cheese, she tells Max she can whip up a batch of enchiladas in no time – much better than anything that comes from a package.

"Save it for tomorrow," Max says, leading Josie back to her easy chair. "Macaroni and cheese may not be good for a steady diet, but sometimes it's just what the doctor ordered."

"Besides, we really like it," Eddie says.

Tía Josie does one of those cartoon double-takes when she realizes Eddie just actually spoke.

"*Ay, mijo,*" she says, throwing her arms around him and laughing. "Then I'll just sit here and rest, like I'm an old fat cat."

28

Tuesday morning Max spends a long time looking through Eddie's drawings.

"What's this mean?" she asks, holding up one of his "Picasso style" drawings.

Eddie shrugs.

"Don't give me that silent treatment, Eddie! I didn't fly seven thousand miles just to play charades with you. Tell me about this drawing."

"It's just . . . something I felt like drawing," he says, staring down at the dark picture.

Max looks at it more closely, from several angles.

"Does it have to do with what Denton did to you?"

"Sort of," Eddie says.

Max points to a heavy black line that starts in the right hand corner of the paper and stretches diagonally over half-way to the left hand corner.

"So, is this Denton's . . . penis?"

"Sort of," Eddie says, still staring at the drawing.

"How about this?" she asks, pointing to a pair of jagged, blood-red lips just above the line.

"A mouth," Eddie says.

Max looks like she could start crying again, but she doesn't.

"It won't happen again," she tells him. "Go get dressed now. You can't sit around all day in your pajamas. It's a school day."

"But . . . I'm not going to school, am I?" he asks, looking confused.

"I suppose not, but get dressed anyway, we've got things to do."

He leaves the room and then we hear the toothbrush start up.

Max reaches for one of Eddie's pencils, purple, and begins writing one of her famous lists on a blank sheet from the sketch pad.

"So, let's see. I've got twelve days left of my two week leave, eleven really, allowing for return travel time, and we've got to figure out . . . "

She's more talking to herself than she is to me. Watching and hearing Max think out loud right now reminds me of how much I've missed that. And her lists – I guess I've missed those, too. It's funny how sometimes you can miss something without really even knowing it.

By the time Eddie's finally finished brushing his teeth and dressing, and dragging Simba in from outside, Max has a list of about twenty-five things to take care of before her leave is up.

"We've got to get back to Hamilton Heights, find a place for you guys to stay, get you back in school. You can't just be hanging out here neglecting your education," Max says, getting up from her chair with the help of her crutches.

She hobbles over to the phone and calls Hector.

"Hector, we've got to get back home to straighten things

out. How's *La Bamba* coming? . . . A week!" Max shouts. "We can't wait a week! . . ."

When Max gets off the phone with Hector she calls Vincent and asks if she can borrow his van. I guess the answer is yes because as soon as she hangs up she tells us to get our stuff together, we'll be leaving soon.

"All of our stuff?" I ask.

"Well, yeah. You want to graduate from Hamilton, don't you? And play soccer?"

"I'm not moving back in with Carmen!" I shout. "And neither is Eddie! She's fuckin' nuts! You can even ask Elena! Or Vincent!"

"Whoa! Calm down! Who said anything about moving back in with Carmen? Do you think I'd let that happen, after all she put you through?"

"She accused me of lying, and of kidnapping Eddie, and of being a bad influence, and of being an Internet porn freak, and . . ."

"Mario! I know!"

Max limps over to me and puts her arms around me.

"Whatever we work out, it won't be with Carmen. It wasn't right to begin with . . . I knew that, but . . ."

"Just let us go back to the apartment," I say.

Max takes a step back and shakes her head.

"Get your stuff together. I want to get on the road so we can get down there before the Armory offices are closed. We can talk about all of this on the way."

"How're we going to get there?"

"Vincent's loaning us his van," Max says.

"Cool," Eddie says. "Can we rent some DVDs before we go?"

Max laughs. "We'll talk about it after you get all your stuff together. Vincent'll be here in about fifteen minutes."

We're just about to the Interstate, where *La Bamba*

broke down. I'm driving because, although Max's leg is better, she still needs to sit with it straight out in front of her most of the time.

Eddie's in the back seat, looking through a stack of DVDs big enough to stock a small Blockbuster's.

"There's nothing good here," he says. "Can't we just rent something good?"

"I'm sure you can find something interesting in that whole pile of things," Max says. "I don't want to take time to stop."

"But these are all Hannah's. There is nothing good here."

"So pretend you're in *La Bamba* where there is no DVD player."

"But there is a DVD player and I want to see something good. That's the whole fun of the trip! I hate this trip without a movie to watch."

This goes on for a while, and I'm hella sick of Eddie's complaining, until I realize how sort of normal it sounds. He's definitely not "shut up" right now.

"Let me look," Max says, reaching back for the DVD carrier.

On the Interstate now, I put the van on cruise control set for seventy miles per hour. It's a totally quiet and smooth ride, and if I want to pass anyone I just jam down the pedal and it zooms forward like it's rocket propelled. At least that's how it seems to me in comparison to *La Bamba*. After a while, I put my mind in cruise control, too, thinking about seeing Jenna again. Maybe I'll be waiting for her at school, at the gate she always leaves from. Maybe she'll come running to me, with her hair all bouncing in slow motion, like in the shampoo commercials . . .

"Mario?"

. . . and she'll throw her arms around me . . .

"Mario!"

Max drags me from my vision back to reality. She's looking at the list.

"You said you called both schools?"

"I called last week and said there'd been a family emergency. I told them we'd be back soon."

"And?"

"And both places wanted to talk to a parent or guardian."

"Did you ask for make-up work?"

"No, I only talked to the attendance woman."

Max goes back to shuffling through the DVDs.

"You might like this," she says, handing one back to Eddie.

He puts it in the player and starts it up.

"Hey! Cool! A Japanese cartoon!"

With Eddie settled in the backseat with the DVD, and Max dozing off in the passenger seat, I sink back into my Jenna vision. It turns out that's all it is though, a vision. A fantasy. In reality, I do go wait for her at the gate. I watch as she walks down the steps of the main building, holding hands with Trevor, talking and laughing. Trevor is the first to see me.

"Hey, look who's here," he says. "What's up?"

I do an imitation of Eddie and shrug my shoulders.

"Oh, hi," Jenna says, walking past me like I barely exist. Which is how I feel – like I barely exist.

Max goes to the Armory and gets us set up with a social worker – Mr. Shields – someone who's going to help us figure out how to "work through our issues." It cracks me up, the way he talks, but he's a nice enough guy. He gave us a voucher for a motel near Eddie's school, because we need a place to stay until we can find something more permanent. He says it'll take a week or so to find a place for us within our school boundaries. He's talking about a foster home, but one that will take both of us. I'm thinking, maybe it'd be okay if I stayed with Walker.

"Hey, Max, what if . . ."

I can't even get the "what if I stay with Walker" words

out of my mouth. It just wouldn't be right. According to Mr. Shields, I've been Eddie's island of emotional security when he was in grave physical and psychological danger, and even with his blown up words I know what he means. So I agree to the foster home thing, even though I'll be eighteen in June and "foster care" sounds like something for little kids.

Wednesday morning Max takes Eddie to school and fills out a form stating that he's to wait for her in the office every day until further notice and that he's not ever to leave with anyone else but me. Then, with Eddie in school, Max comes back for me and we go over to Hamilton, expecting to clear up my absences and get make-up work so I can get caught up in my classes. That doesn't happen.

Because Max had called for an appointment first thing this morning, my counselor, Ms. Ferrin, has grades and comments from each of my teachers, plus a printout of my attendance record. She spreads the papers out on her desk, purses her lips, and says that based on failing grades and missed classes, it would be impossible for me to pass any of my academic classes.

"You missed the major novel test in English. That alone counts for half of your grade."

"Couldn't I take the test now?"

"It's too late. The grade reports are already in."

That sucks. The one time out of all my English classes that I've read an assigned novel and I don't get to take the test. Plot, character, symbolism, ask me anything about *To Kill a Mockingbird* and I'd have it nailed.

The only class I have a passing grade in, a B, is Peer Communications. Ferrin says that returning to Hamilton is not an option. She recommends that I enroll in an Independent Study program, where I can maybe make up enough credit to graduate in June.

"Well, at least you can graduate with your class," Max says.

"It doesn't work that way," Ms. Ferrin says. "If Mario completes the work, he'll receive a diploma, but he'll not graduate on stage at Hamilton High School because he's no longer enrolled here."

"What about soccer?" I ask.

More pursed lips.

"Only students enrolled at Hamilton High School are qualified to play on Hamilton High School teams."

"What about the firefighter training program?"

"That's a partnership with Hamilton High School and if you're not a Hamilton graduate . . ."

In the afternoon I stop by soccer practice.

"Sorry, Mario," Coach Reyes says. "I wish there were a way around that rule, but there isn't. We could sure use you, but only if you're enrolled at Hamilton High."

Outside Java Jive, I watch some new guy through the storefront window. He's concocting drinks at twice my old speed. I don't even bother to go in.

It hits me that I came home to Hamilton Heights to get my old life back, and it takes me less than twenty-four hours to find I have no life here. I have no girlfriend, no school, no soccer team, no job, no future with the fire department.

I call Walker.

"Life sucks!"

"Come on over," he says. "We'll drown your sorrows."

When I get there it seems like Walker's already started drowning my sorrows.

He opens a bottle of something called Third Coast Old Ale and hands it to me.

"Get started," he says, sort of furry-tongued. "Highest alcohol content of any beer on the market. I researched it for PC," he says, laughing.

I take a sip. I already told you, I hate alcohol. But maybe with my life on such a suck-ride it's time to reconsider.

I take another sip.

Walker starts laughing again.

"You drink like a girl, Dude," he says, tipping his bottle up and taking a huge swig. He lets out a big burp and laughs even harder.

"Where is everybody?" I ask.

"Visiting my old gramma."

Somehow, that strikes him as funny, too, and he continues his solitary laugh-fest. Then he turns serious.

"We have to get the empties out of here by nine."

I try to talk with Walker about Jenna, and all that's happened with Eddie, and how I'm out of Hamilton, and soccer, and the whole friggin' mess, but he's a lot more interested in the Third Coast right now.

I turn the radio on to my favorite classic rock station, something I've missed up in the land of mariachis, country stations, and Christian evangelists. Walker wobbles over to the radio and changes the station to some rap-crap. I change it back. Pretty soon, we're in a huge argument about which station to listen to, and which music is best and so instead of staying over with him I'm back at the motel by eight.

Maybe it was my fault. I was in a bad mood anyway because I barely existed. Or maybe it had to do with Walker being half out of it. But I thought the least he could do for me would be to cheer me up with the music of my choice. Not Walker though. It's his way or the highway, so I took the highway.

On the way out he yelled at me that I was no fun anymore and that it was no wonder Jenna preferred Trevor to me. I could forgive him for not taking my troubles very seriously. I could forgive the music thing. But I'm not sure I can forgive him for that last remark.

29

Eddie's all happy to be back in school, and to be hanging around with Brent, and to be having Max pick him up every day. It's almost as if the whole thing with Denton never happened. This morning he even cracked himself up telling Max that stupid joke about a spelling bee being smarter than a talking parrot.

Max is busy running around, checking items off her list. Her leg still bothers her at times, but she can drive now and she's not using crutches anymore.

She goes to see Carmen at the bank where she works, partly because there's a Notary Public there and partly because she knows Carmen won't get all crazy in front of her boss and co-workers. Carmen signs the official papers relinquishing legal guardianship for us and the Notary records it. Max says Carmen told her Denton wasn't really a bad guy. He just needed help.

"Can you believe that?" Max asks me. "After what he did to Eddie? I told her that she was the one who needed help.

'Your head's buried so far beneath the sand, you need to hire a crane to pull it out' I told her. We didn't part on very good terms."

On Thursday, Max drops Eddie off at school and then goes to visit her sergeant's wife out in West Covina. She takes the goofy mac 'n cheese picture, and the picture of the smiling baby with her.

"I'll just tell her he had the baby's picture with him when he was killed. I think she'd like to know that. I'll skip the details, though."

While Max is out, and Eddie's in school, I sit in front of the TV in the small motel room. In the afternoon I decide to try to see Jenna again. I wait by the gate, like before, and this time she's by herself.

"Hi," I say, walking up to meet her.

She nods her head, but keeps walking. I fall in beside her.

"I can get the car tonight," I tell her. "You wanna go do something?"

She stops.

"I don't think so, Mario."

"It's my cousin's car, with a DVD and everything," I say. Like she's ten years old and going to be impressed with a DVD in a car? Like how stupid is that?

"I told Courtney I'd go over to her house tonight."

"Well . . . maybe tomorrow night?"

She shakes her head. In front of the library now, Jenna stops.

"I've got some stuff to do in here, but I'll call you later."

"Promise?" I say.

"Yeah. I promise."

She walks up the steps to the library. I walk back to the motel and the small-screen TV and wait for her call. But here's what I know about Jenna from sad experience. Just because she promised she'd call doesn't mean it'll happen. It does, though, after my eyeballs have practically fallen into my lap from staring so long at the TV. I take my phone outside, away from Max and Eddie, so I can finally have a confidential conversation with Jenna. What I get is not much of a conversation.

It's like she's memorized what she wants to say and can't wait to get it over with. Basically, it's that she just wants to be friends. She cares for me. I'm a good person. Trevor invited her to the winter ball and she said yes. She knows she couldn't depend on me to take her to any of the dances or parties or any of the things she's always looked forward to doing senior year because I'm never around. But Trevor wants to do all of those things, too. She's sorry about what happened to Eddie, poor guy, and she hopes we'll always be friends.

"Sure," I say, and hang up.

What else is there to say? What does a guy say to the old "I hope we'll always be friends" shit? Am I hurt? Yeah, but I've also lost a little something with Jenna. Like if she really liked me as much as she said she did, wouldn't she understand more what I've been going through? Maybe she's not as great as I thought she was.

Late that night, or maybe early in the morning, I'm jolted out of a sound sleep by Max screaming and thrashing around in her bed.

"Max!" I shout, throwing my covers off and rushing over to her. "What's wrong?"

Eddie's awake now, too, and has turned the light on.

"Wake up," I say, shaking her by the shoulders.

She twists away, screaming.

"Max!"

She opens her eyes wide and for an instant I glimpse a look of pure terror.

"Mommy!" Eddie says, looking almost as terrorized himself.

She closes her eyes and shakes her head, back and forth, back and forth. Her pajamas are soaking wet.

Opening her eyes again she looks all around the room, and at us, and smiles weakly.

"Only a dream," she says. "Sorry. Go back to bed, now."

I get back in bed, but Eddie still stands watching her.

"It's okay, Sweetheart. Really. Go back to sleep now."

On Friday, Max and I go to the police station so I can tell them all I know about Denton. Two officers lead us into a windowless room. The guy, Officer Sanchez according to his badge, takes notes, while the woman, Officer Goodridge, asks questions. She keeps going back to what I actually witnessed with my own eyes and asking the same questions over and over again. After telling her about a hundred times how I walked in on Denton forcing Eddie to give him a blow job she says, "Your story's quite consistent."

"I know what I saw."

"I believe you do," she says. "Would you be willing to testify in court?"

"Sure – happy to. More than happy to."

They're very interested in knowing about the other kid that Denton took Eddie to see.

"All I know is his name's Jimmy, he lives in a big house with a pool, Denton fooled around with them and took some pictures. They left in a hurry when they heard a car in the driveway."

"Do you know where the house is?"

"Up in the heights somewhere, I think. Eddie probably knows."

When we pick Eddie up from school, Max tells him the cops need his help. Eddie gets that scrunched up worried look on his face, but he eventually agrees to ride along with the cops as long as we all can go together. So first thing in the morning, the two officers pick us up in an unmarked car and drive us around in the really nice part of town. After driving in circles long enough that I could puke, Eddie finally spots the place.

"You sure?" Goodrich says.

"I remember that statue thing," he says.

"Good. There probably aren't too many other bright pink statues of the Virgin of Guadalupe in this neighborhood," she says.

Sanchez laughs. "That'd be more like my neighborhood."

They take us back to the motel, and ask to come in for just a few minutes.

"There's not much room," Max says.

"We won't be long."

They follow us into our room. Sanchez takes out his notepad. Goodrich motions for Eddie to sit in the one chair in the room. She takes a seat on the rollaway facing Eddie and asks him to tell her everything he remembers about that day. He examines a scratch on the arm of the chair and says nothing.

"Did Jimmy seem to know Denton? Like maybe he'd been there before?"

Eddie nods.

"Did he take pictures, with your clothes off?"

Eddie flashes me one of those "you betrayed me" looks and nods again.

Goodrich asks questions about everything I told her yesterday. Eddie nods or shakes his head in answer but he never looks up from the scratch. When she starts to repeat the questions Max goes over to where Eddie is sitting and puts her arm on his shoulder.

"I think he's had enough," she says.

"Just a few more questions, Ms. Barajas," Goodrich says, taking a breath to ask another.

Max steps in front of Eddie and faces Goodrich.

"He's had enough," Max says, still shielding Eddie from

Goodrich's view.

Goodrich gives Max a long look, like maybe deciding how far to push things. Then she stands up.

"Thank you all for your help," she says.

Sanchez puts his notepad and pen back in his pocket. They hand us cards with their names and numbers, in case any of us remembers anything else. They thank Eddie, especially, for finding the house. They say how important all of this information will be in keeping Denton locked up for decades, where he can't mess with kids like Eddie and Jimmy ever again.

By the time the two cops close the door behind them, Eddie's in the bathroom with the toothbrush buzzing away. The door is locked, and Eddie's not responding to Max's pleas that he open up.

"Come on, Eddie. Let's go get those clean teeth dirty again. We'll go to Dimitri's for lunch," Max calls.

All we hear is that steady damned vroom, vroom, of the toothbrush.

Max forages around in Vincent's van until she finds the little tire-changing crowbar and a hammer.

"Just open up, Eddie, so we don't have to take the door down."

Vroom. Vroom. Vroom.

So we take the door off its hinges. I'm getting really good at this. Maybe it could be a specialty job for me, since the fire-fighting thing has turned to shit.

Eddie's still vrooming away when we take off the door and lean it against the side wall. Max walks in, gently takes the toothbrush from his hand and turns it off. Tears streaming down her cheeks, she leads Eddie out to the rollaway where she pulls him close, assuring him he's safe. His mouth is clean. He's clean . . .

Everything closes in on me. I can't get a breath. I rush past Max and Eddie, out the door, past the blinking vacancy sign, gulping air, pounding the sidewalk, running hard and fast, away from the crappy motel, away from Eddie's damned scrunchy, worried face, away from Max's tears, away from my screwed up life, running, running, until thoughts give way to sensation and all that's left is the next panting breath and the next pounding step.

It is not until I reach the park near Eddie's school, miles from the motel, that exhaustion kicks in. My legs suddenly go weak and I stumble down onto the grass. I should get up and do a walking cool down. I should stretch out my already stiffening muscles. Instead, soaking wet and still breathing heavily, I lie on the grass, staring up at the hazy grey sky, trying to think about nothing.

30

Remember how I said Eddie was happy to be back in school and that it was almost as if the whole thing with Denton never happened? I was wrong. After that day with the sheriffs when he locked himself in the bathroom, he also stopped talking again for the next two days. After that, Max tells me she has a huge favor to ask of me. She suggests we go to Java Jive after we leave Eddie off at school, and talk over a latte. I countered with a Starbucks idea, since I've still not been back to see Sammy.

We got our drinks and sat at a table in the back corner. Max told me she'd decided the foster care plan would be a big mistake.

"Eddie needs to be with people who love him. So do you, for that matter, so I'm asking you to make one more big sacrifice and stay with him in Redville, with *Tío* Hector and *Tía* Josie, just until I get back in September."

She said she knew it wasn't fair to ask me, at my age, to put everything on hold in my own life, but she was so worried

. . . She thought it was crucial for Eddie to be around good men to help offset the awful effects of being around Denton. He needed men he could trust, who would treat him right. He needed *Tío* Hector, and Vincent, and me.

So I went back to Redville with Max and Eddie a few days before her leave was over. Eddie got enrolled at the school where *Tía* Josie works and I'm doing the Independent Study thing to get my high school diploma.

B efore we left Hamilton Heights, Mr. Shields arranged regular meetings with a family counselor, Dr. Patton, in Redville. The three of us went together twice before Max had to leave. Since then, Eddie and I see her separately every other week. On the weeks that we don't see Dr. P. alone, we go together.

In our first session Dr. Patton explained that some people who are sexually molested as children never get over it. Emotionally, they're damaged for life. But it doesn't have to be that way. She told Eddie that even though the memory of what Denton did to him would never really go away, over time it will lose its strength. Eddie's artistic talents, his good heart, and the love in our family will see him through this hard time. Then, while he sat and drew and listened, she asked me and Max both a lot of questions. I thought she was pretty cool not to start right off asking Eddie a bunch of stuff, because he'd probably have stopped talking again if she'd pushed him.

You may be wondering why I go to see Dr. Patton once a week on my own. At first, I thought it was a stupid idea. I wasn't the guy locking myself up and brushing my teeth like a maniac! But I had to admit maybe I was sort of depressed. Did I sometimes feel sad, or empty inside? Did I have feelings of hopelessness? Well, duh! Who in my skin wouldn't?

Had I experienced a loss of interest in things I once enjoyed? Well . . . if not a loss of interest, certainly a loss of opportunity. So, okay, I'm seeing Dr. P. every other week on my own.

   She says both Max and Eddie have something called Post Traumatic Stress Disorder (PTSD). I can't explain it scientifically, but basically it means that Eddie's horrible experiences with Denton, and Max's horrible experiences in Iraq, messed with their minds. Doesn't that suck? It's bad enough to have to live through that shit once, but then it keeps coming back at them. What Dr. P. says is that things will get better with time and effort. I can see that happening with Eddie. I hope it's happening for Max, too.

   Eddie and I email Max every day, just like before, but now we let each other know the good stuff and the bad stuff. Just last week, Max wrote that a roadside bomb had killed another guy in her unit. I wish the killing would stop. I keep telling Max to stay off the roads – not that she has a lot of say in that. I worry about her, though. Not only does she have to experience the living nightmare of being in a war zone, she still sometimes gets one of those shaking, sweating dreams like the one she had in the motel. Still, I'd rather worry than not have a clue about what's going on with her.

   We're doing our part, too, to get beyond the mac 'n cheese talk. A few days ago, Eddie caught this ad for some news report about sexual predators that was going to be on TV. It wasn't even the report – just an announcement for it. But it was enough to send him under the house for three hours. That went in our next email to Max.

   Most of the time, though, things go along pretty smoothly. Eddie likes school up here, even though he misses Brent and some of the other kids at Elm Avenue. He's friends with the boy across the road now, so that's cool. He's back to telling a few jokes, too, so maybe he's going to be okay.

   As for me, even though I let Max think I'd made a great sacrifice by coming back to Redville with Eddie, the truth is, there's nothing much for me down in Hamilton Heights anymore. Walker calls sometimes with news of soccer, or parties, or whatever. Once he told me Jenna and Trevor'd had a big fight and I should call her. After he hung up, I held the phone in my hand for a long time, remembering Jenna's number, thinking about calling, but I didn't do it. That part of my life, with Jenna, and Walker, and the whole Hamilton High scene, seems almost like it happened to someone else.

Up here, besides the Independent Study thing, I'm working two days a week in Vincent's office. I do some filing, and some basic computer search stuff related to trials he's got coming up. It beats turning out the mocha-vanilla bean-decaf with whipped stuff day after day. There's a girl from Redville Community College who works at Vincent's, too. I sort of like her, but I haven't done anything about it yet. She's almost two years older than I am, but I don't think that should make any difference. I've aged a lot the past six months, anyway.

Oh, yeah. I'm playing club soccer, which is way better than playing high school soccer, at least in my opinion.

I did end up testifying against Denton. The trial went on for weeks, but I was just down there for two days, answering the same questions over and over again, both from the defense and from the prosecution. When I was on the stand, Denton threw me some really hard looks, like he was trying to scare me out of saying anything against him. But I looked straight back at him, thinking "you pitiful pervert, in your orange jail suit, your ass is fried." I hope he could read my mind.

I stayed with Walker for those few days of the trial, but we didn't really see much of each other. Between work and soccer and Courtney, and partying, he was pretty busy from after school until late at night. And I was in court all day.

I guess Walker and I are still sort of friends, but in some ways we're sort of strangers, too. He was way more interested in high school stuff than he was in the trial, and I was all caught up in the trial.

About the trial – Vincent knows how to check up on all of that court stuff, so we were able to follow it pretty closely even if we weren't down there sitting in the courtroom. Jimmy's mother testified about how she and Denton dated for a while, until she became suspicious of him coming to her house when she wasn't home and told him to get out of her life.

Jimmy didn't testify, but he gave a deposition about all the stuff Denton had done to him. According to Jimmy, Denton even brought girls over sometimes, and took pictures of them with Jimmy in sex poses. I guess he was making a lot of money off of child pornography. That would explain why he never seemed to have to work at his "landscaping business." Anyway, between molestation and child pornography charges, and his previous record, Denton's been locked away for at least twenty years. Long enough for his filthy dick to fall off is what I hope. That's the good news.

The not-so-good news? Everything I thought was mine – Jenna, a great, final Hamilton soccer season, graduation with my friends, the firefighting course – gone. I still get sort of down about that sometimes. Like just last night, I was sitting out on the porch at Hector and Josie's. The moon was bright, and full, and I remembered that other full moon night, when Jenna and I were parked up in the foothills, back when things were really good with us.

I sat out on the porch for a long time, feeling all hollow inside, watching the Redville moon. But then Eddie came along carrying Simba. He put him on the ground in front of me.

"Look, Mario!"

He had a small rubber ball, about the size of a ping-pong ball, which he threw past Simba, probably not more than ten feet or so.

"Fetch, Simba," he shouted.

Simba got up slowly, waddled over to the ball, picked it up

in his mouth and sauntered back to Eddie.

"See! I told you he'd fetch again!"

Eddie's smile was wide and his eyes were sparkling, and I knew again that I'd done exactly the right thing in getting him away from Denton. If Jenna couldn't understand that and give me some time to get things taken care of, well, maybe she wasn't that much of a loss.

Will I go back to Hamilton Heights after Max gets home? Will I try to get into the firefighter's course next year? I don't know. Vincent told me about a law enforcement course at Redville C. C. that sounds kind of interesting. As much as I've always wanted to do the firefighting thing, I could see being involved in something that would bring guys like Denton down.

In her emails, Max tells me that doing the counseling stuff with Eddie plus working on the GED, playing soccer, and working at Vincent's, is enough. Just take care of now, she says. Maybe she's right, but I want more than "now." So I keep trying to figure out what's next, and knowing that even if everything's turning out a lot different than I expected, other possibilities keep showing up.

31

The night before Max left for Iraq, she took us to the Pancake Barn for dinner – just the three of us out for "one last time." She asked for a booth way in the back, away from everyone else.

I won't bore you with all of the emotional stuff because you already know how it was the first time she left. This was about the same only it was harder because by then we all knew how horrible things in Iraq really were.

During dinner, all of us poking around at our food, Max says she wishes she had more time to talk with me and Eddie about everything in the world – casual talks, a little bit at a time. But since this is her last face-to-face with us for a long time, she's got to cram a lot in. It could be her last face-to-face with us, forever, is what we all know, but nobody wants to say.

So anyway, Max starts talking about "The Lion King," which I think is nearly as wimpy as only talking about mac 'n cheese when the world was falling apart around us. Then she goes into this whole "Circle of Life" thing, about how it moves us all, through despair and hope, through faith and love, 'til we find our place . . . I'm pretty sure you know how the song goes.

Anyway, she says that one of the great powers that moves every single one of us in the circle of life is SEX. That's how she says it, like it's capitalized.

Eddie moves his plate aside, picks up a black crayon and starts drawing. I wish I had something else to do right now, too, 'cause it's sort of disturbing to hear your own mom say "SEX" in a capitalized way.

I concentrate on cutting up what's left of my chicken fried steak into tiny, tiny pieces.

"Let's get this straight," Max says. "We all know how good sex feels. That's a given."

I feel my face heating up with embarrassment and I'm happy my skin is more brown than white, because if it was white it would be turning red. I mean my mom has just said she knows how good sex feels, and I really do not want to go there. Not only that, but she said she knows that I know how good sex feels, and I seriously do not want to go there. And where does that leave Eddie?

As if she's read my mind she says to Eddie, "Maybe, at first, some of what Denton did with you felt pretty good, before he got rough and mean."

Eddie grabs a clean sheet of paper and starts furiously drawing horizontal black lines from one side of the paper to the other.

"There's no shame in that, Eddie. It's a natural physical response. I imagine Mario and Jenna did some things that felt pretty good, too, when they were together."

Dang! Does she have to get so personal?

"Those feelings are part of the power that keeps the circle of life turning, and they're a gift to us from the universe. The trouble is, some people, like Denton, make terrible use of that power, and they don't care who they hurt, or how badly, for the sake of some selfish sensation."

Max looks at us for a kind of long time.

"Eddie, I don't want you to let what happened with Denton sour you on sex. Or have you rushing to repeat those sensations, either.

"And Mario . . ."

The waitress stops by our table with a dessert menu and says she'll be right back.

Eddie looks up from yet another drawing. This one, I notice, is of a lion. A black lion.

"Know why the lion crossed the road?" he asks.

Max and I both look at him blankly.

"'Cause chickens hadn't been invented yet."

His remarks are so not related to the conversation, at first it's like we haven't even heard him,

"Get it? Why'd the lion . . ."

Max starts laughing, and then I do too. When the waitress comes for our dessert order all we can do is laugh. Max takes Eddie's paper and crayon, writes "NO THANKS" on the back of his drawing, and we laugh all the harder, not because it's the greatest joke ever, but because it's definitely time to lighten up.

Max finally gets it together enough to pay the bill and the three of us walk out to the newly repaired *La Bamba*. I get behind the wheel to drive us back to Hector's. When we're all in the car, doors closed, windows up, I let loose with a rumbler fart. Max and Eddie both get their windows open as fast as they can, waving the air in front of them. I adjust the rearview mirror to reflect Eddie. He's laughing so hard he's practically doubled over. I step on the accelerator and pick up speed as quickly as possible, the better to air out the car. Whoever said people can't smell their own farts was soooo wrong!

Late that night, I drag my pillow and blankets from the

sofa into the bedroom where Max and Eddie are sleeping. I make a place on the floor, just like that first night Max was back. I lie awake, stretched out between them, listening to the crickets, and the soft steady breathing from Eddie and Max, breathing in rhythm, together. I try to match their rhythm and after a minute or so it works. The crickets' songs, the slight breeze from the barely open window, the light scent of eucalyptus, the three of us breathing in unison – all of this I store carefully, in a special compartment deep within me, so it will be there, safe, when I need it.

NOVELS BY MARILYN REYNOLDS
True to Life Series from Hamilton High

DETOUR FOR EMMY — Classic novel about Emmy, pregnant at 15. Read by tens of thousands of teens. American Library Association Best Books for Young Adults List; South Carolina Young Adult Book Award.

LOVE RULES — A testament to the power of love — in family, in friendships, and in teen couples, whether gay or straight, of the same ethnicity or not. It is a testament to the power of gay/straight alliances in working toward the safety of all students.

NO MORE SAD GOODBYES — "For all the sadness in it, Autumn and her baby's story is ultimately one of love and hope. It's a very positive presentation of adoption, especially open adoption." *Kliatt.*

IF YOU LOVED ME — Are love and sex synonymous? Must Lauren break her promise to herself in order to keep Tyler's love? " . . . engaging, thought-provoking read, recommended for reluctant readers." *BookList.*

BABY HELP — Melissa doesn't consider herself abused — after all, Rudy only hits her occasionally when he's drinking . . . until she realizes the effect his abuse is having on their child.

TOO SOON FOR JEFF — Jeff Browning is a senior at Hamilton High, a nationally ranked debater, and reluctant father of Christy Calderon's unborn baby. Best Books for Young Adults List; Quick Pick Recommendation for Young Adult Reluctant Readers; ABC After-School TV Special.

BUT WHAT ABOUT ME? — Erica pours more and more of her heart and soul into helping boyfriend Danny get his life back on track. But the more she tries to help him, the more she loses sight of her own dreams. It takes a tragic turn of events to show Erica that she can't "save" Danny, and that she is losing herself in the process of trying.

TELLING — When twelve-year-old Cassie is accosted and fondled by the father of the children for whom she babysits, she feels dirty and confused.

BEYOND DREAMS — Six short stories dealing with situations faced by teenagers — drinking and driving, racism, school failure, abortion, partner abuse, aging relative. ". . . book will hit home with teens."

Visit your bookstore — or order directly from Morning Glory Press
6595 San Haroldo Way, Buena Park, CA 90620. 1.888.612.8254.
Free catalog on request.
Visit our web site at **www.morningglorypress.com**

ABOUT

THE

AUTHOR

In addition to *Shut Up!*, Marilyn Reynolds is the author of eight other young adult novels: *No More Sad Goodbyes, If You Loved Me, Love Rules, Baby Help, But What About Me? Too Soon for Jeff, Detour for Emmy,* and *Telling,* and a book of short stories, *Beyond Dreams,* all part of the popular **True-to-Life Series from Hamilton High.** She is also the author of *I Won't Read and You Can't Make Me: Reaching Reluctant Teen Readers.*

Besides her books for teens, Reynolds has a variety of published personal essays to her credit, and was nominated for an Emmy Award for the ABC Afterschool Special teleplay of *Too Soon for Jeff.*

Reynolds is a seasoned educator who has worked for more than twenty-five years with teenagers facing a multitude of crises. Her extensive background with young adults includes teaching reluctant learners and at-risk teens at an alternative high school in Southern California. She often is a guest speaker and seminar leader for programs and organizations that serve teens, parents, teachers, and writers.

When she is not reading, writing novels, or participating in conferences, Reynolds enjoys walks along the American River, visits from children and grandchildren, and movies and dinners out. She and her husband, Mike, live in northern California.

ORDER FORM

Morning Glory Press
6595 San Haroldo Way, Buena Park, CA 90620
714.828.1998; 1.888.612.8254   Fax 714.828.2049
For complete catalog, contact Morning Glory Press

		Price	Total
Novels by Marilyn Reynolds:			
__ *Shut Up!*	978-1-932538-88-5	9.95	_____
__ Hardcover	978-1-932538-93-9	15.95	_____
__ *No More Sad Goodbyes*	978-1-932538-71-7	9.95	_____
__ Hardcover	978-1-932538-72-4	15.95	_____
__ *Love Rules*	1-885356-76-5	9.95	_____
__ *If You Loved Me*	1-885356-55-2	8.95	_____
__ *Baby Help*	1-885356-27-7	8.95	_____
__ *But What About Me?*	1-885356-10-2	8.95	_____
__ *Too Soon for Jeff*	0-930934-91-1	9.95	_____
__ *Detour for Emmy*	0-930934-76-8	9.95	_____
__ *Telling*	1-885356-03-x	8.95	_____
__ *Beyond Dreams*	1-885356-00-5	8.95	_____

Also by Marilyn Reynolds

__ *I Won't Read and You Can't Make Me*

		Price	Total
	0-325-00605-9	17.00	_____

Other titles (non-fiction) for Young Adults

		Price	Total
__ *Breaking Free from Partner Abuse*	1-885356-53-6	8.95	_____
__ *Moving On*	1-885356-81-1	4.95	_____
__ *Will the Dollars Stretch?*	1-885356-78-1	7.95	_____
__ *Dreams to Reality*	978-1-932538-36-6	14.95	_____
__ *The Softer Side of Hip-Hop*	978-1-932538-83-0	9.95	_____
__ *Mommy, I'm Hungry!*	978-1-932538-51-9	12.95	_____
__ *Nurturing Your Newborn*	978-1-932538-20-8	7.95	_____
__ *Your Pregnancy/Newborn Journey*	1-932538-00-3	12.95	_____
__ *Your Baby's First Year*	1-932538-03-8	12.95	_____
__ *The Challenge of Toddlers*	1-932538-06-2	12.95	_____
__ *Discipline from Birth to Three*	1-932538-09-7	12.95	_____
__ **Spanish editions of above six titles**	Each —	12.95	_____
__ *Teen Dads: Rights, Responsibilities and Joys*			
	978-1-932538-86-1	12.95	_____

TOTAL _____

Add postage: 10% of total—Min., $3.50; 30%, Canada _____
California residents add 7.75% sales tax _____

TOTAL _____

Ask about quantity discounts, Teacher, Student Guides/Workbooks.
Prepayment requested. School/library purchase orders accepted.
If not satisfied, return in 15 days for refund.

NAME _____ PHONE_____

ADDRESS _____

_____